NEVER AFTERS

ALSO BY KIRSTYN MCDERMOTT

Perfections

Madigan Mine

Caution: Contains Small Parts

Triquetra

Hard Places

NEVER AFTERS

KIRSTYN MCDERMOTT

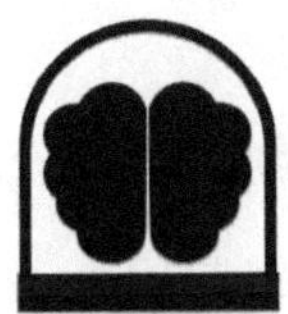

Brain Jar Press
PO Box 6687
Upper Mt Gravatt, QLD, 4122
Australia
www.BrainJarPress.com

Cover design by Peter Ball
Cover Image: *Woman in Victorian Dress,* Fotolit2/DepositPhoto.

ISBN: 978-1-922479-84-6 (Ebook) | 978-1-922479-83-9 (Paperback)

CONTENTS

BURNT SUGAR

My brother stumbles through the back gate while I'm still in the hen-house, plucking smooth, warm eggs from dirty straw.

"Them old girls earn their keep this morning?" He tugs at my skirts, flips them up about my wrinkled knees like he always does when he's in his cups, or climbing out of them, like we're still children and always will be. My hands are full; I can't swat him away.

"More than some," I say, passing him a handful of eggs.

He makes a face but takes them, cradles them to his chest. I don't ask where he's been all night, or how many coppers I'll need to fork over to redeem his goodwill at the pub. I hope he took up with Berta this time; she looks kindly upon him, for reasons no doubt best left a mystery to sisters, and would have covered his feet as he slept. My brother is always cold.

I find one last egg to tuck into my apron, then head back to the house. The speckled hen with the gammy leg is pecking around near the steps. Hopeful for scraps, she hops towards us, making gentle bok-bok noises. Behind me, my brother lets loose a cry; I turn too late to catch the eggs as they fall from his hands.

"Hansel!"

He looks down at the bright yellow yolks smearing the ground and the toes of his boots. "That bird looked at me slant," he says. He wipes at one boot with the sole of the other.

The speckled hen makes a rush but I shout and shoo her off. Once they get a taste for eggs, they'll crack open every last one that's laid. I make my brother stomp the whole mess into the mud, churning yolk and white and bits of shell together till there's nothing to be gleaned by even the most persistent of beaks. Four eggs gone to waste, which means fewer cakes today. I'll have to make up the loss with boiled sweets and slabs of fudge.

"Sorry, Gretel," my brother says.

"Don't you fret on it." It's been so long since a *chicken* spooked him, I'd stopped paying attention. Fat and flightless, yes, but birds nevertheless. I lay a hand on his shoulder, squeeze my fingers around his knobbly old bones. "Come inside, you. I expect our Dagmar might have put some bacon aside from breakfast."

"Might there be some cinder toffee put aside as well?" My brother's grin is gap-toothed and yellowed, and grows ever more such with each passing year. I'm certain I'll bury him without a single pearl in his head.

"There might."

Mounting the steps, I look back over my shoulder. The speckled hen is scratching around in the mud. Three of her sisters stalk over to see what she's found, their russet-brown plumage fluffed with interest, but she hops away before their greedy beaks can take a piece of her.

"Birds," my brother snorts.

"Birds," I agree, and push him inside.

She was our mother, the woman who led us into the woods, I'm almost certain of it.

I have only two clear memories from Before.

One is the recollection of her large, strong hands about my waist, lifting me up so that I might see the robin redbreast perched on the woodpile outside our window. Her body is soft and smells of fresh-baked bread. The sun is warm on my face. There are pretty yellow curtains. As she holds me, she hums a tune which I've not heard since and which I could not, in good faith, reproduce today.

In the other, she's feeding me a salty broth. I have a sore tooth, or a sore throat, or a fever, and it hurts to eat. She blows on each spoonful before holding it to my lips. *Open wide*, she says. *Else you'll waste away to shadows*. I couldn't tell you the precise flavour of the soup. Some days I imagine it was chicken; at other times I can summon nothing but the greasy taste of mutton to my tongue.

In neither scene can I picture my mother's face.

I worry that memories wear thin, like cloth. That in my desire to hold on to them, in my attempts to retrieve more and more details with which to patch the holes, I'm not carrying out repair work so much as embroidering new threads over the top. Embellishing, with what seems most meet.

My brother, for instance, is adamant that our curtains were never yellow. That they were nothing more than sackcloth hammered in place with rusty tacks. He's equally adamant that the woman was our stepmother. No *real* mother could abandon her own children like that, he insists. Alone in the woods with nothing but a hunk of stale crust in their trembling hands. Certainly not *twice*.

(I never bring our father into such conversations, though he led us into the trees sure as she did. I never ask why his absolution was so readily granted.)

But she *was* our mother. And, sometimes, she was very kind.

I'll never know why she (and our father) abandoned us. By the time my brother and I found our way home from the witch's house, pockets bulging with stolen gems, our mother was dead and buried. From that moment on, all words were my father's to wield and he found none but ill to speak of her.

These days, with the weight and the wisdom of too many seasons behind me, I'm given to suspect foul play. Her death seemed so convenient, his delight in being loosed from the shackles of marriage so bold. The bruises earned in failing to boil water enough for his bath, or by darning his socks without due neatness of stitch, have long since faded but I feel their shadows still. I never speak of such things to my brother; he won't hear any slight against the man who raised us. (The man who abandoned us. Twice.) And next winter our father himself will have been in the churchyard for three decades, so there is nothing to be gained from that quarter.

But I do think he killed our mother. I'm almost certain of it.

The small iron bell above the door jangles and Dagmar leaves off kneading the pastry for her strudels. I stay in my chair by the window, the mid-morning sun warm on my cheek, peering through half-shuttered lashes as the dark-skinned girl approaches the counter. She'd be tall if it wasn't for the way she carries herself, stoop-shouldered and hunched as though she's even older than I am. She's scrawny too, with wrists that a firm handshake might very well snap, and her hair is doing its best to escape the messy, crow-black braids that confine it.

"Miss?" Dagmar wipes floured palms on her apron.

The girl turns and there's no amount of hunching that can hide the growing swell of her belly, not from those that know how to see. "Day-old bread?" she asks.

"Not that kind of bakery, love. We make cakes here, and confections."

"Day-old cake, then?"

Dagmar looks her up and down, then smiles kindly. "Might be something I can find out back, you give me a minute or two." As the woman bustles through the curtain that leads to our living quarters, I already know she's planning to wrap up the fruit slice which was meant for her supper, though it was only pulled from the oven this morning.

The girl wanders the length of the store, darting glances my way as quick as silverfish in sunlight. My lower back tingles with the faint, familiar press of unseen hands but I keep myself still, keep my breathing deep and even. I'm a harmless old woman dozing in her favourite rocker; pay me no mind.

On the counter top, a tray of toffee apples harden to a glossy, irresistible red.

She grabs two or three in each hand before scurrying to the door, left cannily ajar. A graceful hook of her foot, a bump of her hip, and she's through, the bell sounding alarums even as Dagmar returns with a loaf-shaped bundle in her arms.

"Little mouse!" Dagmar turns to me, bewildered. "I was hardly about to ask for coin."

I push myself to my feet, knees creaking along with the old wooden chair. "Little mouse with a sweet tooth."

"Those apples will come as a shock then, once she gets past the shell."

I rub my lips together, recalling the fruit I ate sliced while dunking its fellows into the vat of bubbling, molten sugar. So crisp the flesh, so tart, yet near too sweet for my tongue. I'd rather pickled onions by the jar full, green tomato relish or liquorice, double-salted. Some days, I could drink my own weight in vinegar, such is my craving for sour.

There's a commotion outside, raised voices and the scuffing of boots, followed by a keen-edged shriek. The door flies open again and my brother marches across the threshold, dragging the weeping, dishevelled girl by her braids.

"Caught her!" His eyes are afire, his mouth snarled in triumph.

Dagmar steps forward. "You turn that poor creature loose."

"She's a thief," my brother says, his words slurring into one another. "See?" He wrenches the girl's arm around to show us the sole remaining toffee apple still clenched in a determined fist. The rest are scattered in a trail behind her, lying out on the wooden stoop and rolling in the filth of the street. Ruined beyond return.

"Let her go, Hansel," I tell him.

He glares at me, then pushes the girl to the floor. She cries out, both hands reaching to break her fall, and the toffee apple hits the boards with a dull, sugar-splitting crack. My brother grins. "Dirty thief," he says, and spits on her.

In three quick paces I'm on him, my palm stinging hot across his cheek.

His eyes grow wide, shock and hurt and fury all vying for best seat.

"Go," I tell him. "Leave now and don't come back till there's not one drop of grog left to wring from your sorry self. Don't bother coming back at all, you ever gonna lay hands on someone who didn't lay hands on you first." Dagmar is right by my side now, solid and strong.

"She's a *thief*," my brother repeats. "She *stole* from us."

"There's some of us know a thing or two about thieving." It's a struggle to keep my voice low, to resist the further urging of those hands at my back. "But we've nothing worse here than a girl with a hungry belly. And we do know worse, don't we, brother?"

He makes no reply to that, only grinds his jaw back and forth, swaying a little on his feet.

"Go on, Hansel," Dagmar says softly. "Take a walk, suck some fresh air into your lungs."

My brother points a bony finger at my chest. "World's full of bints with hungry bellies. You can't be feeding every last fucken one of them." He nods, happy with his last words; I keep my mouth shut tight, happy to let him have them. As he leaves, he slams the door so hard behind him that the glass lids of the sweet jars rattle like old teeth.

Dagmar is already helping the girl to her feet.

"Are you hurt?" I ask her.

She shakes her head, brushes off her skirt. "That man your brother?"

"Don't concern yourself with him; he's been drinking."

"And when he's not been drinking?"

"Then he's still my brother."

The girl regards me warily. One hand rests on her midsection.

"You have a fella?" Dagmar asks. "Someone taking care of you?"

"No." That narrow chin juts forward. Defiant, like the prow of a tall ship coming into harbour. "I take care of myself."

"That's good," I say. "And where do you take care of yourself?"

"I find places."

"The elms have yellowed; the snows aren't far behind."

The girl shrugs. "I'll find warm places."

"Seems you don't hold the whole bushel on stubborn," Dagmar says to me. She smiles and takes the girl gently by the hand. "First, little mouse, you need to get some fruit slice and a strong pot of tea into yourself. Then you can help me finish the strudels."

"Strudels? No, I —"

Dagmar clicks her tongue sharply. "Fruit slice. Tea. Strudels. Then run away and find all the warm places you please. If that's what you please."

The girl looks at me, her face thin with suspicion.

"Do you have a name at least?" I ask.

"Rezia."

"Re-zzz-ia." I like the feel of the word as I speak it, the buzz of that small, trapped hiss behind my teeth. "There's an extra cot and room to spare, for as long as you need use of it. In return, we would have your busy hands helping us in the kitchen and around the store. This isn't charity, young lady, it's trade; fair, square and simple." I mimic her earlier shrug. "The choice is yours."

The girl is still frowning, but I've no further patience to press the point.

"Fruit loaf, tea and strudels," Dagmar says. "You're a skinny little mouse, but no matter. A few months round here will soon see you good and fat and strong."

There's a queer pang in my heart as the two of them disappear behind the curtain. I said near those same words to Dagmar herself when she first slipped into my store all those years ago, shifty-eyed and spindle-shanked, more grime than girl till I got a washcloth to her. Only it wasn't a handful of sour toffee apples the little urchin stole and scoffed right out on my own back steps, too starved to run any further. Not toffee apples or any kind of candy, but a fresh-baked tray of gingerbread.

It's been her favourite ever since.

I consider going after my brother with a bag of peppermint humbugs, but I'm tired and it's easier to let myself be steered back to the chair instead. I close my eyes and listen to the sound of tea-making and know that soon Dagmar will bring me a cup of my favourite blend, spiced and steaming, and that I'll continue to sit here, and rock, as those hands move in gentle, approving circles over my back.

It's always easier.

Despite what our father said when I brought it home from the witch's house, the Book isn't bound in the skin of children. It's deer hide, rubbed dark and smooth by countless years of careful, crafty handling, and the pages within are finest vellum.

It belonged to the witch, though she wasn't the first to own it, nor even the second, and now it is mine.

On the day we came back, our father wrenched it from my tiny hands and, cursing the Devil and all the women who cavort with him, threw it onto the fire. I expected the Book to shriek, to scream bloody murder, but it made not even a whimper. As it burned to ash, the stench of scorching sugar filled our little cottage. My brother closed his eyes and licked his lips. Rubies tumbled from his loosened fists. I vomited all down the front of my apron.

The look of disgust on our father's face was short-lived but I saw it. I see it, still.

That night, after all the stolen gems had been counted and gloated over and locked away safe in his sturdy wooden chest, our father tucked us into our beds. He stroked our hair and kissed our faces as he bade us good night, his bristled whiskers scratching at our cheeks. *All one family again*, he told us. *And you, Gretel, you be the lady of the house now.*

My brother fell asleep almost immediately.

But I slid my hand under the pillow, seeking out the hard, foreign shape I felt beneath my skull. My fingers bumped against unblemished leather, brushed across feathered vellum edges. My skin sparked. And I heard them once more, those familiar bookish whispers curling through my ears with the rustle of late autumn leaves. Unintelligible, yet soothing all the same. Coaxing me as they'd done all those weeks in the witch's house. Promises sly and soft: soon, I would know; soon, I would understand; soon, I would *be*.

I'd wanted to rescue my brother, of course I had. My terror for him, and for myself, for the both of us ending up cooked and plated like stray spring lambs, had been real. But that wasn't why I'd pushed the witch into the oven. It wasn't why I'd slammed the iron door with a clang that will echo to my last living breath, or why I'd bolted it against her pounding and her screams.

Content with itself, the Book warmed its covers against my palm.

In the darkness, the smell of burnt sugar lingered. It coated the back of my throat, no matter how many times I swallowed.

It lingers with me, still. The smell of a witch, roasting.

· · ·

I wake up choking and roll over to spit a ruby into my palm, thankful at least that I didn't swallow the thing. There's no magic in awaiting a return of *that* nature; several doses of cod liver oil and a close inspection of the chamber pot will do nicely.

I feel a faint, insistent pressing on my back. Though it's dark outside, I sit up and nudge my feet into their slippers. I could find my way in this house with both eyes plucked from my head yet I move with care, having no wish to disturb the sleep of my companions on the other side of the room. With Rezia's belly grown so full, Dagmar has taken to the cot, skidding it right up beside her old bed in case she's needed in the night. I can hear the wispy sound of her breathing as I pass.

Rezia is not asleep. Her eyes glitter like pebbles in the moonlight.

I raise a finger to my lips. I'm seldom able to nod off again when I wake in the small hours and the girl is used to me creeping about at night. Often I plod downstairs and begin preparations for the day's baking. Sometimes I simply rock in my chair and watch the gradual lightening of the sky till the others rouse themselves. Tonight, I light a candle from the stove's embers before making my way to the little closet beneath the stairs where I keep the Book and my father's wooden chest and other sundry things.

There's no lock on the door, and no need for one; it opens to my touch alone.

The Book sees to that, I believe.

Once inside, I drop the ruby into the chest with the rest of the gems. It took its time coming back, this one; I almost suspected it lost. The Book has its roost on a little table wedged into one end of the closet. It waits for me there, exuding an air not so much of patience as inevitability. I lower myself to the three-legged stool that is one of the last sticks of furniture remaining from the cottage where my brother and I lived as children, and open the front cover. Turn to the place where I record the jewels and their travels. Dip goose feather into ink pot and make a small cross next to the most recent entry. All home, all accounted for.

Hands stroke along my spine.

The Book whispers and gloats.

I leaf through the recipes and culinary notes that fill the bulk of its pages, carefully inscribed by several different hands including, most recently, my own. One is newly blank save for a title, *Half-Sour Pickles*. Frowning, I begin to copy down the recipe for the third time. The Book seems to abhor any dish that isn't sweet, but I'm determined to have my favourites recorded and can rewrite them just as quickly as it wipes the pages clean. Perhaps this time the words will be left unmolested.

My half-sour pickles, in particular, are exquisite. The secret is whole coriander seed and a single drop of blood squeezed from my thumb.

A series of moans fall through the cracks in the staircase above my head. I pause to listen, lifting the quill from the page. My brother was struck poorly this week and refuses to leave his bed, refuses even to allow the town surgeon to visit his sickroom for fear of the leeches that might be pressed into service. Our father was much the same way, near the end. There comes another moan, followed by the dull thud of fist against wall.

I hold my breath. I wait.

Till, at last, it comes: Dagmar's resigned and heavy tread as she feels her way through the dark to my brother's room. She will bring him watered wine, if that's what's needed, and sop the fever from his brow with a cold cloth. She will listen to his complaints about the owls that watch from the eaves and reassure him that they possess no fingers with which to unlatch a window. She will tell him that he's safe and she will hold his hand and stay with him till he sleeps again, or till dawn breaks, whichever comes first.

Dagmar has far more patience with my brother these days than I'm able to scrape together. Too many fractious years have seen my own reserves all but exhausted; what little remains must be prudently rationed, doled out only in times of direst need. Not even this crafty Book can deliver a formula for patience, it seems, nor do I know of any merchant who sells it by the pound. With Dagmar, my brother is in good, gentle hands. She is a kinder woman than I've ever been, and some day I'll find the courage to thank her for it.

Beneath my hand, the Book murmurs and wheedles.

It desires me to turn to its end pages, to study once more the wavering, indecipherable script that will shimmer and swell even as my eyes move over it. I've never been able to read what's written there; even the letters, if such queer scribbles can be called such, are foreign to me. All I've ever gained from such attempts are migraines fit to cripple an ox.

I bow my head and continue with the recipe.

Tonight, no matter how sweetly the Book coaxes, I am stubborn. Tonight, I refuse.

That first time, our father had taken two handfuls of opals, turquoises and pearls to a gem merchant three towns away. I doubt he made the best possible trade, but he did well enough to return with plentiful supplies of food and ale, as well as chickens and a milking cow. My brother received a fine hunting bow that he never learned to use properly and for me there was a smart velvet coat, forest green with the softest fox-fur trim, that lasted two winters before I outgrew it.

A month passed and I was out in the yard feeding the chickens when there came an unpleasant popping sensation in my ears. My mouth was suddenly full and, as I parted my lips in surprise, all those pearls spilled to the ground as though from a broken necklace. It was all I could do to beat the excited birds to them.

(When our father later slaughtered an egg-bound hen, I found a pearl in her gizzard. It astonished me, the thought of such a precious thing rolling around inside her all that time, unsuspected.)

The rest of the gems trickled back over the next year or so, landing on my tongue alone or in pairs at any time of the night or day. I could find neither rhyme nor reason for their return, so I simply squirrelled them away in various secret hidey-holes. I never told my father; even at that young age I could sense the peril that infinite wealth might hold for a man such as he. I never told my brother, either.

Nowadays, there's only one merchant I trust with such trade. A southern man with sun-scorched cheeks and a smile I once found winsome, now feel more as a comfort, he travels through our town each spring. We tumbled together often enough in our younger years and, though it never came to more than that, I can still bring to mind the taste of his sweat-salted skin. He accepts my gems in exchange for all manner of goods, some mundane, some wondrous strange, and as much coin as he might spare. I suspect he knows something of their nature, though the subject has never been broached between us, and his reputation has not suffered from their goblin ways.

(I suspect he knows something of magic in *many* of its sly and slippery forms, but we do not talk of this.)

There was a time, one fate-addled summer, when my bloods briefly stopped and I thought I might have something more precious, more startling, than rubies to present on his next visit, but it wasn't to be. The town had a herbalist and midwife by the name of Eufemia back then – a soothsayer as well, according to some – and she helped me through the pain and the mess of it. Afterwards, she gave me a small clay urn with its stopper newly sealed with wax.

Might fetch some use, such a woman as ye be.

She touched a finger to her nose, and her eyes drilled right to the core of me. I had no wish, and no small terror, to know what she saw. I put the urn away in a low, dark cupboard and didn't so much as look at it till the following spring.

There was no tumbling with my merchant that year, winsome smile or no. I showed him the urn and told him the story, and we held hands and wept a little together. Then we buried the urn beneath a yew tree and never spoke of it again. That might have been the season for me to suggest he loose his mules and settle his restless bones into my store a while; or for him to pat the seat at his side and ask if I would care to see some more of the world as he travelled it. But he didn't ask, and neither did I, and the moment passed as moments do.

Six jewels glitter in my cupped palm: three rubies, two sapphires, and an emerald, small but clear in colour. Enough to send greying eyebrows skyward on a face well-schooled in discretion.

"An uncommon abundance," my merchant says, holding out his hand. One by one, he lifts each gem to the light, squinting through his appraiser's glass. He has seen the rubies and sapphires before, though naturally will not remark on this fact; the emerald I have never shown him. Long ago, my father traded it for the ramshackle house on the edge of town where we all lived for thirteen years till he died. It didn't pop into my mouth till he was buried.

"I find myself with uncommon needs." I push the plate of spice-cakes towards him. He brought me the recipe himself, picked up on his travels along with the vital ingredients, though over the years I've stretched it out of true.

My merchant smiles. "Sweetening the deal?" He chooses a cake and nibbles from one side. His smile broadens.

I tell him what I require, as well as what I would merely wish to have should he manage to come across such items. Only once has he ever failed me, on a request of such exceeding whimsy and so little consequence, I would be churlish to count it against him.

He nods as I speak, pulling on his beard from time to time. I can all but hear the intricate gear-wheels of his mind moving through their tallies and calculations. There is nothing on my list that cannot be provided, he assures me finally. Though certain things will take some time, if I have it to spare. Sadly, he is not carrying sufficient coin on his person, but can arrange delivery of the balance via a trusted colleague. I'm agreeable to all of this, and more than grateful, and so we touch cups and drink tea to seal our terms.

Out in the front of the store, the bell rings and I hear Dagmar greeting a customer. There is laughter between them and talk of shortbread.

My merchant rests his cup on its saucer. "When I arrived, there were three crows perched upon your roof."

"My brother is dying," I tell him.

"The tide rolls out, so that it may roll in once more."

I've never seen any ocean, and have little patience for pretty words just now, so I sip my tea and say nothing. After a moment, he reaches into his robe and places a small cloth-wrapped object on the table between us, nodding for me to take it. There is a muffled tinkling noise as I unwind the swaddling, and soon I'm holding a miniature sceptre of some strangeness, its brass handle decorated with several tiny bells. At its end is mounted a polished orange shaft about the size and shape of my index finger, bent at the tip as though caught in the act of summoning.

"Red coral," my merchant says. "For when the little one's teeth begin to cut."

Rezia has been closeted upstairs all morning. Her son, barely a week old now, hasn't made so much as a whimper. The beaming man at my table almost certainly winnowed his way through the full harvest of town gossip before coming here, but I'm not about to point out such mundanities. In truth, I'm as fond of the aura of mystery he cultivates as he is himself. I smile and shake the device; the sound of bells is high-pitched but not unpleasant. "Are children's rattles made so fine now?"

"At court, such a gift would be commonplace."

"Here, it is anything *but* commonplace." I wrap the rattle up once more and assure him that Rezia will be delighted. Then, holding the teapot in both hands, I refill our cups. Despite my care, I leave a trail of drops on the tablecloth between his saucer and mine; discarded, discoloured pearls that neither one of us will ever retrieve.

My brother died with skin as yellow as pulled taffy. He died thirsty, begging for water but unable to keep even a single swallow in his stomach. The surgeon, dour and wholly unsurprised, pronounced the patient's organs too full of drink already. My brother, he said, was a sponge grown too sodden to sop anything more. It was past the time even for leeches.

I offered feverfew leaves for my brother to grind between his gums, though judging by the manner in which he writhed upon his bed, this remedy did little to dull the pain.

Still, I sat with him, and Dagmar sat with me, and together we witnessed the last breath rattle from within his ribs.

We stripped him, the two of us, then bathed his body with lavender water. His poor belly was swollen fit to give birth, but no meat clung to his bones, and we could move him well enough to change the linens. We would not allow Rezia to come into the room or help in any way; it might bring a curse on her milk, and she has her son to consider.

Dagmar is down in the yard now, burning his soiled garments before nightfall. I can smell the smoke through the open window.

I sit with my brother, alone.

There are tears pricking at my eyes, but I'm afraid to let them loose. Afraid they will fall not for my brother, but for myself. Not from sorrow, but from anger, and from relief. Shame has been a hook in my heart so long, it's startling to feel its tug afresh.

"Hansel." His name catches on my tongue. I clear my throat. "Hansel, do not fret. Look." From my apron pocket, I pull handfuls of small, white stones. Gathered the night before our father moved us into town, I've kept them safe and hidden all these years. A memento of the cottage in the woods which was our home when we were young.

Before and, for a short time, After.

"The curtains were yellow, Hansel. I'm certain of it."

I lay the stones on his bare torso, making a spiral that unfurls from his navel outward. The last is the smallest, barely a pebble, and I warm it between my palms. Then I part his lips and push it gently into his mouth.

"There, my brother," I whisper. "Now you may find your way home at last."

I sit with him, alone, till the room grows dark and I can hear Dagmar creaking up the stairs to fetch me. Outside, an owl screeches. I do not weep.

The almond crescents almost land on the floor as a sudden, sharp push knocks me forward. I take a steadying breath and slide the baking tray onto the bench. The hands are still at my back, pressing, pressing. "Rezia, come turn these out for me."

The young woman sets aside her broom and hurries over. Dagmar, separating eggs at the other end of the bench, throws me a glance. Her brow is furrowed. "Are you not well, Gretel?"

"Well enough," I mutter, already pushing past the curtain. For all her concern, Dagmar knows better than to follow.

I march straight to the staircase closet; there's little profit in pretending I could go anywhere else. The Book is on its table, looking the same as it ever did, and yet somehow utterly different. There is a *liveliness* about it now, like it might begin to throb or glow beneath my touch. My stomach lurches. Sweat beads along my hairline. I sink down upon my stool and turn to the very back of the Book. And, with that, everything changes.

Though the language remains unfamiliar, its squiggled letters like none that I've ever before seen, I find myself now able to read it. My fingers glide over each new line; the pages are warm as flesh through which the blood still flows. The Book whispers, whispers, and I open my mouth to its words. My throat fills with them. My heart, my lungs, my womb.

Touch me in this moment and I will begin to throb. I will glow.

Everything has changed.

Dagmar grabs me in a fierce hug. Her breath tickles my ear. "Must you go?" As though we haven't had this conversation several times over the past month, the past week, the past hour.

"I must," I say again, disentangling myself from her arms.

"I can't think how we're going to fare without you."

"You have all my recipes by heart, Dagmar, and several of your own. The store will fare just fine."

"I'm not meaning the store, you stubborn old goose."

Smiling, I turn and busy myself with checking the cart one last time. It holds everything I'll need – my merchant, as always, having remained true to his word – and will serve as both transport and bed till I reach my destination, wherever that may turn out to be. The mule I bought cheaply from a local horse trader; she is old and white, a colour many consider to be ill luck in her breed. Her name is Pearl, which seems a portent of sorts.

Wrapped in oilskin and tucked safe beneath the driver's seat, the Book murmurs to me. Hands press at my back, then pinch. The sun will soon raise itself over the roofs of the town; time skips ahead of us. I pull a small sack from my apron pocket and hand it to Dagmar. "This will keep you in good stead."

As she peers inside, her eyes widen. "Oh. Oh, my."

"People like sweets, but they don't buy enough to keep two women and a young child from the poor house. Trade those jewels as you need, but only with the merchant who travels up from the south. You will come to no harm with him, I promise."

"No, Gretel, they're yours. You should take them."

I push her outstretched hands away. "I have all that I need."

We embrace again and I look up over her shoulder at the bedroom window, propped open to catch the summer breeze. Rezia stands within its frame, the babe propped on her hip. She's angry with me for leaving and refused to come down this morning to say farewell, but now she lifts her hand, fingers stretching in a small, sad wave.

My throat cinches tight. I raise my own hand in return.

"Come back when it pleases you," Dagmar says, helping me up onto the cart. "You'll always be wanted here, Gretel. Never think it otherwise."

I nod, my throat too dry for words, and slap the reins lightly across Pearl's back. The mule lurches into motion and I steer her down the road that leads west, away from town, out into the woods. Her white rump gleams in the sunlight.

I don't look back, not even once.

We travel too many days for me to keep track.

Three times, the cart wheel becomes bogged and I have to lay twigs and pine needles for the wheels to bite onto. Three times, the woods become impregnable, impassable, and we need to go back some ways before making further progress. Three times, Pearl stops altogether and waits with trembling flanks and ears a'twitch till some unseen danger passes us by.

I've no clear direction in mind, save where the hands guide me.

We fetch up at last in a clearing deep in the heart of the forest. A brook runs nearby, its waters swift and clean, from which Pearl happily drinks her fill. I snack on salted pork and black olives, sucking the brine from my fingers when I'm done.

My new oven is heavy and black. Nothing a good mule can't lower from the cart with the aid of winch and pulley. Only when the oven is safely sited do I unwrap the Book and breathe in the sweet scent of its binding. The first page I'll need is right at the back and I read through it with care, as I have each and every evening for the past week. These sorts of words are slippery; they have a cunning all their own. I would not like to underestimate them.

At last I feel ready.

I fill the oven's belly with slow-burning coals and stoke it to life.

Then I begin to bake, and to build.

Time slinks past unnoticed in my little house by the brook. I bake and carry out repairs as needed. (Some deer possess a surprisingly sweet tooth; there's a squirrel nearby with an eye for candied cherries.) My cupboards always seem to contain the required ingredients, though I never go to market, nor even know where a market might be found.

I sleep, perhaps more than I should, but never dream.

Occasionally, a gem will pop into my mouth and I think of Dagmar and Rezia and the little babe, who surely can't be a babe any longer. I don't remember the colour of his eyes, or his hair. I can barely recall the shape of his mother's smile. So I put the gem away into the chest with the others, and think of other things.

I read the Book. I feel myself expanding.

One winter morning, I trudge out to the stable to find Pearl dead, her white legs long and stiff. It's cold and the ground is frozen so I retreat back into my house. The oven is warm. The cupboards are full. I don't step outside again till spring and, when I do, Pearl is gone. Not even her bones are left. I don't know if wolves came scavenging during the snows, or if this is all the Book's doing, but I'm saddened nonetheless.

I would have liked to bury my mule. I would have liked a grave by which to sit.

Instead, I choose the largest, smoothest pearl from my father's wooden chest and plant it outside the stable. After three days a small shrub grows there. Its leaves are a bright, flagrant green and sugar cubes dangle from its branches.

The Book is displeased at my misuse of its magic. For one full cycle of the moon, my joints swell and my limbs ache and I find it a struggle to move very far from my bed. Anything I eat is soon brought back up again, along with some things that I did not eat at all.

By the time I'm well, the little shrub has withered and died.

. . .

I disregard the noises outside, assuming them to be the predations of yet another deer, till there comes such a violent shove to the small of my back that I stumble and almost fall. My mouth opens and words, which have never been mine to speak, march smartly out of it.

"Nibble, nibble little mouse; who is nibbling at my house?"

The noises cease and a tiny, tremulous voice calls, "The wind, the wind; 'tis only the wind."

For several petrified moments, I can't move, can't think. Then those hands are steering me to the door and I seem to watch, near outside myself, as my own traitorous fingers reach for the latch, and lift it, and pull.

Two children stare at me, jaws agape. The boy, a shrewd-faced lad of perhaps eight or nine, drops the hunk of gingerbread on which he was chewing and takes a protective step towards his sister. The girl is a year or two younger, with eyes round as harvest moons and tangled yellow hair that hasn't seen a comb for days.

"We was hungry," the boy whines.

There's a pinch at the base of my spine. "Poor children." I hold out my hands to the both of them. "Come inside and I'll feed you all that your hearts desire."

Although somewhat out of practice, I do my best. Buttermilk pancakes sprinkled with sugar and piled high with cream and strawberries. Stewed apples and roasted walnuts drizzled with caramel sauce. Vanilla sponge fingers dipped into warm custard. The girl has a lovely smile, a little shy, but mostly grateful. Despite my trepidations, I feel myself warming to her. Around a mouthful of sugar, she asks why I'm not dining with them.

"I don't like sweets. I never eat them."

"Never?"

"Not since I was your age."

The boy doesn't say a word, just sets himself to chewing and swallowing as though the dinner table is a battlefield, laid out for him to conquer. His eyes are as greedy as his stomach; I see them dart about the place, taking stock of my humble belongings. I see them linger on the wooden chest in the corner. Its lid is closed but unlocked.

After the children are finished eating, I wipe their sticky faces and tuck them into my own bed where they snuggle together like a pair of pigeons. I settle into my rocking chair with a crocheted rug draped over my knees. Too perturbed to sleep, I doze but fitfully, and so overhear the boy when he begins to whisper.

He warns his sister not to be so nice to me. I'm nothing but an ugly old witch, who will eat them for her supper. She starts to cry but he shushes her, tells her not to be such a baby, that good little girls are brave and strong and do what their brothers say. In the morning they will sneak off, taking the old wooden chest with them. He's heard about witches from stories; the chest will be full of treasure and their papa will be pleased. The girl wants to know what will happen if the witch catches them stealing from her.

We'll hit her right in her ugly face, he says. *And then we'll burn her. That's what you do with witches who eat children.*

My blood curdles with rage. I wait till I'm sure they're both sound asleep before sneaking over to the bed. The little glutton has gorged himself on so much of my food, he barely makes a murmur as I lift him in my arms and carry him from the house. The stable is dry and not too cold this time of year, and I make sure to bar the door against his escape. At dawn, I take the boy a plate of eggs with buttered toast and find him hunched on a pile of straw in the corner, head in hands. His eyes, when he looks up at me, are red-rimmed and frightened.

"What you gonna do with me?" he asks.

"You?" I point my finger through the bars. "Why, I'm going to fatten you up and have you for my supper." Then I run back to the house before he can see me laughing.

As soon as she awakes, the girl asks after her brother. I tell her that he was naughty and needed to be taught a lesson, but that she is a good girl and can stay with me in the house to help cook and clean, and to learn many fine and wondrous things. And that she can have more pancakes for breakfast if she likes, or else bacon and eggs and fresh-fried tomatoes, red and soft as her heart.

"Whatever you want, child. Tell me and I'll make it for you quick as wishing."

She crosses her arms over her chest. "I ain't hungry."

The girl tells me her name is Gretel. (Of course.)

Her brother is Hansel. (Of course, of course.)

She's very bright, if willful at times, and picks up her letters with remarkable speed. The only pages we have for writing are in the Book, which cleans itself of our lessons each day as if it were nothing more than a schoolhouse slate. Such tricks have ceased to startle, and the girl has taken to reading recipes out loud to me while we cook together. She still makes mistakes, of course, and shows occasional flashes of temper when corrected.

Her brother is dim, but thinks me even dimmer. He continues to believe that he's destined for the stew-pot and thrusts a gnawed chicken bone through the stable bars at me whenever I demand to inspect his finger for fat. If I even think of letting him loose, there is such a pinching at the base of my spine, I can't breathe for the pain.

(This does not excuse the teasing; I don't know why I do that.)

The hands keep a constant pressure on my back, guiding and guarding my movements, though the Book no longer whispers to me. It no longer throbs, or glows. I worry about those pages at the end. I worry that, should I look at them again, I will see only mad, unintelligible scribbling.

My worry is a cage; it closes ever tighter about me.

I've caught the girl staring at the Book, face slack-jawed and blank. When I shake her thin shoulders, her eyes snap back into focus and her gaze sharpens. Her smile has lost its shyness, and its gratitude. I treat her as kindly as I can.

At night, I lie in bed and listen. My house is too quiet. The girl sleeps curled into a ball at my side, the bony ridges of her spine turned against me.

I have never been so afraid.

. . .

There's a crow in the tree outside my kitchen window, its feathers gleaming blue in the morning light. It catches my eye and clacks its flat, black beak. Pretending not to notice the bird, I return my attention to the bread dough on my table and begin to punch down. There's great satisfaction in how it yields and spreads beneath my fists. When my wrists start to ache, I shape the dough into a loaf and set it aside to proof.

At the other end of the table, the girl sits with a hand on the cover of the Book, her fingers idly stroking the leather.

"Shall I warm you some milk with honey?" I ask.

She shakes her head.

"Then we should start your lessons."

Her gaze, when it fixes upon me, is dull and vacant.

Hands press now at my back, nudging me towards the oven. "But first we will bake." I'm at a loss to explain these words, that trip so casually from my tongue. "Will you creep into the oven, Gretel, and make sure it's hot enough for the bread?"

The girl pushes back her chair, rises to her feet. "I don't know how I'm to do it."

"You silly goose!" I want to slap both hands over my mouth, but such an effort is beyond me. All I can do – all I am *allowed* to do – is stand before the oven and draw the bolt. The iron door swings open. A gust of heat washes over me; the fire is well stoked.

"It looks too small." The girl moves around the table. "I don't think I could fit in there."

"It's big enough," I hear myself say. Strong hands turn me around, pushing at my hips, my shoulders, my neck. "Look, I could get myself in." They bend me over, thrust my head forward. Sweat runs down my face; my eyebrows start to singe. There is a rightness to this moment, I feel it. To the vast, inexorable clockwork turning and grinding and falling at last, again, into place. There is a rightness to *me*, to all I have done, and will do once more. I cling to such certainty; it's all that remains.

And yet, as those bare feet sneak up behind me, there comes a stubborn twist of hope.

That *this* time the girl will make a different choice.

That *this* time —

"Stop." The word is scarcely more than a croak, but it's mine. "Stop," I repeat, louder this time, reaching out to grasp both sides of the oven. Hot iron sears my flesh as I struggle against the force that holds me. "Stop." My throat bleeds hoarse from my screams. Sweat slicks my face. Teeth clenched, I drag myself upright and slam the oven door shut. Bolt it, to be safe. Only then, hands curled raw against my breast, do I turn to find the girl not two paces from me. Her eyes are wide and wet with shock. She is so small.

(I was so small.)

"Stop," I whisper. "Enough."

Ignoring the pain that seethes along my arms, I drag the girl back over to the table, back over to the Book. Her face contorts with dread, with fascination. It's like looking into a mirror. "Don't touch," I warn, slapping her little hand away. "Its claws are sunk too deep in you already." Before my nerve can fail, I open the Book to a blank page. Tear it out quick as pulling a child's tooth.

The Book shrieks even louder than the girl does.

I slam the covers closed then push the damnable thing to the floor. "Enough from you," I tell it. "More than enough, to speak it plain." That sets the Book to muttering, a brittle string of sounds like the crunch of dead twigs beneath a boot. Perhaps I've broken something, or fixed it. Perhaps that is one and the same.

Though my poor fingers won't stop trembling, the page folds easily into the shape of a bird with wings outstretched and a thin, upright tail. There's more than a little of my blood smeared within its creases already, but I dab two more red dots in place of eyes. "Fly," I say, blowing lightly across its back. The bird flutters to life, trilling sweetly, and swoops twice about the house before coming to land on the girl's shoulder.

"Oh," she says, astonished. "Dear little thing!"

"It will show you the way home, if you ask it." Drained, I wave towards the wooden chest in the corner. "Fill your apron pockets, then free your brother and leave. Once you are safe, unfold the little bird and put it away; it's fragile and not a toy for children." I glare at the Book by my feet. "Few things are."

The girl follows my gaze; her young face hardens in longing. I remember.

"Listen." I grasp her by the chin, despite the pain and swell of nausea this action brings with it. "When you are grown, when you are a woman and know your own mind, if not your own heart, then you may find your way back to us, if you still wish it. You only need fold the little bird up again and whisper in its ear. It will lead you to me, and to the Book, which I promise to keep safe till that day."

She looks at me doubtfully. But her eyes at least are bright.

"Trust me, Gretel." I let her go then, and wipe away the smudge of my blood from her face. "Please, this once, let me make this choice for us both."

The girl took all the jewels that she could carry, more than enough to keep her family in comfort for years to come. I wonder about her father, whether he is a more honourable man than mine, whether the girl will still have a mother when she and her brother come scampering home with their stories of witches ensconced in gingerbread houses.

And I wonder if there is any sense to make from such questions at all.

The Book is still sulking; it does nothing but grumble.

After three days of sleep and salves, my hands are healed enough to bind in strips of vinegar-boiled cloth as I set about the slow, painful work of packing up what meagre possessions I wish to take with me. I try not to think about my fingers and how the tightening scars have hooked them into talons. How two on my left hand and three on my right have all but melted together in the healing like over-spread biscuits on an oven tray. The finer skills of baking, I fear, will now be lost to me.

I leave the Book till last. It warms beneath my touch as I wrap it in its oilcloth; my hands spark and tingle. "Behave yourself," I admonish. But when I peel back the cloth to see, my injured skin seems pinker and shinier, and the pain has lessened measurably. "Cruel thing, to wait so long!"

The Book hisses at me.

It makes a fair point. I did leave it lying on the floor all this time, abandoned with wounds of its own to nurse. We have both shown a measure of cruelty; who am I to judge which way the scale leans? Still, I do not trust the thing and am careful to wrap it well before placing it into my pack.

I'll shuffle my way back to town, eventually, I don't doubt that. My hands may be crooked and near to useless, but I know how to follow the stars and to watch for moss on the north side of trees. More than anything, I wish to see Dagmar again, and Rezia too. I wish to see how tall and strong the babe has grown. I wish to sit in my rocking chair by the window and listen for the creaking of mule carts in the spring.

All these things mean home to me, and I need no trail of breadcrumbs to find them.

As I leave, I break off a chunk of gingerbread from the roof. It smells as fresh as the day it was baked, though without my presence I fear the rest of the house will soon crumble away. Only the oven will remain, standing black and cold and alone in the heart of the forest. Perhaps it will be found some day, by a woodsman or a traveller straying from the path, and perhaps they will take it with them as a gift for their wife, or for their daughter. I hope so. It's a good oven, well-made and resilient, and it deserves a second life.

THE NEW WIFE

The chamber floor is clotted with blood, and my fine silk slippers skid on the tiles, soaking themselves scarlet. Dove grey, they were, shot through with brightest blue: the colour of the vast and changeable oceans they travelled to reach my soft little feet; the colour of my absent husband's beard. Faint, I hold on to the marble basin that stands in the centre of the room and try not to consider its gruesome contents.

Will I ever be rid of what I've seen in this place? Will —

I need to leave.

I need to fetch my brothers from the inn where I pray they're still staying, and rouse the town guard as well. Bring them all, muskets and sabres and neat black moustaches, bring them to this wretched basement so they may see for themselves what breed of monster it is I have married.

My brothers will know what to do; they will keep me safe from his wrath.

The door is shut, though I don't remember closing it; the handle turns but doesn't yield. I press my ear to the dark wood, expecting — what? The sound of breathing from the other side? A rumble of laughter, low and limned with cruelty, or the eager, ominous shuffle of boots on stone? All these things, and none of them, and it's none of them I hear. My heart settles its fearful pace. The door had swung shut behind me, that's all. Swung shut and locked itself, as some doors are made to do, with my mind too consumed by horrors to pay heed.

But where's the key? Not in my hands or the pockets of my skirts, though I pat frantically through the voluminous folds, turning about to retrace my steps until I spy the thing, bright and golden, all but floating in the middle of a gleaming, viscous pool.

The blood wipes off easily enough. The brass polishes clean.

Until, lifting key to lock — oh, me! — that dauntless red seeps back again. And again, and again; no matter how vigorous my attempts to vanquish the stain, it will not budge for more than the span of a desperate, long-held breath.

"There'll be no hiding that, my dear. Not from him."

The woman drifts loose of the shadows, her pale throat bearing a gash so deep I can see the flash of bone through the pulse and twitch of severed flesh. Blood drips from the wound as she moves; the bodice of her lilac gown shines as dark as the skin of bruised plums. She bears some resemblance to the corpse on the far wall, the one whose yellow hair is matted dull with cobwebs.

"You'll not be rid of it," the woman says, "no matter how much rubbing you do."

Her voice isn't the voice of any living soul. I can feel it in my teeth.

"Who are *you* to speak so boldly to me?" I draw myself upright, hitch my shoulders straight and pray my trembling falls beneath her notice. "Here, in my own home, uninvited and ... and ... shabby as a beggar-maid."

The woman laughs, throat agape. Then —

— she is standing right before me, narrow face scarce inches from my own. I cry out and stumble backwards till my spine is pressed against the door.

"Your home?" the woman sneers. "*I* married the man to whom this house belongs. *I* dressed the dining room windows with drapes of fine damask, and brought as dowry the silverware with which you eat your supper. This is *my* home, little girl, and I shall speak as bold as I please within its walls."

"We all married him, Charlotte." A second figure comes into view.

She wears a mint-green dress and holds both hands to her stomach; blood oozes through the splay of her fingers. "We're all his wives, with this one no different for breathing."

The first woman, the woman called Charlotte, snorts. "That's all the difference in the world, Gabrielle." Grey eyes glitter within dark and hollow sockets. I think of the brooch my mother gave me the night before my wedding, delicate marquisette passed down from *her* mother, and *her* mother before that, the only item of value I could bring to the marriage — apart from the throb of maidenhood between my thighs, a bauble my husband swiftly claimed.

"A petty distinction," Gabrielle says, "with so little time for it to matter."

My jaw clenches as I notice the shapes of two other women behind her, with a third hovering at their heels. "How — how many of you are there?"

Charlotte turns to follow my gaze. "This is the whole of us. Five wives, soon to be six."

"Seven." The voice is soft and tremulous.

"Six," Charlotte repeats firmly.

A short, slim figure glides forth. Her hair is a limp and sodden mass of brunette curls, and I can only guess at how pretty her face must have been before someone stove in the left side of her skull. My husband adores a pretty face above all else; he's told me so on several occasions. The slim woman shakes her head; her left eye bulges and rolls in a strange and sickening fashion. "Seven," she insists.

Instantly, the two remaining women are by her side. "Hush, Marie-Catherine," says the one wrapped in a jonquil robe, the one whose neck is ringed by a livid scorch of rope. She wraps an arm around Marie-Catherine's shoulders. The other woman, tall with broad, gentle hips swathed in blushing pink, bends to whisper into Marie-Catherine's ear. She folds her arms like wings behind her back and my eyes are drawn to her wrists, their stumps raw and red and dripping.

Bile rises in my throat and I swallow, sagging against the door as my vision wavers and fogs.

"What an innocent we have found," Charlotte says. "A babe in the woods!"

The woman in pink turns her head to regard me with a mild, incurious gaze. Then she opens her mouth, wide and wet and dark, and coughs a bloody chunk of gore onto the tiles at her feet. There is no time to look away, no time to dodge the knowing of it.

"Marie-Jeanne, really." Quick as blinking, the woman in the jonquil robe scoops the tongue up from the floor, holds it to her companion's mouth the way a groom might offer an apple to a horse, fingers stretched flat and steady. Marie-Jeanne accepts it, sucks the severed piece of flesh through thin, pale lips and smiles. Blood smears her chin. The woman in the jonquil robe cleans it away with a lace-edged handkerchief tugged from her sleeve.

"Enough parlour games," Charlotte snaps.

Marie-Jeanne grins at me, her teeth red.

"Poor little dove," says the woman in the jonquil robe.

Charlotte rolls her eyes. "That's sympathy gone to waste, Henriette. The snivelling wretch brought it on herself, same as we all did."

It's enough to goad my voice from hiding. "Was it me who did all this?" I wave at the bodies hung about the chamber walls, those deathly still relics of the women gathered before me. "Was it my hand that slit your throat?"

"'Twas your hand that opened the door, *little dove*. 'Tis your hand that holds the key this very moment."

I glance down, finding the stain even brighter now against the brass, glossy and gleaming and fresh. "Help me." The words crack on my tongue, and I swallow hard as I hold the key out, this soiled and paltry offering. "Help me clean it."

"It will never come clean," Charlotte says. "Not till your own blood is spilled."

The woman in the jonquil robe, the woman called Henriette, smiles at me. "As ours has been spilled. As we deserved." Her voice is kind, and so are her eyes. "Do not fret; it will likely be swift."

Beside her, Marie-Jeanne shakes her head and extends her stumps.

Henriette squeezes the woman's shoulder. "He does not take the time these days, dearheart. He is quick about it." She looks at Charlotte, whose bone-white fingers are now at her own wounded throat, fiddling with a clean-cut edge. "Too quick."

"But I've done nothing wrong," I say.

Gabrielle steps forward, bloody hands still clutching her midsection as though holding herself together, as though holding herself within. "You've seen him for what he is."

"You broke your promise," Henriette says.

"You disobeyed." Charlotte leans in close to me, nose wrinkling. "No one to blame but yourself. He asked one thing of you, forbade you but one room in this whole great house, and yet here you stand before us, a scarce two days since he left."

"I withstood temptation a whole fortnight," Henriette informs me.

"I had the key in the lock while the wheels of his coach still rattled down the drive," Gabrielle says.

Charlotte favours her with a withering glare. "Yes, yes. We are all aware of your unmitigated haste."

The key is warm in my hand, slick and dagger-sly, and I thrust it in Charlotte's direction. "But he *gave* us the key — he wanted us to come in here, can't you see? It was a trap."

"It was a test," Charlotte says. "And none of us worthy of his faith. Six wives, and not a one as loyal as even the most dejected cur."

"Seven," whispers Marie-Catherine.

"Henriette, can you not have that mad creature keep her peace?"

"Hush now, dearheart." Henriette pats Marie-Catherine's cheek and rearranges the woman's curls to better fill the sickening hollow in the side of her head. "It will be over again soon."

Seven. This time the number catches, an insistent child tugging on the ragged hem of my thoughts, and I push past the women, push *through* the women, their forms offering less impediment than morning fog on a carriageway. My index finger shakes as I count the corpses in the room, count them and match what remains of their garments to the gowns worn by their spectral counterparts.

Seven.

"Who is she?" I point to a small, crumpled pile of dark blue fabric in the corner. How many years before she rotted down to bones?

"No one that need concern you," Charlotte says.

"She isn't here. Why isn't she here?"

Marie-Catherine lifts her head in my direction. Her right eye holds my gaze; the left rolls dangerously in its misshapen socket. "First."

"Need I tear out your damnable tongue myself?" Charlotte turns on the woman with hands outstretched, fingers curled to fearsome claws, but Henriette steps neatly between them. The expression on her face could shatter steel.

I stare at Marie-Catherine. "First ... wife?"

The barest glimmer of a smile lifts the corner of her mouth.

"First wife," I repeat, speaking to Charlotte now, and to the rest of them. "And what did *she* do then, to deserve such a fate? What could she possibly have seen that he needed to silence her for it?"

Charlotte glowers. "Perhaps that is why she is not here." She flicks a seething glance towards Marie-Catherine, who shrinks down into her own hunched shoulders. "Perhaps that is why *we do not speak of her.*"

Gabrielle glides forward and takes Charlotte by the hand. "Save your words," she tells me. "There will be more time for talking amongst ourselves later. More time and less confusion, you shall see."

"Run along, lovely," Henriette urges. "He won't be long now."

Expectation sharpens their features as they herd me towards the chamber door. Charlotte, Gabrielle, Henriette and even poor Marie-Jeanne, mouth pressed to a red-lipped smirk, all of them ushering me on my way. *Count the hours left to you, lovely. He will be coming, little dove. Listen for the rattle of coach wheel on cobbles. Await the clatter of iron-shod hooves.* Only Marie-Catherine lingers behind, watchful face half-hidden by blood-draggled curls, slim hands wringing themselves into knots.

My younger brother, Charles, does the same thing when he's anxious.

My brothers. Oh, my brothers, *my brothers.*

I could weep with the relief of it. "I don't need your help," I tell the wives, unlocking the door and pulling it open. "My brothers are in town awaiting orders from their garrison. Once I fetch them, they'll see to it my husband is hanged for these vile crimes. Hanged, or worse."

Charlotte cocks her head. "Brothers, is it? Off you go then, little dove."

"You — you can all stay here and rot." I lock the door behind me and shove the key deep into my skirt pocket. Though the wives do not follow, their laughter pursues me all the way down the corridor, crowding my head with scorn and bitter glee.

I cannot leave the house.

It matters not which manner of egress I try — the heavy oak of the entrance door, the delicate glass that would on any other day usher me into the gardens, even this rude kitchen door by which my servant-girl Suzette comes and goes — the result is the same. As soon as I attempt to pass, my vision blurs and darkens, all breath is sucked from my lungs, and I find myself propelled backward, buffeted by an unseen storm within that roils and gusts and threatens to tear me asunder.

Palm pressed to my chest, I slump onto the slate tiles and wait for my heart to slow.

This house is a trap — a trap for wives, I fear, sprung by the same murderous sorcery that governs the key. My husband must surely be the Devil, or else has made the most vile of pacts with him. Tears prick afresh, but I don't bother to wipe them away. "Oh, my brothers," I whisper, "if only you could know your wretched sister's plight. If only you could hear her prayers."

In the hearth on the other side of the kitchen, a fire burns low beneath the soup-pot that Suzette has left to simmer. Thick, meaty aromas fill the air, and my stomach churns.

Run along, lovely. He won't be long now.

On the morning after my wedding night, I came downstairs to find my husband crouched by the fireplace in the parlour room, feeding the garments that I had so carefully packed and brought with me into the flames. My objections he silenced with a smile, and with a thumb pressed firm against my lips. *What need do you have of such rags, oh my beloved, when I can clothe you in finery beyond your dreams?* He kept me by his side, one arm encircling my waist, while he burned the remainder of my things. The fire raged so high and so hot I half-feared it would burst its confines and latch onto the hem of my robe, but my husband leaned ever closer, his face flushed and gleaming.

By the time he was done, nothing remained but ash.

Taking a deep breath, I push myself to my feet. Though I may not be able to escape this house, I can light a fire.

The flames consume the slippers with ardour, the slippers and my gown as well, its hem dragged red with trespass. But the stain on the key holds fast, glows with even greater vibrancy amid the lick and crackle of the flames, and my hands shake as they reach for yet more wood. If only I'd not sent Suzette to the village so laden with errands, if only I'd not been so eager to have the mansion — with *all* its rooms — entirely to myself. The girl might be sullen and not very bright, but she can stoke a fire with heat enough to bead the coldest brow.

Heat enough, surely, to burn blood from brass.

Failing that, she might know a scullery trick to do with salt or soured milk or such, some cunning ploy to clean the key as easily as she did my bridal linens, and — oh!

The front door opens with a sly creak then snicks closed again as my husband's voice booms down the entrance hall. "Beloved, I am home." Not due! Not due for many a day but still, these are his words, and these his boots, treading with ominous deliberation upon the floorboards. "Beloved, oh my beloved, where are you hiding yourself?"

Within the embers, the key gleams smug and sure.

There'll be no hiding that, child. Not from him.

I thrust the poker into a log burned near to crumbling and it groans apart, smothers my would-be telltale beneath cinders and ash. A hasty burial but needs must do; I'm not some mewling kitten, to be damned for curiosity. Forcing my mouth into a smile, lips catching dry over teeth, I turn to face my husband as he strides through the parlour door. It's not possible for him to have grown taller, for those shoulders to have broadened and bulked, and yet here he stands, looming over me in the manner of a bear roused from slumber, its once drowsy eyes now keen with appetite.

My hands tighten around the poker.

"Beloved," he says. "You have lost all your pretty colour!"

"You startled me. I had not expected you back so soon."

He reaches out and brushes the backs of his fingers over my cheek; it takes all of my will not to flinch. A messenger met him on horseback, he explains, with word that those matters of business which were to draw him abroad have been fortuitously resolved, and so of course he hastened back to be with his bride. Am I not happy to see him, he wants to know, plump lips pouting through the blue of his beard. Am I not elated to have my husband home again?

"But, of course," I assure him. "I only regret having been caught so unprepared." I smooth my hair and swish the hem of the dressing robe I'd donned before consigning my stained garments to the flames. Fortuitous news, fortuitous timing — or yet more of my husband's devilry.

He holds out his hand. "I'll have my keys."

I take the heavy, jangling ring from my pocket and place it in his palm.

"And the other one, oh my beloved?"

"Oh, that — that's tucked away safe upstairs in my rooms." I flutter my lashes as I've seen my mother do when trying to shave some coins from the price of a mutton leg. "Why would I have need to carry a thing I am forbidden to use?"

His smile stretches, as thin as the blade on a paring knife. "Fetch it for me."

I don't realise that I've glanced towards the fireplace until it's too late. Only for a moment, for less than a moment, but more than enough to catch his notice and he's upon me in two quick paces, one blunt-nailed hand seizing my wrist, the other wresting the poker from my grasp as he drags me over to the hearth. Ignoring my pleas and protestations, he pushes aside the burning logs and lumps of coal, scattering ash in a fine grey cloud, until, oh, there it lies — the wretched key, glistening with blood so bright it might have been fresh-spilled.

"Villainy!" My husband's eyes blaze as dark as brimstone. "Villainy and lies!"

I plead for him to let me loose, beggarly words that trip and thicken on my tongue. The door was barely opened, I assure him, and barely a single step did I take across the threshold, so dark was the forbidden room and cold as well, and so I saw nothing, if there even was a thing to see and this not some cruel trick that husbands play on new wives to test their love.

"Their obedience," he corrects me. "To test their obedience."

I lower my gaze. "I've been obedient in all else. As I shall continue to be, if only you can forgive me this one small transgression." He makes no reply at first and still I stand with head neatly bowed, trying not to consider the nakedness of my scalp, the fragility of bone beneath.

"Fetch my key," he says at last, releasing his hold on my wrist. His voice is softer now, edged with an anticipation that I recognise from our wedding night, but when I reach for the poker, my husband shakes his head and swings the tool beyond my reach. He nods at my hand, at my fingers bare and trembling. "Fetch it, beloved."

"It will burn me."

"Not if you are innocent as you claim. Have you not heard of such trials?"

"Those are for witches!"

"And adulteresses, and heretics, and liars of all stripes." He nods towards the fireplace and slaps the poker against the flat of his palm. "But if you are a Godly woman…"

Without allowing myself time to think, I crouch and scoop the key from the ashes, intending to cast the thing immediately at his feet, but my husband moves with viper speed, snatching my fist in his own and squeezing so tight I cannot tell which hurts more, the crush of bone against bone, or the sear of brass into flesh.

For an eternity, such agony is the entire sum of my being.

When I can no longer scream, when the only sound that can claw its way from my throat is a cracked and broken whimper, he tosses me aside, allowing me to crumple to the floor with my poor hand curled to my breast. The key falls at last from my grasp, still bloody and bright, awaiting the death that shall cleanse it.

"You are all alike," my husband mutters. "Wicked, wicked women." He raises the poker above his head. Such a sharp point it has, and so savage that little spike that juts out near its tip like the fighting spur on a rooster. Strange, how I've never had cause before to notice. So strange.

Close your eyes, little dove.

And I do.

But the expected blow does not land. Instead, there comes the thump of booted feet and urgent, shouted voices, and I lift my head to see — oh! my answered prayers! — my brothers storming into the parlour with sabres drawn and gleaming.

"What is the meaning of this?" Pierre demands of my husband. Charles moves to approach me, but our older brother stays him with an outstretched arm.

"Your sister lacks obedience," my husband says. "She requires instruction, which you cannot deny is both my right and my duty to administer. In truth, young sirs, you furnished me a spoiled, irresponsible child — am I expected to leave her untempered?"

The moment swells, thickens with indecision. Even Charles seems to hesitate, and I cannot bear it, cannot bear the thought of them, my own brothers, deferring and retreating and leaving me to the mercy of this monster. I lift my hand, brandishing the bleeding, seeping wound like a witch's mark. "He killed them," I croak. "His other wives, he killed them all."

With a roar, my husband sinks his boot deep into my stomach. I gasp, my throat closing on breathless space. I cannot move, can do no more than curl on the rug, eyes fixed on the newly raised poker—

Close your eyes, little dove.

—and then my brothers are upon him.

Steel flashes, slicing through flesh. Again, and again, until that massive frame falters and finally falls to the floor beside me. He gapes, my husband, mouth opening and closing like a trout on the block, his life pooling thick and red and hot, spilling and spreading across the fine Turkish weave upon which we both lie. His eyes, I notice for the first time, are as blue as his beard. And how they burn, even now, even with his last breath, how they burn!

At night, the halls of this great house are as dark and cold as the tombs of kings, and the flame from my candle provides little warmth. The front door looms before me, its whorled carvings of leaf and flower seeming to shiver in the flickering light as I place the candlestick on the floor, nudging it to one side with my toe. My injured right hand is useless, bound in swathes of linen that Suzette changes three times a day. The wound will not stop bleeding, though the army surgeon whom Charles fetched dismissed it as a trivial thing, so concerned was he about my nerves.

I have been confined to bed now for five days, during which time my brothers have kept themselves busy, dealing with the constabulary and other long-nosed men of law, spurning the ever inquisitive villagers, those men and women and tribes of eager-eyed children all salivating for a glimpse of the slaughterhouse.

Charles tells me nothing, of course, but Suzette has no such qualms.

Witchcraft, Madame, that's all the talk at market. Witchcraft and sorcery and how his lordship must've made some high bargain with the Devil, getting away with it as long as he did, or maybe how he was the Devil, and maybe — those muddy brown eyes flicking up to meet my own, as sly as pennies for the dead — *maybe how you've had dealings yourself, being as how you're the only one left alive of all them poor ladies, and not once shown your face since they brung out all them bodies. Not that I believe such talk, Madame, not I that knows you.*

Her words chill me. Who can guess what gossip the girl takes with her to market, what flames she likely fans for the sake of new-found infamy? I wish her gone and have said as much to Charles, but he insists there is no one else in the village who will come work here. Still, I do not trust Suzette and the close, appraising manner with which she looks at every scrap of chattel in this house. She looks at me most keenly of all.

The brass handle is cool beneath my touch. It turns easily, the door swinging inward with the barest sigh. Outside, the moonless sky is dark and the world is silent and unstirring.

Though I take slow and careful steps, the instant my foot touches the threshold it comes, just as it did before, a tremendous pressure as painful as stays pulled past bearing. I slam the door, then press my back against it, dragging air into my lungs. I had hoped that my husband's sorcery would have dissipated with his death. My brothers have been able to come and go at will these past few days, and so has Suzette. But as for myself —

"We cannot leave," a voice whispers from the dark. The woman with the stoved-in face — Marie-Catherine? Marie-Jeanne? — is right beside me. She sees me staring, ducks her head and reaches up to pull more of those sodden brunette curls over the injured side. Embarrassed, I shift my gaze to the dress she wears, those billows of pale peach silk with tiny pink roses stitched around the hem. Such fine work would have come at no small expense.

"You're still here," I say. "I had thought, with your bodies laid to rest..."

My brothers took care of such matters with all due haste. They contacted the families of my husband's former wives, what families could be found, and saw to it that their lost daughters, their lost sisters, were returned to them. Only the bones in the blue dress, the oldest bones, the bones of the first wife, remained unidentified. They could find no record of her among my husband's papers and no one in the village owned to ever being aware of her existence. She is buried, her grave marked but bearing no name, in the churchyard. At my insistence, the vicar's purse was weighted with enough coin to ensure a proper Christian burial. It was the least, the very least, our husband's money could do.

"We cannot leave," the woman says again. "We wore the ring. We used the key."

"But he's dead now." Dead and burned to greasy ash on a pyre with all the village circled around, spitting and singing hymns to the sky. Suzette told me that, her tone deadpan yet somehow conveying an unsavoury glee. "Shouldn't his spells die with him?"

She shakes her head. "Not spells. Worse than spells. Colder."

"Marie-Catherine, here you are!" The woman in the jonquil robe, the one with the hideous rope burn around her neck, drifts towards us from the other end of the hall. "Come, dearheart, leave this lady in peace." She puts an arm around Marie-Catherine's shoulders and touches her cheek with a gentle hand.

"Henriette?"

She looks at me with one eyebrow arched.

"That is your name? Henriette?"

"It is."

"Can you help me? I want — I need to leave this place."

"Wants and needs hold no water. You made your bed, same as the rest of us."

"But I'm not like you. I'm not dead." The expression on her face is so piteous, so motherly, even though she could not have been more than a year or two my elder when last she drew a living breath, that I falter, finding no words save the echo of those already spoken which, less assured now, splinter on my tongue. "I am *not* dead."

"No," Henriette says, her voice kind. "Not yet."

At her side, Marie-Catherine shivers and laces thin fingers together as though in prayer. Prayer, or supplication. "Not safe."

"Yes, dearheart, I know." Henriette raises a finger to her lips, stares straight at me and —

— vanishes. The two of them, simply gone.

A damp and bone-numbing chill seeps in to the hall, bringing with it a blackness so dense it crushes the light of my candle to a pinprick and a silence that robs all sound from the world save the unmistakable hiss of a single indrawn breath.

"Beloved," my husband whispers into my ear. "Where is my key?"

Hysteria, the surgeon deems it, with my brothers in whole-hearted agreement. What else could have compelled me to wander barefoot through the house in the middle of the night? What else could explain the bloodcurdling screams that dragged them from their beds and led them to find me huddled in the entrance hall, fingers knotted in my hair and babbling all manner of nonsense about ghosts and graves and husbands back from the dead? Hysteria accounts too for the seeping wound on my hand, the brand still as fresh as the moment my husband made it — *why, the poor girl's body cannot even heal itself when her nerves are in such disarray!*

I remain confined to bed-rest in my rooms. Suzette changes my dressings and brings me beef consommé with millet bread for supper.

"Did you really see him, Madame?" she asks one evening, gaze firmly fixed on the bandage she is wrapping around my palm. Several strands of straw-coloured hair have worked their way loose from her bun to lie untidily along the nape of her neck; I resist the urge to take one between my thumb and forefinger and yank. Instead I tell her that it was merely a nightmare, the product of a mind curdled with horror and grief — a mind that is fully itself once again, I hasten to add.

"You haven't seen any wraiths since?"

Though my spine itches, I do not so much as glance at the window where Marie-Catherine has taken to standing, gaze fixed to the world outside. "No," I tell Suzette. "I have not."

Once the girl leaves, disappointed no doubt at being denied fresh gossip to dole out in the village, I turn to the creature I swore I did not see and ask her once again why, in the whole of this great and miserable house, it is my bedchamber she has chosen to frequent. I do not expect a response, or least not one that makes any kind of sense, but Marie-Catherine tilts her head and stares at me from beneath her curls. Her left eye still bulges from its shattered socket, but I no longer find myself sickened by its roll and sway; how soon atrocities become commonplace.

"Safe," she murmurs.

My palm, I notice, is already spotted afresh with red.

"She said that it's safe," I tell Henriette when she appears later that night, as she always does, to fret and fuss over her friend. "What does she mean?"

"He doesn't come into this room; she's safe from his torment in here."

"He torments her?"

Henriette favours me with a patient, sidelong stare. "Did you suppose yourself his favourite? That he waits faithful and forlorn for you to emerge from this chamber in which you have so neatly ensconced yourself?" A faint smile curves her mouth. "He torments us all. We can no more escape him in his present state than when we were alive. Not him, and not this house."

Now I know the meaning of those sounds I have too often heard of late, have too often pretended not to hear, just as my brothers pay them no obvious mind: moans and distant wails; running feet and roars of pursuit; belaboured breaths and sobs choked back in terror.

"In his present state... but has our husband not always imprisoned you?"

"He paid us no mind after our deaths; perhaps he did not even know we remained until now." Henriette frowns. "The key is cursed, and has bound all who made use of it to this house — including our husband."

"But how, when the damned thing belongs to him?"

"The butcher seldom forges his own blade." Henriette adjusts her jonquil robe, pulls the collar close about her throat so that the rope burn is all but hidden. "I cannot guess at its workings, but the key's magic does not belong to him, nor does he control it. I feel sure of that — as sure as we must now, again, bear the brunt of his ire."

Because of me, the woman does not say, because of my brothers and the doom they brought with them to this house. But had they not arrived with their sabres flashing, why then I would be as dead as Henriette and the other wives, would be lurking in the shadows the same as they once did, sharpening my tongue in anticipation of yet another wife being carried across the threshold.

And another. And another.

Though I'm loath to think of us all rubbing shoulder-to-shoulder like sardines packed in brine, I ask Henriette why the other wives do not retreat here as Marie-Catherine has done, if this room is so safe, if the thing that was our husband does not cross its threshold.

"Should we spend eternity confined to just one room? He cannot torment us all at once and turns must be taken." She surveys her surroundings and shudders. "Besides, it is... unpleasant here. This room repels at every moment."

I follow her gaze, taking in the fine and lavish furnishings I've come to know so well: the billowy blue curtains draped around my bed, its linens matched down to the last hand-stitched cornflower; the soft, padded chairs embroidered with birds and berries that surround the little table upon which I take my afternoon tea; the pale lilac drapes, now closed against the night outside. Layers of former lives, of former *wives*, meant I have never been truly at home here — or anywhere else in the house, for that matter — though since my husband's death... yes, there is something more. A constant prickle and itch, along with a vague pressure at my temples that occasionally deepens to mild nausea. Discomforting, surely, but repellent?

"It doesn't feel so terrible to me," I say. "Considering the alternative."

Henriette regards me with equanimity, one hand caressing the mark on her neck. "When you are dead, you know your place — and you know where your place is *not*."

"Marie-Catherine seems to find it agreeable."

"Perhaps only more so than the alternative." Henriette rubs her companion's back in slow and soothing circles. "Her poor mind has fractured over time; it seeps sense as a cracked vase seeps water."

"Such unkind words!"

"Such *honest* words. What use have we now for any other sort?"

From somewhere deep in the house there echoes a faint, shocked cry. Henriette straightens her shoulders and, in the span of a blink, vanishes from sight. On a rescue mission, perhaps, or else simply spurred to a more palatable hiding place, I cannot tell. I do not understand the wives and their workings any more than I understand the curse that keeps us all in this prison-house. A prickling of tears takes me by surprise, and I wipe at them savagely, pressing the heels of my hands into my eyes hard enough to spark stars.

At her place by the window, Marie-Catherine whispers a single word. "Safe."

My brothers are leaving, recalled to their garrison by orders they would ignore at their peril. Pierre, winding his pocketwatch by the parlour door, seems eager to depart, even as Charles expresses once again his reluctance to abandon me to the haunts and horrors that remain in the house. He speaks figuratively, of course. Neither of my brothers give any indication that they too can see Marie-Jeanne by the fireplace, her severed hands dripping onto the spot where my husband — our husband — was slain. The rug she stands upon has been hauled down from one of the attic rooms, worn in places and clashing with the curtains, to serve as stand-in for the new carpet ordered several days ago.

I endeavour to ignore Marie-Jeanne, thankful that she is at least keeping her tongue inside her mouth this morning.

"I have sent word to Anne," Charles is saying. "I have asked her to come."

"Why?" He has my full attention now. Not our sister, not here. "What need has she to visit?"

Again, he tells me how worried they are, he and Pierre both, how hesitant they are to leave me alone with my poor nerves so frail. My hand that remains unhealed, my refusal to leave the house even to stroll on a brotherly arm through the gardens, the troubling manner in which I have begun to stare at shadows and start at the smallest creak or sigh — all these things weigh on their minds. No, it is best that Anne come stay awhile to help me manage things.

"Our sister has a head for household affairs," Pierre adds, his voice as flat and sharp as the blade that hangs by his hip.

"But she has our mother to care for," I protest.

"Our mother can come with her. It's not as though there isn't the room."

"Just see," Charles says. "The company of other women will do you the world of good."

Behind him, Marie-Jeanne bares a red and toothsome grin.

"I've meant to ask you, Charles... that day... what made you come here?"

My brother looks uncomfortable. "I felt that we should." He moves his fingers over the nape of his neck. "There was a tickle, almost, as of someone breathing soft and close, and I felt... I felt you needed us. I cannot explain it any better."

"What does it matter?" Pierre says, clearly impatient. "You should be grateful, sister, and not question the workings of providence."

Providence, I would not think to question. The workings of wives, however, is another matter.

At the entrance door, my brothers both embrace me and, as Charles bestows a kiss upon each cheek, I look over his shoulder at the outside world, so big and bright and forbidden. A carriage with two sleek bay geldings in harness, far fancier than any our family could previously have afforded to hire, waits for them on the drive. Behind me, upstairs, someone wails.

Pierre unhooks my husband's keyring from his belt and passes to it me. "For the lady of the house." His bow is courteous but gently mocking. Anne will be here before long, that bow reminds me. Anne, with her head for household affairs.

"A key is missing," I point out.

"Your girl has it," Charles says. "There was... a stain; she was instructed to clean it."

We are not to speak of what the stain might be, his anxious face begs me, nor of which particular door the key unlocks.

I watch until the carriage disappears behind the trees that line a curve in the drive, until I can no longer hear the sound of the horses' hooves, just as I did on the morning my husband laid out his dreadful trap for me. Oh, would that I could revisit that day! That I could but take his keys, all of his keys, and leave them nestled harmless in my pocket, untried and untainted, while I sat by the fire with my needlework or played on the piano in the music room or wandered the grounds with a slim volume of poetry in hand. That I could but return them unsullied, so he might gaze at me with lustful eyes and call me his beloved and bear me up the stairs to his bed. I would put up with even that to wind back this particular clock.

If only I had kept my promise —

But no, for I remember too the gleam of bone amid rags of dark and dusty blue. The nameless wife, the first wife, who could have found nothing in that room but her own demise.

There would always have been another trap.

I summon Suzette to ask for the little brass key my brothers gave her. She tells me that it has been soaking in vinegar for a week, and it certainly smells as much when she brings it.

"It's a strange thing, Madame, these marks not coming away." The girl wipes the key on her apron one last time before handing it over. "Looks like blood — fresh blood at that — only no blood I know'll hold so quick to metal, not after a vinegar bath. I tried lye as well, and boiling in lemon juice."

"Never mind." I snatch the key from her fingers and thread it back on to its ring with the others where it gleams as bold as Suzette's ill-hidden smile. "Find me paper, pen and ink," I tell her. "I shall be in my room."

It's laborious and frustrating, crafting the letter to Anne with only the use of my clumsy left hand. The ink smears beneath my skin until I learn to turn the page at just the right angle, and the resulting letters appear to have been scratched out by an orphan child. Still, I persevere, advising my sister that there is no need for her to endure the disruption of such a long and arduous journey, let alone to uproot our poor invalid mother. Our brothers worry for no reason. Other than my injured hand, which is admittedly slow to heal, I am in good health and have the company of a jovial and stalwart housekeeper. They should visit when our mother is feeling better, perhaps in the spring when the gardens will be in glorious bloom. In the spring, yes. I shall send for them then.

My throat tightens around a sob as I seal the letter and ring for Suzette. I hope my missive is enough. I hope the money I will also dispatch will reassure rather than alarm. I hope they both reach my sister in time.

She cannot come here. This house is not safe for women, living or otherwise.

I can feel when our husband is nearby. When he is, as Gabrielle puts it, *on the stalk*. If there is any one of us he favours most, it's Gabrielle with her wide doe-eyes and trembling lip, that mint-green gown billowing behind her as she flees through the halls. A miasma of desperation, of sad and submissive eagerness, surrounds the young woman — the youngest of us all, if only by measure of years spent breathing — and perhaps this is what lures him. A weakness, a softness at her core. Gabrielle is nothing if not pliant.

I have come to recognise the chill that precedes him, the rushing in my ears and the shiver of gooseflesh along my arms. I have come to know when to run. He is bolder now that my brothers have left, but Marie-Catherine is right: he never enters my bedchamber. Still, I cannot remain locked in that room for the remainder of my life. I try all the outer doors each morning, hoping that the curse will at last have waned and I will once more be able to step outside. It has not happened yet.

This morning, I've resolved to do something more.

The broad oak desk in my husband's study is filled with papers, ledgers and notebooks of which I can make little sense, but I search through it all regardless, hoping to find some clue to free myself from his magic. I shall move onto the library next, though I hold little hope of finding some black-spined grimoire sitting helpfully on the shelf.

"Those investments won't mature for some time yet, little dove."

Startled, I drop the ledger I am holding onto the floor. Charlotte is standing by my elbow, her mouth creased in a thin smile.

"I wish you would not do that."

"Do what?"

"Appear like that, without warning."

"'Tis my house, little dove. I shall *appear* how and where I like."

Ignoring her, I retrieve the ledger and run my finger down the columns of numbers and notations.

"Most will not be honoured in any case," Charlotte says. "Not with our husband now in his grave."

"Surely, that matters not? His estate must have a claim."

"So naive, little dove." She laughs, the gash in her throat raw and gaping. "Do you suppose a man such as he made his fortune wholly within the law? Or that all those with whom he dealt hold faith with contracts and courts? Press your claims, should you even understand them, and you might find your pretty head lopped neatly from your shoulders after all."

"Better that than starving to death in the streets!"

Charlotte snorts. Histrionics will help no one, she scolds, and besides, it is not as bad as that. There is a modest income to be derived from legal channels, and the hoard in my husband's safe will stretch a long way if we are frugal — longer, if we are canny. She guides me through the ledgers, pointing out which dealings should be surrendered as a loss and which paltry number might still be revived. Few of our husband's former associates will deign to deal with me, a naive widow so young and fresh, but some might yet be convinced. The secret, she says, is to be bold. But not, she cautions, *too* bold.

Her eyes glitter like jewels. Her face glows. Surrounded by figures and forecasts, Charlotte is a woman in her element.

"I... I thought you hated me," I say at last. "And here you are being so helpful."

She straightens, that skeletal smile back on her lips. "I do not especially like you, 'tis true. I do not especially like anyone in this house. But we *are* in this house, the six of us birds of a tarnished feather, with yours the only hands able to carry a coin or sign name to paper to ensure we keep it. I am not so foolish, nor so proud, as to deny this obvious fact. Nor do I intend to be evicted from my own home, even if I have little say in whom I share it with."

Umbrage is instinctive, a nasty rebuke landing so swift on my tongue I scarce have time to swallow it down. "You have a practical mind," I tell Charlotte instead, returning her smile with an icy offering of my own.

"An uncommon thing in a woman, my father was wont to say, with much the same acerbic tone as you would throw at me. But uncommon things are valuable, little dove, more so than empty pleasantries, simpering friendships or the broken vows of wives." She regards me for a moment longer, that narrow face veiled by something akin to sympathy, before vanishing with as little fanfare as she appeared.

I close the ledgers and stack them neatly on the desk. We are not to be friends, then, Charlotte and myself, nor enemies neither — and I find myself strangely relieved. There is a weightlessness in speaking the truth precisely as one wishes, in casting aside all mannered artifice and guile. A cruelty perhaps, if one chooses to hear it, but also a kindness.

Henriette is right.

Among the dead and the exiled, what use are any words but honest ones?

It's on the upstairs landing that I spy them — Gabrielle with her spine bent over the banister and our husband with one hand clutching her throat, the other plunged wrist-deep in her belly. Her mewling cries are those a stray kitten might make when caught by savage children, soft and plaintive, absent any hope of rescue, and it is these cries more than anything that propel me up the stairs with neither thought nor hesitation.

"Leave her be," I yell, brandishing the book I went to fetch from the library.

He turns, his mouth a gaping maw within that nest of frightful blue. My legs weaken, my stomach rolls, and — oh! — how I wish I'd simply scuttled on my way as I have so many times before upon hearing him at his games. But his hand drips red onto Gabrielle's green dress, and with each heave of her chest a coil of flesh, too pink, too glossy, peeks from the wound in her stomach. Bile burns at the back of my throat, hot and harsh and ashamed.

It is one thing to hear; it is quite another to witness.

"Leave her be," I say again, cursing the quaver in my voice. "Leave us all be."

Time stretches to a thin, taut line beneath my husband's regard.

Be bold, but not too bold.

I lift my chin, refusing to drop my gaze from his.

Then the moment snaps and he charges, his furious bellow filling my entire being with terror. I cry out, cringing behind the book as he launches a bloody fist right at my face — right *through* my face — a swift and wintry frost all that marks its passing.

Shocked, I touch my cheek. Already the flesh is warm again.

Leaning in close, my husband lets loose another ghastly roar. His mouth is black and hollow, his breath stinking of iron left to rust and rot, but this time I do not flinch. He is no longer a man before whom I must scrape and simper lest I be taught the lessons of his wrath, no longer a man who controls my fate, my fortune, with neatly manicured paws.

No longer a *man* at all.

"Ghoul," I whisper. "Leave me be."

Only after he vanishes do I realise what was changed about my husband, why he was so incoherent in his rage. His tongue — his tongue is wholly missing.

It is clear that none of the wives wish to be here, save Marie-Catherine of course, who stands in customary stillness by the window. Charlotte paces, hands on hips; Gabrielle mutters words of prayer beneath her breath; Marie-Jeanne pushes her tongue between her teeth at regular intervals, before sucking it noisily back in again. I try not to look at her.

Henriette, whom I convinced to gather them all together in my bedchamber, casts me an anxious glance.

I clear my throat. "We share a common problem, the six of us."

"Seven," Marie-Catherine whispers.

Charlotte rolls her eyes. "For pity's sake."

"Wait, please. Listen." She raises a doubtful brow but makes no further motion to leave. It's a minor benediction on her part, this stretching of patience, and I hurriedly continue. "Our husband makes sport of us all, some more so than others." A nod for Gabrielle, who accepts it with a wan and trembling smile. "It is obscene; we should not stand for it."

"You speak as though we have a choice in the matter, little dove."

"I speak because we *do* have a choice in the matter. We can refuse."

Henriette shakes her head. "That might be true for you, with breath still in your body and flesh he cannot touch, but the rest of us are not so fortunate. We run, we hide, we go mad. Those are our choices."

"No, Henriette, you are wrong. Our husband once had the advantage, yes, but death has robbed him of that. He is no stronger now than any of you. He cannot hold his money, or his position, or any kind of authority over your necks any longer. Do you not see? He has no power but that which we allow him to take from us."

"Perhaps that is power enough," Henriette says, her voice subdued.

"He *is* still stronger," Gabrielle insists. "You, he can only frighten. Us, he can *hurt*."

"And you can hurt him."

"Preposterous!" Charlotte says. "These are but foolish guesses, and 'tis we who will bear the brunt of their falsehood. He is beyond our ability to harm or hinder."

"But one of you ripped out his tongue!" The women stare at me, shocked. I turn to Marie-Jeanne, who bares red-stained teeth in a smug and gory smile. "Was it you? Did you find such a gruesome revenge only fitting?"

"And how would she have done it?" Charlotte demands, striding forward to grasp Marie-Jeanne by the wrist. She holds up the woman's bloody stump. "With what instruments?"

"Then you, Henriette? Or Gabrielle?"

The two women shake their heads. Henriette seems to blanch at the mere suggestion, but Gabrielle frowns. "He has... wounds from time to time," she says, surveying her companions with a cautious glance. "But I would have never thought that one of you —"

"It was *not* one of us!" Charlotte snaps.

"One of us," Marie-Catherine echoes from her place by the window.

And, at that moment, there comes the faint but unmistakable creak of a floorboard from outside my bedchamber.

Three indignant strides see me to the door. As I swing it open, the girl leaning on the other side stumbles and nearly falls into the room. Grabbing Suzette by the upper arm, my fingers digging into her flesh with more ferocity than is entirely needed, I demand to know the reason for her clumsy espionage. More grist for the village gossip mill perhaps, or is it my brothers who are so keen to have her report — no matter, for whatever she believes she has heard, she is most assuredly mistaken.

Suzette glares at me. "It's not just what I *hear*, Madame." Her gaze shifts then, with slow deliberation, first to Charlotte, then to each of the other wives in succession, before sliding back to connect once more with my own.

I am stunned. "You — you can see them? For how long?"

"Been seeing wraiths since 'fore I had words to tell about them."

"Why didn't you say?"

The girl shrugs her shoulder, pointedly, and I let loose her arm. "Wasn't sure about you, was I? Wasn't gonna say nothing that would see me sent packing from here, or locked up in the madhouse, or worse."

Charlotte sniffs loudly. "This one is nothing more than a servant. She has no business here."

"And you're nothing more than a *lady* stupid enough to get her own throat slit."

"Suzette! How dare you speak that way!"

The girl sketches a curtsy so shallow her skirts barely skim the ground. "Beg pardon, Madame, but wraiths got no cause to feel superior to any living soul, no more than we got cause to humour them to think so. It's what you said: there's no position in being dead."

Charlotte's eyes are narrowed and dark. "I shall not stand for such insolence."

"Then leave. This house belongs to Madame, now. Leave it — if any of you are able."

My hand strikes, its mark blooming bright on the girl's cheek, though the blow was awkward and would scarce have hurt near as much as intended. "You are the one who shall leave," I tell her. "*I* will not tolerate such ill manners towards any person in my home, living or otherwise. Collect your belongings and depart this hour."

Suzette rubs at her face. "I can help."

"In what manner?"

She looks around the room once more, capturing the attention of each of us in turn, and when finally she replies, it's with a voice as quiet and unruffled as a millpond. "I can help you be rid of him for good."

Oh, how I wish to believe her — but what would a lowly village girl know about ghosts, let alone the unfinished business that lingers between husbands and wives? She has not used the key; for all she thinks she can see, she is not privy to everything that has happened in this house.

"I have had my fill of nonsense for one day," Charlotte says.

"Look." From her apron pocket, Suzette retrieves a golden ball no bigger than a pigeon egg and holds it up to the light.

I lean closer. "What have you there?"

"An ambuscade." She turns the thing over in her fingers. It's not a perfect sphere, its surface being marred with various dents and scratches, but there is nevertheless such an enticing, luminous quality about the little ball that I find myself reaching out a hand, wanting to hold it for myself. Quickly, Suzette tucks it back into her pocket. "It's a trap — for wraiths."

The other wives have crowded close. Even Marie-Catherine, though she has not moved from her customary position, is watching with newly focused eyes.

"Where on earth did you find such a thing?" Charlotte asks.

Henriette licks her lips. "How does it work?"

"Can we see it again?" Gabrielle pushes even closer. "Please?"

Suzette shakes her head. "I made it for him, not for you."

"*You* made it?" I am incredulous, that those same blunt fingers which each day bind my bandages fat as a winter mitten could manage such work. More like it is some bauble she has stumbled across, scooped up sly and spun a story around, though to what purpose I cannot imagine.

"If I can speak it plain, Madame, my father's a wraithwright. I learned more'n how to chop wood and slaughter chickens by watching his hands at work."

I've heard tales of such men — those who seek out haunted places, who are summoned to cleanse a stubborn, spectral stain — but assumed the most salacious details to be wholly imagined, pressed to the cause of scaring young children out of their wits, as my brothers oft delighted in doing. Of course, the once-solid floors upon which I used to so thoughtlessly tread have themselves seemed less reliable of late.

"Your father is a wraithwright."

"Yes, Madame. As was his before him."

"With the mantle now being passed on to your young shoulders, we are to suppose?"

A flicker of anger darkens her face. "He's looking for a 'prentice. Says that girls can't be what he is, that only boys got the knack for it, but that don't make sense. If only a wright can see a wraith, then aren't I one by any natural reckoning?"

"Only if I am as well, Suzette. Which I very much doubt."

"Beg pardon, Madame, but all you can see is *these* wraiths." She waves her hand around the room, mindless of the manner in which it slices right through Gabrielle's face, so close has the woman sidled in order to peek inside Suzette's apron pocket. "And that's only 'cause you're linked to them, like pearls on a string, linked to them and linked to him. It's why they're wanting my ambuscade, because of him, because it's made with —"

The girl bites off her own words, snatching her lower lip between her teeth.

"Made with what?" I grab the girl by the arm again and pull her close, then reach into her apron with my wounded hand. My fingertips flex and scrabble, shooting pain along my arm as they scoop out the ambuscade and hold it right in her face. "What did you use, Suzette?"

Around us, the wives hover and coo. *Look, dearheart, how it gleams. Can we touch it? I want to touch it.* The girl struggles to free herself, but I hold fast, demanding to know what dark magic she employed in the making of such a device — but even as I speak the words, I want to swallow them back, or I want to swallow the ambuscade, to feel it slide smooth and golden down my gullet, to know the weight of it nestled deep within my belly.

I could weep at the thought.

"Madame, here, let me take it." Her words a whisper now, gentle as a mother cat as she prises the ball from my hand. My bandage is soaked through, and she wipes the blood from the ambuscade's gilded surface before secreting it once more in her apron. "I made it from his wedding ring. His wedding ring, mixed with other scraps."

Charlotte glares at the girl. "A common thief as well, then, to steal from a dead man's hand."

"He wasn't using it no longer."

"Are we to take the words of a thief for truth? It seems an ugly bauble, and ill-made. I doubt it even works as she says."

Suzette smiles at the woman before her. "Good thing *pretty* doesn't stand for all."

"Enough," I tell the both of them.

Beside me, Henriette wets her lips. "Do you think he *could* be trapped?"

She is asking the question of me, but it's Suzette who answers. "Of course he can be trapped. Any wraith can be trapped if a person has the knowing of it. Only..." Her gaze falters for the first time since I dragged her into my bedchamber. "Only, I can't do it on my own."

She's tried to catch our husband herself, the girl explains, many times over, but he seems wholly distracted, casting about like a hound on a scent. It will take the wives and myself, the six of us — "Seven," says Marie-Catherine, largely ignored — to help corner him, to focus his attention on the ambuscade and remove all other temptation from within his grasp.

"But how do we do such a thing?" Henriette asks.

"Refuse him," Suzette says, glancing at me. "It's not really true, what Madame said before. He is still stronger than any one of you, and more powerful — he brung that through from life. But not together, not if you all stand against him at once."

Charlotte has been pacing the room with long, slow strides. Now she stops and taps a finger against her lips. "Perhaps the upstart creature seeks to ensnare us all."

Henriette shakes her head. "If that were true, she would hardly be sounding a warning."

"Do we trust her?" Gabrielle whispers. "Do we dare?"

Marie-Jeanne spits her severed tongue on to the floor and grins.

Charlotte stares at Suzette for a moment longer, brow creased with indecision, before turning to me. "I don't entirely *dis*believe the girl, but if we assist her and she fails, what fate then befalls those of us still trapped in this house with a husband whose wrath will burn even hotter?"

"I am trapped here as well, Charlotte. If he can be captured, then we might all of us be freed. At the very least, we will be free of *him*."

"We are his wives, little dove. We shall never be free of him."

With that, she is gone, followed soon after by Henriette and Gabrielle, who offers me an apologetic wave in parting. Marie-Jeanne leaves her tongue behind, and it remains for several seconds before vanishing on its own. Suzette crouches to touch a flattened palm to the empty, unmarred carpet where it lay. By the window, Marie-Catherine stares at the girl, unmoving.

"Seven," she says. "Never free."

That evening I make my way to the kitchen where I find Suzette muttering to herself as she rolls out a pie crust. The girl's sleeves are pushed up to her elbows, and I'm taken aback by the sight of those strong, bare arms working the dough. My mother used to make pies for us, before my father died and she herself became too ill, too weak for such exertions. I remember the clouds of flour that settled on the table and how Anne and I used to write our names in their soft, white leavings. My throat tightens and I clear it noisily.

By her bench, Suzette startles. "Beg pardon, Madame." She claps her palms together before wiping them on her apron. "I didn't see you."

"I've been pondering our current circumstances," I tell her. "It seems quite fortunate, provident even, that just as the need arises for a person with very *particular* expertise, why, here you are with your little trinket."

The girl picks up the rolling pin once more. "What work do you suppose there is for a wraithwright's daughter down in the village? I've only got this job 'cause no one else wanted it no more, not since the last housekeeper come back with stories of thumps and bumps and bloodcurdling screams in the night."

"Before my husband died, I myself heard nothing untoward."

"Folks like to talk big. When something isn't right with a place but they got nothing to show for it, they make it up themselves, or their imagination does. A wraithwright knows to keep an ear out, knows what stories to listen for."

"Tell me the truth."

"What truth would you be after, Madame?"

"You say you have come to trap my husband's wraith and yet you were part of this household well before I arrived, let alone before he died."

The girl folds the dough over itself before starting to roll it afresh.

"You came for the others, Suzette, did you not? For the wives?"

"I guessed there'd be a wraith here, from what folks were saying. Figured I could snare myself one to prove to Pa I could do it."

"Did you know my husband murdered them? Did you know he was planning to murder *me*?"

"No!" She seems roundly shocked at the suggestion. "They kept to themselves before he started chasing them about. I wasn't even sure who they were."

"But you suspected."

Suzette kneads the dough into a ball and pounds it onto the benchtop. "And if I did? His lordship with his title and his coin and his sly old words? Who'd have believed the likes of me over all that? Wives die all over, Madame — that's the truth you're so keen on digging out. Wives die, and the world keeps to its path."

She glares at me, cheeks flushed and fingers clenched deep in the dough, and I wonder at how a girl her age grows to be so fierce. Perhaps all children of wraithwrights are thus, born with fearsome natures to a fearsome world.

"Such an odd word when you think on it."

"Beg pardon, Madame?

"Wraithwright," I tell her. "Wraith-hunter would seem more appropriate, wraith-trapper even, if that be what such a person does. Why *wright*? What is it that's *made*?"

"Ambuscades are made. And places — they're made safe."

Her gaze flickers to the bench and back; one blink and I would have missed it.

"If you want my assistance, Suzette, or the assistance of any in this house, you would do well to speak plainly."

She gnaws on her lip. "We're not supposed to tell. It's not for ordinary folk to know."

"What is it about this situation that seems *ordinary* to you?"

"The ambuscade, it's used..." She begins to work the dough once more, her hands gentler now and careful. "It's used to make other things. Important things, valuable things."

"Such as?"

"Depends what's trapped inside. My father, he made a needle once, never laid a bad stitch. The Royal Seamstress has it, he says, but that might not be true. And, up north, I heard there was a knife made would always find a man's heart, no matter how clumsy the aim. That's rare, though, and needs a mighty powerful wraith. Most of the time it's smaller things, charms and wards — but better than you'd get with cottage magic."

"How is it done?"

"I don't know that part of it."

"Suzette..."

"I swear, Madame, on my life. I know how to craft an ambuscade fairly well but that other work..." She shrugs, but this time her gaze holds firm with mine. "That's not for anyone but wrights and 'prentices — which I'll never be 'less I bring my Pa a wraith of my own."

I cross my arms over my chest. "Then let us hope the others may yet be convinced."

"You'll talk with them, then? Persuade them?"

"Me?" Laughter comes unbidden and I cough, covering my mouth with my hand. The bandage, I notice, will need changing before dinner.

"You are not a good judge of station, are you, Suzette? My words will persuade none of them, so lowly am I in their estimation. Why, I am not even dead!"

"But a wife, same as them. You still wear your wedding ring."

Frowning, I consider the slim gold band that adorns my finger. I cannot think why I have not removed it, why I have not even thought to remove it before now. It slips over my knuckle with only minor persuasion and falls onto the flour-strewn benchtop with a small puff of white. I tell Suzette to destroy it, to melt it down, or sell it and keep the coin for herself — I care not so long as I never see it again. Already, I feel lighter, closer to the girl I was before my husband ever laid his monstrous eye on me.

At the kitchen door, I turn. "One final matter, Suzette, and heed me well."

"Yes, Madame?"

"If but one of these women comes to any harm in making use of your ambuscade, you shall deeply regret ever crossing the threshold of this house. That, I promise."

"I promise, too, Madame." Her voice is solemn. "It's only *him* I want now."

Next morning, while Suzette is attending to my bandages, Charlotte appears in my bedchamber. "We are resolved to assist you," she tells me in proud, clipped tones. "This is our home, and we will no longer be chased through it like curs in need of lashing. We will no longer hide."

"You are all agreed on this?"

Charlotte glances towards Marie-Catherine, stationed by the window as usual, and sniffs. "Almost all." She makes a small movement with her chin, and Henriette materialises at her side, followed by a grinning Marie-Jeanne.

It takes Gabrielle a few moments longer and, when she does appear, her face is worried and drawn, and she has both arms hugged tightly about her waist. Blood seeps fresh over her cuffs. "What if the trap doesn't work?" she whispers. "What if—"

"It will work," Suzette says. "If we all band together, we can catch him."

Gabrielle looks doubtful. "I'm frightened."

"We're all of us frightened, dearheart." Henriette places a hand on the other woman's shoulder. "That is precisely why we must make the attempt."

"Compose yourself, Gabrielle," Charlotte says, her voice softer and kinder than I have ever heard it. "If we succeed, you need never bear the brunt of our husband's desires again — not you nor any one of us. This place is not our home if we are forced to live in it as prey."

Gabrielle nods. "It may as well be our prison."

"And we our own bailiffs."

The exchange has a well-worn quality to it, as though these same words have been trod over for many an hour. Still, Charlotte seems satisfied as she turns to thrust a finger towards Suzette. "You, girl, bring forth that bauble of yours and teach us its workings."

I marvel at her bearing; if not for the handicap of her sex, Charlotte would have made a fine general, able to cajole and command in equal measure. With all agreed, it seems, we fall to strategy. Suzette and Charlotte jar and scrape against each other's hulls, but the girl manages to curb her temper more times than not, and the other woman allows the lack of deference she receives to pass, if not unnoticed, then mostly unremarked. At one point, Marie-Jeanne catches my eye and, with a wink, pokes her tongue out between her teeth. Gruesome as her visage is, I find myself smiling.

Over by the window, Marie-Catherine ignores us completely.

Later, after the wives have departed to prepare themselves as best they can, Suzette retrieves what appears to be a necklace from her pocket. It is a decidedly unattractive thing — a blunt and battered piece of gold strung on leather thong. "I made this for you, Madame, for you to wear."

Trying to mask my dismay, I accept it from her hand. "Suzette, I..."

"It's a talisman, to keep you safe. To keep you hidden from what would hurt you." The girl licks her lips. "I used your wedding band."

Holding it up to the light, I notice a series of symbols scratched into one side. I have no idea what they mean, or what their purpose might entail, but I take a strange kind of comfort in their shaky, ill-carved lines.

"Pretty doesn't stand for all," Suzette says in a low and hopeful voice.

I smile and pass the necklace back to her. "Please, my hand is too clumsy for knots." Sitting very still, I close my eyes as Suzette ties the thong around my throat. Her breath, so close and warm on the nape of my neck, feels like something akin to trust.

The basement chamber is no less cold than when first I stepped across its threshold, but this time at least it is clean — an improvement no doubt due to Suzette, on her hands and knees with a hard-bristled brush and bucket after bucket of tepid water hauled down the stairs, scrubbing until all blood was banished. Such a grisly chore and yet here she stands, round face so stoic in the flicker of candlelight you would suspect her to have witnessed no sight in her young life more gruesome than a sackful of drowned puppies.

Charlotte offers me a curt nod, then leads Henriette and Marie-Jeanne into the shadows on the far side of the chamber where they all but disappear. Marie-Catherine, as suspected, has refused to take part — although *refused* is perhaps too deliberate a word to describe the habitual silence she keeps — and Gabrielle is on the stalk.

If indeed a deer can ever be said to be truly stalking a wolf.

"I would see it again."

Suzette opens her fist to show me the ambuscade nestled within. "Please, Madame, stop fretting." She closes her fingers around the lumpy golden ball once more and drops her hand to her side. "It'll be made right, I swear."

"*If* Gabrielle can find him. *If* she can lure him down —"

There resounds a roar from beyond the chamber door, and then the two of them come flying in: Gabrielle with arms outstretched and mint-green dress sailing in her wake, our husband barely a pace behind. His fingers tangle in her hair, wrenching her back against his chest, and she cries out in pain and shock, her eyes wide with terror. I scarce have time to note the new alteration to his visage, those scarlet slashes running so deep through his cheek that the bone glistens white within, before the others are upon him.

Screeching like Valkyries from their corner, they descend with teeth bared and fingers hooked, Charlotte leading the charge but Marie-Jeanne and Henriette fast at her heels, and Gabrielle too now turning upon her attacker. The four of them rend and pummel and tear until our husband lets loose a guttural wail and makes to retreat — to no avail, for wherever he turns there is yet another wife, the full force of her fury unleashed at last upon the man who has trapped her all these years, who has refused her the peace that death promises in preference to his own vile pleasures.

"See here," Suzette steps forward, holding the ambuscade on her outstretched palm. "See! See here!"

And see he does, those great blue eyes round as dinner plates heaped full with longing, with desire bolder than I have witnessed before. He endeavours to wrest himself free, but the wives will not relent, so enraptured are they now in their own vengeful pursuit that all our careful plans seem tossed awry.

"Charlotte!" The name shoots from my lips almost of its own volition, it seems, and I shout it again, and again, until finally the woman turns her head to fix me with a glazed and ill-focused stare. "Charlotte," I say once more, my tone lower now, "Charlotte, please. *Stop.*"

She blinks and shakes her head. Then withdraws, placing a hand on Henriette's shoulder as she does so, pulling the other woman back with her, and their husband, my husband, *our husband no more*, takes his opportunity and —

— is gone.

In Suzette's hand, the ambuscade gleams brighter than the candle flame.

"Is he... ?"

The girl nods. "He's trapped. It's done." She looks up, grinning wide, and an immense wave of relief shudders through me. Until — oh! — her face contorts, mouth set in a grimace as though someone has caught each side in fish-hooks and is pulling downward, pulling her whole body down to the flagstones where she begins to flail and fit.

Crouching at her side, I grasp the girl by the shoulders and try to still her thrashing while the wives hover about us like all-too-anxious aunts.

"What is happening to her? Why does she writhe like that?"

"Is this his doing?"

"But he is trapped — see how the ambuscade glows."

"Perhaps he is stronger than she thought."

"And furious, oh! How furious he will be with us!"

As suddenly as she began, Suzette stops her shaking and stares at me, a thin line of saliva suspended from her lower lip. Her eyes are raw, their whites shot through with blood, their pupils huge and black.

"Suzette, what is the matter?"

I flinch as she raises her fist, and the ambuscade is in her mouth before I realise her purpose — but realise it I do or, more truly, recognise it: that queer desire to subsume the thing into myself, and so my own fingers follow it, doing battle with tongue and teeth until at last I grasp the thing, all slippery and slick, and wrench it from her. As the girl moans and falls back, her sudden fire extinguished, there comes a curious, fleeting pressure against my sternum, like the muzzle of a disappointed hound, snuffling and searching and moving swiftly on. Beneath the bodice of my gown, the talisman grows warm.

Suzette drags herself several paces, chest heaving, then vomits into the corner. The smell of urine wafts from her skirts.

"What was that?" I ask her. "What did he do to you?"

The girl swallows, wipes at her mouth. "Not him," she croaks at last. "That was *her*."

Behind us, the chamber door slams shut with a sharp, resounding crack that I feel to the marrow of my bones.

First Wife. Whose name is lost, whose family is unknown. Whose honour will remain besmirched.

"But *where* is she?" Charlotte asks. "None of us has ever so much as sensed her presence in this house."

"She's everywhere." Suzette frowns, rubs her lips together. "She... she *is* this house. She's soaked into every tile and floorboard, every nail and window pane; you can't sense her no more than a fish knows the water it swims in." The girl looks at me. "But, Madame, I reckon your bedchamber's her very heart. I reckon that's why the others don't like it there, why your husband's wraith couldn't pass its threshold."

"Marie-Catherine likes it there," Gabrielle retorts.

Henriette shakes her head. "I do not think she likes it; I think she endures it."

"Can you make an ambuscade for her — for First Wife?" I ask.

"She's not a wraith," Suzette says. "She's not any kind of thing I know how to snare."

There comes another loud crash from upstairs, the third or fourth since the door was locked against us, and I jump as I have each time before. All of it is First Wife's doing, according to Suzette: the blood on the key, which now refuses to turn in the lock, and how all of us have been kept prisoner in this house; no one who dies here gets to leave, nor does any living wife once she sates her curiosity with a peek into the one place her husband forbade her. For if it was to be *her* fate, this matrimonial murder most foul, most unfair, then why should any other suffer less? No one shall leave, not any of us and certainly not her husband. Too many years have been spent in patient anticipation, waiting for the right time, for the right wife to bring with her the necessary tools for her husband's demise.

She wishes to take her time tearing him to pieces.

"She's nothing but pain and rage and hate," the girl says. "You hurt a person bad enough, they stop being a person at all. Vengeance is all she is now."

"And we have robbed her of even that." I squeeze the ambuscade in my good fist. Suzette has left the tiny globe in my keeping; the talisman I wear seems to veil it well enough — from both First Wife and my own urges. "She waited all this time and we took him from her."

"You cannot know any of this," Charlotte says. "'Tis nothing more than idle speculation."

Suzette glares at the woman. "You try having her inside o' you, squirming 'bout like a belly full o' polecats all fixing to sink their fangs. I know what she is now, and what she wants. I know it more'n anyone here and I won't be having it said elsewise."

"It's worse than it ever was," Gabrielle wails. "We had the whole house to hide from him, and now we're trapped in this awful room where... where..." As she begins to sob, Marie-Jeanne drifts to her side. She presses her cheek against the other woman's shoulder and hums, a soft and comforting tune that I remember my mother singing to me as a child. Gabrielle clutches Marie-Jeanne's arm and sobs harder.

She is right. This is worse. We cannot stay here, two living women and four dead ones — eventually to be six dead if we cannot figure an exit from this chamber that stinks of vomit and urine and fear. Wrestling with Suzette has caused the wound in my right hand to bleed most generously, and my mouth is dry with thirst.

"We have to reason with her," I say. "It makes no sense to punish us along with him; we are his victims as much as she was."

"You can't reason with what she is, Madame."

"Then perhaps we can bargain." I march across to the marble basin, scrubbed as clean now as the rest of the room.

"Madame, no!"

Ignoring the girl, I place the ambuscade in the empty bowl where it rolls a little before coming to rest in the centre. "First Wife," I whisper. The stale air presses close about me, and I clear my throat. "First Wife, see what I have here." The room chills, the skin on my arms itches.

She is listening.

"You may have him," I tell her. "You may have him all to yourself. But first you must deliver us our liberty." I glance behind me: the wives, clustered together, are watching. "All of us, those with breath and those without. For we are as you find yourself — most grievously wronged."

The air tears apart with a shriek as the basin is lifted two clear feet above the floor then thrown against the wall with such force that the marble shatters, sending pieces ricocheting across the room. I touch a hand to my cheek; it comes away red. Gabrielle is weeping again, and Suzette is crawling through the rubble, fingers frantically searching, until — there! — a faint glow, and I hasten to her side, crouching to take hold of her wrist. "Do not touch it! Remember the last time." Instead, I retrieve the thing myself, dust it clean on my skirts.

"First Wife." My voice is stronger now. "Release us from this place, from this house, and we shall surrender our husband to your keeping. You cannot retrieve him yourself now; you must realise that. If you keep us locked in this chamber until we are all of us wraiths, what will that gain you?"

Nothing, for near too long. Gabrielle begins to speak but Suzette shushes her. My temples throb.

"You have my word," I say. The bandage on my injured hand is half undone. Wincing, I unwrap it the rest of the way, cross my wounded palm to my breast. "My blood oath, as one wife to another. He was your husband first; he will be yours to the last."

The pressure in my head eases, the chill lifts from the room.

And the great chamber door creaks open.

The house is in utter disarray. Drapery has been torn from the windows and furniture flung about as though by a giant's fist, while the dining room chandelier glitters in shards on the table, and half the balustrade lies in splinters over the stairs. Suzette and I pick our way with care. Charlotte and the other wives glide easily in our wake.

"Why destroy the house now?" I mutter. "She hasn't so much as blown a candle out before."

"She *is* the house, Madame. Would you pull out your own hair? Your own fingernails? She must be desperate to be tearing herself apart."

"Desperate?" Charlotte snorts. "Spiteful, perhaps."

"Spite's got nothing to do with it," Suzette says. "It's fury and frustration that makes her mad."

"But if she can do all this..." I wave at the destruction around us. "Why did she not dispense with our husband years ago? He was a man; murderous and evil, but still a man. His neck would have broken clean as any other's."

Suzette rubs at her forehead. "I don't think she could. It felt like... like his death made her this way, made her stronger. Made her... *full*." Her voice lowers to a whisper. "Let's leave, Madame. Break a window if that's what's needed, but please... let's leave now."

Charlotte clears her throat. "Is it *she* or merely us that you suppose hard of hearing?"

"Enough," I say. "Suzette, let us be done with this." Though clearly miserable, the girl nods. I touch her shoulder. "It's the only way. She will allow none of us to leave otherwise, which will likely be the least of our troubles."

The bedchamber is so cold my breath frosts the air. The ceiling-high window where Marie-Catherine stands watch is shattered, its curtains torn on the jagged splinters caught in the wooden frame. Their tattered shreds flap and tussle in the winter breeze, and yet she does not move from their path, does nothing but turn her head as our motley brigade enters the room, her gaze shifting through us and past us just as surely as the curtains slice through her spectral form. Henriette rushes to her side, clasps one of Marie-Catherine's hands within her own, but whatever words she finds to whisper into her friend's ear remain unacknowledged.

Gently, I push Suzette forward. For the first time, there is more than just discomfort in this chamber; I can sense the profound unease of which the wives have spoken. The skin on the back of my neck prickles, and I recall the last time I saw Charles and the way his fingers scratched at the air over his own nape, and wonder if the phantom breath of which he spoke felt equally chill. Was it really true that none of my predecessors had brothers or fathers nearby at their moment of need — or, rather, at *hers*? I do not wish to think upon the number of wives who might have followed had I, too, been bereft of kin to summon to her vengeful cause. The poker my husband wielded had such a sharp hook; I would not have made a pretty wraith.

Sitting cross-legged on the floor, Suzette smooths her skirts neatly about herself before holding out her hand. With only the barest hesitation, I lean over and place the ambuscade upon her palm.

Whatever dread event I was expecting, it does not manifest. The room remains cold. The wind continues to blow through the broken window. The wives keep watch in silence.

Letting loose a long, tremulous breath, Suzette closes her eyes and rolls the ambuscade between her hands as though it is a tiny ball of dough. All the while she mutters, words that rumble low and deep, their meaning well beyond my comprehension, and after a time the sphere seems to elongate between her palms, its shape stretching well beyond true. It glows brighter than before, brighter than the first peek of dawn, and the warmth it radiates draws me closer, closer, until I am crouching right beside the girl, fixed to the working of her hands. Their motions are wondrous strange.

When first it appears, the crack is thinner than an eyelash and scarce as long, and as I watch a fine tendril of mist snakes forth, describing a lazy spiral towards the ceiling.

"Suzette, look…"

The girl's eyes widen, as though she did not truly anticipate the success of her ministrations. Then she shakes her head, tears welling. "No," she whispers. "I won't let it go. I thought I could, but… I need him." And her hands close tight.

"You must continue. We have given our word."

"Your word, not mine." The girl drops her gaze. "I'm not a wife; I didn't use the key. *I* could leave."

Even as I reach for her, desperately trying to prise her fingers apart with my own — because she cannot leave, she *cannot* — Suzette lets forth an awful moan and starts to shake, her body rocking violently back and forth. First Wife, wronged and wrathful — surely, this time she will not release the girl.

"Suzette," I shout, inches from her face. "Let him loose. Let him loose now!"

The talisman sways between us, and I wrench it over my head, cheeks chafed by the leather thong, in the hope that it will shield Suzette from First Wife as well as it does me. But there is no time to give it to her: the moment the necklace leaves my person, that wrathful focus narrows and pivots and then —

— I'm flying across the room, slamming against the wall with such force I fear I may never breathe again.

The talisman falls from my hand.

One of the wives screams.

Suzette is shrieking as well, and I wrap my arms around my head, trying to blot it out, trying to blot everything out, the noise and the sharp new pain that pierces my side with each hard-drawn gasp, until —

— silence. Or nearly so, just a faint, delicate keening.

Marie-Catherine kneels before Suzette, who is swaying only slightly now with lips parted slack around the reedy noise she makes. "Stop," the woman murmurs as she stares into the girl's terrified eyes, into the eyes of the being that hides within. "Stop now. It is done. It is done."

Suzette's hands fall open.

The ambuscade tumbles, bounces, and —

splits

— and here he comes, my husband, our husband, *her* husband, coalescing in mid-air with the tormented roar of a lion caged. Wheeling around, he takes all of us in, his wives, and that vicious snarl narrows to a sneer. I force myself to my feet, determined to stand between whatever evil he intends and the women upon whom he would visit it. But no need — oh! — no need, for that same force which tossed me as readily as an autumn leaf now ensnares him in its grip and tears him quite asunder.

Blood falls, red and dry as spectral rain. The whole house shudders and shakes. And falls into satisfied silence.

I stumble over to where Suzette lies, curled tight and whimpering. "Hush, come now." Teeth clenched against the stabbing pain in my side, I pull the girl to her feet. "We must leave."

She coughs. "There's no rush, Madame. She has what she wants."

"My husband? Did you not see? She has done away with him simple as blinking — she will vent her wrath on us next."

"No, she merely plays — a cat with a mouse. As she has done before."

I consider his missing tongue, and the deep scratches in his cheeks. Charlotte steps forward. "You cannot kill what is already dead, little dove."

"And if she seeks other mice with which to play?"

"This is my home. I intend to remain here."

"And you, Marie-Catherine?"

The woman in the pale peach dress smiles and pushes her hair away from her face. Her mutilated eye is no easier to witness. "We are safe. We are *all* safe." The ghost of a smile flashes across her mouth. "All but *him*."

"Madame!" Suzette grabs my right wrist, her face alight with wonder. "See!"

And I do. For the first time since my husband pressed his burning key into my palm — *her* key, *her* tireless wounded magic all this time — the sore has ceased its constant bleeding. A clear fluid still weeps from its centre, but the edges are miraculously crusted and dry.

My hand, at long last — my poor little hand is healing.

It should come as less of a surprise to me that the remains of my husband's wealth smooths many paths. It kept him in wives for years, after all, kept both the curious and the priggish from his door in equal measure. And of course it paved the neat and slippery road upon which I found my own self, skating with girlish naivety into his arms on the promise of a life easier led — a most cardinal sin, judging by the sanctimonious looks Suzette and I receive upon stumbling into the village, to wish for safety, for security, to value such things above the luxurious romance of love.

But for the midwife who stitched the cut in my cheek and fussed over my fractured ribs, who provided a basin of warm water for the both of us to bathe the grime from our bodies, a coin pressed into her palm means a new roof for her cottage and several young chickens to provide her with eggs each morning.

For the constabulary to whom I reported the ransacking of my house by brigands unknown, and who undertook with oaths solemnly sworn to keep regular watch over the premises in my most understandable absence, a handful of gold will procure two swift steeds for the stables.

For the men engaged to repair the windows and board up the premises, as well as for the broad-shouldered warden who will stalk the grounds with his dogs of a night, my husband's money makes plentiful the food on their dinner tables and well-made the clothes on the backs of their families.

I was never alone in my desire for security.

Across from me in our newly acquired carriage, Suzette slumps and snores. The girl is exhausted and I do not begrudge her the rest I cannot yet find for myself, so tumultuous are my thoughts. Two letters awaited me in the village for several days, both from my sister, Anne. The first advised that our mother's illness had worsened considerably and, though it pained her to defy the urgent summons of our dear brother, neither she nor our mother would be able to visit. If it were at all possible, might I come to them for a few days instead? The second, scrawled in obvious haste, expressed relief that I no longer had need of her immediate presence and thanked me for the sum I had sent — she suspected it might be put to use in part in the arrangement of our mother's funeral, so dire is her condition. She failed to understand why I had not sent word, why I had not come.

I hope our mother is still alive; I hope the four horses pulling us through the night are fast enough.

If not, I hope Anne will forgive me.

"You should sleep, dearheart," Henriette says. She has sat beside me for the entire distance, gaze fixed to the rushing world beyond the window. Even now, when there are only stars and the shadows of branches to see, she does not look away. Gabrielle and Marie-Jeanne flit in and out of the carriage as suits their whims, perching at times upon the roof or squeezing in beside our oblivious coachman. My talisman, fashioned from the wedding band our husband gave and took from each of us in turn, is enough to provide them an anchor — though for how long Suzette cannot say. *Wraiths without a place get windblown, Madame. Only the dead know what happens after that.* Even so, none of the three wished to remain behind in the house where they had been so gruesomely murdered. Perhaps they will like the home I will share once again with my mother and sister. Perhaps they will find an anchor there.

"I see too many things when I close my eyes," I say to Henriette.

"They will diminish in time," she replies. "I can assure you of that."

I trace a finger over the key-shaped scar in my palm and think of First Wife, stalking her husband for eternity, tearing him to vengeful shreds over and over again and, with him, what remains of herself. I think of Charlotte and Marie-Catherine, and hope they are safe. I have promised to keep the house for them, and for First Wife, as long as I am able.

Some things will never diminish. Some wounds will never heal.

I close my eyes regardless and wait for sleep. If the wind does not blow too harshly, I might yet find for myself a place in this world.

AFTER MIDNIGHT

And so it comes to this: sequestered in one of the guest wings of the palace, where my stepsisters have stayed before me, while SHE is safely ensconced in my own chambers. The *Queen's* Chambers — but although HER son may indeed be King one day, SHE shall never be Queen. ~~Not while I breathe~~.

Perhaps those are not words I should commit to paper, lest the Fates be tempted too sorely.

I have been told nothing about HER other than what SHE has in HER belly. The future of the kingdom, my husband insists. It would be no small irony indeed if what came out in the end was nothing more than another squalling girl-child, as useless as he deems the three daughters I have given him.

No, not useless, not entirely: he has already married off H—, our eldest, to cement an alliance in the west; negotiations for the hand of L — remain unresolved but promising. As for dear little S—, I fear she will end her days a spinster. Even now, although nine years of age, she can barely speak a sensible sentence and has proven a dullard when it comes to learning her letters. She can count and, in fact, counting is almost all that she does with her days — counts the flowers in the garden, the tiles on the floor in the hall, the boiled eggs that are brought to the table for breakfast. If she were prettier, her proclivities might not prove an obstacle but, with her flat features and perpetual scowl, she has only her father's name to recommend her — and who will care overly about the third princess in line once there is a prince waiting to ascend the throne?

No, she will likely remain with me until the end of her days. Or mine.

"You are Queen," my husband assured me. "You will always be Queen." Not, *my* Queen, I note. He has not called me that for many a year.

Oh, there have been others — pretty girls with hope and fancy in their eyes; silly girls easily appeased by a fistful of gold once he tires of them. There may even have been other illegitimacies, although I have been spared the knowledge of them. I have had my dalliances as well, of course. There is no shortage of fine young men with honour enough to guarantee silence.

We have been discreet, my husband and I. Although the first bloom of love may have faded as fast as a midnight frost, we have no wish to humiliate each other nor to bring suspicion upon our alliance. He was once the Prince who lifted me from the hearth, brushed the ashes from my skirts and restored me to my true station — he has always recognised my worth.

Besides, there are too few ways to rid oneself of an unwanted Queen, especially one who has cultivated the adoration of her subjects, who has inspired story after fanciful story of pumpkins turned to coaches and mice to prancing horses.

Even one whose womb has borne no fruit for almost a decade.

It is the perfect subterfuge, my husband says. This girl, according to both the wise woman whose head will roll if she is wrong and the King's physician whose head will remain neatly atop his shoulders no matter the outcome, this girl carries a *son*. An heir. The bloodline must flow forward, and my husband is unready to relinquish power to his cousin, already furnished with three strapping boys. *His* children should inherit the crown, he has said many a time. It should be *his* children, *his* grandchildren, with no shadow cast over succession.

For my part, I understand too well the need to employ all means an end may justify. If I had been in my stepmother's shoes all those years ago, I too may have butchered the feet of my daughters in order to place them upon the very throne where I have found a perch. At the side of the King, I am safe. I am powerful. I am assured of neither sweeping a hearth nor counting a single lentil ever again. Would that not be worth a pesky toe or two?

Enough of such thoughts. Dinner is late and my stomach pinches. A guest in this wing has never been treated so ill before, I warrant. But I shall wait until the sun has completely set before ringing the bell a second time. I have learned nothing if not patience over the course of my life. Patience, and timing.

G— herself brought me my meal last night, having been the only one of my Ladies to have been retained. In service to the Royal Family for most of her life, I suppose she has been deemed the most trustworthy.

The girl has been furnished with an entirely new retinue, a trio of young women from across the sea who speak barely a word of our tongue but whose lands are famed for their advances in midwifery. It is a plausible enough story for Court, or so we hope — a long awaited conception followed by complications and thus a prolonged but necessary confinement. The midwives, naturally, will be dismissed the moment the child is born — the moment *before* he is placed into my waiting arms. Paid well for their services and their secrecy — if indeed they even suspect the secret they keep — and waved off home.

I enquired of G— as to HER health. Does SHE sicken in the morning as I did with all three of my girls? Do HER ankles grow fat? Has SHE the butterfly rash that ruddied my face with each of my pregnancies?

"SHE does well enough, Majesty," was all G— would say. Was it my imagination, or did that *Majesty* have an edge to it? Although I pressed her, as she brushed out my hair and readied me for bed, she continued to deflect my questions about all that goes on in the Queen's Chambers, of all that SHE does with HER days.

SHE does well enough, Majesty.

"It's only four more moons," G— told me with a smile I could not decipher.

Four moons! I took but three nights to hook my Prince's heart. What could SHE do with so much time? ~~What could~~

No. I must stop this. I am the Queen. Mother of the Princesses. Soon to be Mother of the Prince and Heir Apparent, whom I will raise as my own flesh and blood ~~if it kills me~~. My own flesh and blood — I can afford nothing less. When it comes to being a stepmother, however secret the role, I have had ample tuition in what *not* to do. ~~And even if she~~

No, I will not write it down. I will not even think it.

I am Queen. *I will always be Queen.* Woe betide any STRUMPET who seeks to dislodge me from my throne.

I have checked — they have not locked the door to this wing, although there is a guard posted outside the door. He stood to attention when I poked out my head and stuttered a nervous, "M'lady?" before I ducked back inside. He is young, that guard, and he has a pretty face. Clearly a fresh recruit. I do not know whether to be affronted by the assumption that I require a mere child to keep me in place, or relieved. But of course, he is here to ensure that no curious soul enters these quarters, rather than preventing myself from leaving them. I wonder who they have told him it is that he guards. If I desired it, I could wait until the lad grows drowsy and dim. It would be nothing to slip past him then.

But some cards are best kept in hand.

At least these rooms are warm. I have stoked the fire well, using the logs that G— piled beside the hearth earlier this evening. It is not work for a *Queen* but one does not entirely forget the skills of one's youth, no matter how repellent their memory.

Still, I wish I were in my rightful chambers. The windows to the south overlook the Queen's Garden and allow for a view of the hazel tree that I ordered moved there from my father's house. ~~She~~ It does not seem to have thrived as ~~she~~ it did where it was first planted, but I could not bear to leave ~~her~~ it behind when I came to live in the palace. The pigeons that once nested in its branches flew away years ago. Perhaps the tree misses them, and pines. I wish I could see it now. I wish I could steal out into the moonlight and press my brow against its trunk.

Tomorrow, I will demand that the remainder of my library be brought to these rooms. I am certain that SHE will not be in need of it. I doubt very much that SHE has even been taught her letters.

They have brought less than a quarter of my books.

G— said the removal of any greater number from the Queen's Chambers might cause suspicion. I did not care for the manner in which she spoke, not meeting my eye, as she arranged them on their little shelf.

I am certain that she is keeping something from me.

The strangest thing — last night, in the middle of the night, I was awakened by a sharp pain in my foot. I sat myself up and saw, by the guttering light of the fire, a movement beneath the bedclothes. Then came another pain, like the bite of a small, sharp-toothed creature and I admit to crying out in surprise. I whipped off the coverings and there, perched with its little paws together in an attitude of prayer, was a rat. He was a large fellow, with a streak of silver down his spine.

I am not afraid of vermin, but nor did I wish to suffer another nip, and so I moved to kick my furry visitor away. The curious, bright-eyed expression with which it held my gaze, however, gave me pause. Head cocked to one side, the rodent wrinkled its nose at me then made a high-pitched chittering noise and scampered from the bed to vanish into the shadows beneath it.

Only then did I see what it had left behind.

The ring was the one my mother had given me before she died. It had been her mother's ring before her and I had worn it on a chain about my neck until my father remarried. My stepmother, catching sight of it one morning as I cleaned, deemed the thing too precious for a child to wear as a mere bauble and took it away — for safe-keeping, she said. I had not laid eyes on it since. I have no idea how the rodent came by the ring, nor why it decided to return it to me. It sits easily on my index finger now and I like how the small ruby in its setting sparkles when I hold it to the light.

Regardless, I made sure to remove it when G— came with my breakfast. The woman has a sharp eye and a mind made to keep inventory; she would spot the ring immediately and know it had not come from the Queen's Jewels. Then she would ask questions and might mention it to someone else, to my husband even. But it is my ring, and I would keep it a secret. The Queen should be allowed a secret or two, although heaven knows it has been years since my every possession, my every step and sigh, was solely my own.

I inquired after my stepmother and G— gave me a surprised glance. Why did I care to know about that woman, she wanted to know. As far as she was aware, my stepmother was still living with my father, growing ever poorer under his roof and withering title.

"But has she not paid a visit to the palace recently?" I asked.

"Not since the royal wedding," G— said.

I smiled to hear it. My stepmother knows how unwelcome she is and would not dare curry further disfavour.

I am glad to have my mother's ring once more, whatever the means by which it reached me. Later, I shall ask to be escorted to the Queen's Garden. I wish to visit the hazel tree. It is spring; perhaps the birds have returned.

The rat continues to bring me gifts, waking me in the witching hour with a nibble on my toes. Pieces of jewellery from my own collection — not ones that I had worn often, but still mine — among others I do not recognise. Gold rings and bracelets, studded with gems; necklaces and chokers, both ornate and plain. Even a brooch that appears to be carved from jet. I dare not wear any of it. There is, however, a small compartment in my dresser and I have hidden it all inside, beneath one of my embroidered shawls.

Despite my demands, I have not been permitted to leave these rooms, even briefly. When my husband first came to me with his plans, we discussed such matters and decided that I would be allowed a modest walk of the grounds at dawn or at dusk — alone and incognito — so that I might take in the fresh air — but this has not yet come to pass.

G— is adamant that there is too great a risk. I might be seen and recognised. She reminds me, as though I am a simpleton, of the ruse in which we all now take part, so necessary to protect the future heir, my future *son*. No one outside the innermost circle of the court must know that I am not the child's mother.

"The Crown must be secure," she says.

"Your husband has enemies," she says.

"Any whiff of illegitimacy would be a threat," she says.

I have heard these words so many times; they are beginning to wear thin to my ears.

I fear I will go insane in these rooms. This morning I burst into tears for no reason while G— dressed my hair. ~~I could not stop crying~~. She appeared frightened and tried to comfort me. I have crescents in my palms, so tightly did I clench my fists.

But one good thing has come of it — my husband visited with me this afternoon for almost an hour. We sat and he held my hand in his and told me again that he worried for me and that it pained his heart to see me so fretful. I would always be Queen, he assured me, I would always be the mother to his children — *all* of his children — and I had nothing to fear. Three more moons and this confinement would be over. Three more moons and I would have a new baby boy to love. A new baby *prince*.

Did I not realise how important my role would be? Mother to the Prince. His eyes were kind as he pleaded with me.

"Why can SHE not be here instead?" I found myself asking. I hated the whine in my voice. I shudder, even now, to remember it. But I continued nevertheless — why should I be the one banished from my own chambers, from my beloved garden and the rest of the palace, while SHE is free to roam at will? It was not fair.

My husband frowned and regarded me as though I were a child.

He assured me that SHE is not free, any more than I am. SHE is confined to the Queen's Chambers, as much as I am confined to these accommodations, with rumours of ill health spread daily. HER new ladies in waiting are the only ones to see HER, with the King's physician as intermediary, and he leads them to believe that the woman they wait upon is the Queen.

"No one must know, my darling. It is the most important secret you will ever keep."

I felt foolish, the blood rushing to my cheeks. I knew this, every word of it. How could I have forgotten? While he was here, I felt calm and reassured. I could look into his eyes and see only sincerity and warmth. The strength I have always seen in him. But now my rooms are empty and I find myself fretting once more. ~~If only~~

Part of me wishes I had not agreed to this subterfuge. I had not expected the confinement to be such a trial. I wish I had my daughters with me — even S— would be a comfort, if not a thrilling conversationalist. I hope they are all happy on their tour abroad and that their tutors and governess are taking good care of them. But I also hope that they miss me as I miss them, and that they think of me as they lie on their pillows each night, and keep me in their prayers.

Me, and their soon-to-be little brother.

If I am not to leave these rooms until the birth, I think I shall go mad with only my own company to keep. I told G— as much and she merely smiled.

"Your own company is fine company," she said. "Anybody would be glad of it."

I have read all the books.

I am sick to death of embroidery.

I find myself sleeping too much and too soundly, woken only by the nibble of a rat's tooth on my toes, or the gentle shake of a shoulder by G — when she brings me my meals.

"Do you attend upon HER so solicitously?" I asked of her this morning.

"I attend upon her as she needs, Majesty."

"And does my husband attend upon HER also? As she needs?"

G— paused at that, before saying that I must not fret myself to pieces. The King attends upon HER daily, I was told, as propriety demands. What would the palace think if he did not visit his ill Queen during her confinement? G— assures me that I need not to worry. All is proceeding to plan.

I am trying not to worry.

But it has never been *my* plan. I merely acquiesced to play my part.

The rats have not been to visit for days. It is strange to write it, but I find myself missing him.

Of all the unexpected things — a visit from my younger step-sister!

Balancing a heavily laden tea-tray, G— escorted her to my rooms this evening. Even hidden beneath a veil and a cloak of midnight blue, I recognised M— by her tread before a word was even spoke, by that limp which has remained her whole life, despite the golden toe she had cast for herself after her marriage.

Why was she here, I demanded to know the moment that G— withdrew. I kept my voice low, not wishing the guard beyond the door to overhear.

"I have often visited you," she replied. "*Sister.*"

The emphasis on that last was not lost on me but I held my tongue, examining as I always do the shape of her nose, the furrow that deepens between her eyebrows whenever she frowns, even the shape of her fingers as they lift a teacup to her mouth. As the years pass, she looks more and more like me. Like my father. Like her father. We have never spoken of it directly but we both know the truth. A half-measure of the same blood runs through our veins; her older sister's as well, no doubt, although the resemblance is not as perceptible. Little wonder, then, that my father remarried so quickly after my mother's death. To a woman with many hard-worn years under her belt, no less, and two mewling daughters dragged along in her wake.

Both my step-sisters are older than me, a fact I have contemplated often. Why did he marry my mother if he loved another — loved her enough to bring her into his home after so many years apart? Did he love my mother at all? Was the match with her a more advantageous one?

I could ask him if I truly wished to know. But what has passed cannot be undone and forgiveness is only for those who ~~desire~~ deserve it. I do not count my father among that number. He who cast me aside as though I were naught but a soiled rag, or a stone that became stuck in his shoe during an ill-fated journey. My step-mother I can almost understand, coming into a second-hand nest with one scrappy chick left to tend — but my father, oh! My father turned his back and left me to her. Left me in the cinders and the ash, and then called me *filth*. No, not even in my mother's memory will I talk to that man again. Let him rot.

But come, I digress.

M— knows of the plot, it seems, having been instrumental in its architecture. SHE who bears my husband's son was employed in her very household! Came into this palace under her auspices! M— saw how my husband looked at the girl, took careful note no doubt, and when SHE began to show, sat HER down and questioned HER. It was M—, I learned, who brought the WRETCH here a second time, brought HER to my husband's attention once again. I am livid at the thought.

"I did not think this would come to pass," M— told me, gesturing to the room around us. The girl was a good maidservant and my step-sister only wanted to help HER. M— liked HER and hoped SHE would one day be her Lady's Matron. The expectation was merely that the King would correct his error with coin enough to allow the girl to keep and care for the child — not that it would be stolen from HER under royal fiat. But my husband's physician stepped in with whispered words and, before M— could protest, the girl was whisked away.

"Why come to me?" I asked her coldly. "What benefit does it bring you?"

M— put down her teacup with care, although her fingers trembled and the cup clattered rudely against the saucer.

"You do not have to allow the situation to continue," she said. "You have the power to put a stop to it all and demand the girl go free."

I was taken aback by the sudden tears that glossed her eyes. My step-sister who, as a young woman, had taken a carving knife to her own toes in hope of securing a future for herself, weeping over a servant! Irritated, I demanded that she dispense with these ill-veiled lies and tell me the truth. What did she really want?

Lowering her head, M— dabbed at her eyes with a lace-trimmed handkerchief. "I love her," she said. "I would do anything for her." I can still hear the catch and shudder in her voice as she spoke those words.

"As a daughter," I ventured when I found my speech again. "As you would love a daughter?" My step-sister had proved barren after all; it would be no great shock to find her motherly affection spoiling for an object.

But M— merely held my gaze and said, again, "I love her. Not as a daughter; not as a sister."

There has been talk seeping from her household for years. I had her married off to an old, cantankerous Lord who, folks whispered snidely, cared more for hunting and drinking and gambling than he did for women. I herded both my step-sisters into marriages that would see them well-kept, and which would be advantageous to the Crown, but I cared little for what happiness might result. In truth, I took a certain satisfaction in seeing them attached to men I would not deign so much as to spit upon. Although there has been no issue from the marriage (unlike my older step-sister with her brood of six), Lord F— seems not to care. He has brothers to whom his estate may pass, should there be anything left of it upon his death. My husband sits a card sharp at the gambling tables; much of Lord F—'s losses flow to the royal coffers. The arrangement is satisfactory to all.

I had dismissed the rumours that surrounded M— until now. A childless woman in a loveless marriage — of course there would be speculation of dalliances. Although the talk of pretty young chambermaids spending the night in her rooms ...

This evening, I looked into her face and knew the stories to be true.

Was she so lonely, I wanted to know, that she would seek solace in the arms of a girl? Were there no pretty boys in her household, no handsome young groom or guard to summon to her bed?

She smiled then, a chill and callow grin that I did not care to see. "Not at present," she replied. "But I shall make sure to install a worthy selection for when next you come to call."

I blushed at that, my cheeks growing hotter yet with annoyance. I hate to blush, or weep, or show any signs of weakness, especially before my step-sisters. My victory over them, and over my step-mother, is tarnished by such displays.

I told M— that there was nothing I could do, that what has been set in motion cannot now be stilled, not when the hand of the Crown itself drives it on. Why should she care, in the end? The girl would be returned to her in a matter of moons, empty-bellied and ready for the play-pen once more.

M— winced at that and, for the fleetest of moments, I regretted my cruelty. But she brought this upon herself; she brought it upon us all.

"You are not so naive," M— said in a low voice. "I know you are not."

"Neither are you," I retorted. Did she think that, even if I ~~could help them~~ helped them, she and the girl might run away like a pair of wayward lovers? That they might set up house and hearth to raise the baby together? I have heard of such *Sapphic* arrangements in other, less civilised, lands but not here. What did she think could come of my interference but a public flogging? Or worse?

M— narrowed her eyes. "Don't presume the hearts of others to be as mercenary as your own, sister." She assured me that the girl does indeed return her feelings, but even if that were not the case, it would make no difference to her actions now. She does not wish to surrender her baby; this situation had been forced upon her as much as it had on me. Surely I must see that? Surely I must too feel impelled to assist a young woman in need?

I stared at her, willing ice and steel into my gaze. "It is not her baby to keep. 'Twas my husband's seed that planted it; by rights, he shall reap the harvest."

My step-sister left soon afterward, first gathering herself into her cloak and veil. She did not look at me again and I did not turn to see her leave but waited, spine straight, until I heard the door close softly behind her. Her accusations are preposterous! Of course the girl will be dismissed once ~~her the~~ my baby is born. With a purse full of gold, no doubt, and a head full of plans to seduce some ~~other foolish~~ unwitting wretch. Such girls forge careers lying upon their backs; this one is different only in that she will make delivery of a Prince. I would not have thought M— so foolish as to be seduced by such a creature.

I certainly am not.

G— arrived just now to assist me with my bath, but I sent her away.

I do not wish to speak to her, nor to any other person. The jug of water she left behind grows cold beside the basin. I will not bathe tonight. I am Queen and can do as I wish.

The rat returned tonight and brought with him several friends. They nipped at my toes until I awoke, then scampered from the bed and scuttled over to the door where they waited with noses twitching, seeming for all the world like strange miniature dogs begging to be let outside. My toes were bleeding and left marks behind on the floor. The door, unlocked as always, opened almost soundlessly on its well-oiled hinges. The same young guard was slumped on the ground, dozing.

Carefully, following the lead of the rats, I tiptoed past him.

The palace was quiet, and cold. The little rodents led me through the halls, their claws clicking on the bare stone as they hugged the walls. I kept to the carpets that lined the centre of the halls, wishing that I had thought to wear my slippers. It was not long before we were near ~~the Queen's~~ my chambers. Peering around a corner, I could see two guards standing either side of the door; neither looked the slightest bit drowsy. I stepped back, uncertain, my mouth suddenly dry. But ~~one of the rats~~ the rat with the white stripe tugged at the hem of my nightgown, urging me back the way I had come. Dutifully, I followed the bold little creature and soon found myself facing a small, lamplit alcove that I must have passed a thousand times without notice. A framed tapestry hung on the recessed wall; autumn fruits stitched by a patient hand.

Several of the rats chittered below, half scrambling up the wall. The striped rat bit my toe again and I hissed at it, using much strength of will not to raise my foot and stomp the insolent creature flat. The rodent stared at me with bright dark eyes, then looked towards the tapestry and then, I swear, the little fellow *nodded*. Carefully, I lifted the frame from the wall — and gasped. Behind was a hole, no bigger than my wedding ring and shining with a pale yellow light. I pressed a cheek against the stone wall and peered through.

It was ~~the Queen's bedchamber~~ my bedchamber that I looked upon, with HER lying in my bed, lit by an array of candles. I could see her hair splayed on the pillow, her delicate hand clutching the coverlet. And oh! SHE looks like me! My pen shakes even as I put these words down, I am so overcome with ~~fear~~ anger. SHE could be my younger sister — not the cuckoos who came into my home after the death of my mother, but a *full-blooded* sister — or even a *younger* self.

She has the same yellow hair that was my pride before the grey came creeping in. The same figure too, I would warrant — wide of hip with a cinched-in waist so perfectly sized for a ~~princely~~ *kingly* hand to wrap about. Are HER eyes the same brilliant emerald green that I see in my looking glass? Have I judged wrong in thinking the girl so dispensable? Until I looked upon HER, I did not question my husband's interest in anything other than HER issue. ~~But what if he~~

I must remember — I have no friends in this palace. My ladies in waiting are all dismissed and there is only G— who has more loyalty to my husband and to *his* children — no matter the womb from which they spill — than to myself.

SHE looks like me. SHE

I had to leave off just now, to arise and pace and pace until the churning in my stomach quelled. For there is more here to record.

From my secret vantage in the alcove, I could view half the bedchamber. I felt ill then thinking of who else may know about this spyhole, of who may have watched me over the years, and what they might have witnessed. I did not tarry any longer but replaced the tapestry and hurried back to these dull quarters where I am now confined. No dozen fat candles to guard my sleeping self! No coverlet made of fine damask! ~~No~~

Still, be still. There is more.

The young guard was awake and emerging from my room as I rounded the corner. We almost bumped into each other and, startled, I struck his cheek.

What right did he have to enter my private rooms, I demanded to know. What was he seeking? On whose behalf?

The young man looked aghast. He had only nodded off for a moment, he stammered, but had woken to find the door ajar, only entering to ascertain my own safety after his knocking went unheeded. He swallowed hard, more nervous than I have ever known a grown man to be. He was only concerned for me, he said, and was exceedingly grateful to find me now returned, and unharmed.

I pressed a finger to his mouth. "You were asleep longer than a moment, dear boy; I have been gone half the night. What would your captain say if he knew how derelict you have been in your duty? Why, any brigand might have slipped by you and cut my throat!" The boy was ashen. He began to reply but I hushed him with a shake of my head. I would say nothing, I assured him, and neither would he. So long as the rats do not find sudden use of their tongues, who will know?

"We have a secret now," I whispered. "Do you know who it is that you protect, and why?"

"You—you are cousin to the Queen," he said.

"And so my secrets are hers as well." I leaned close and brushed my lips against his cheek. "It is quite a thing to keep a secret for a Queen, and to have her keep one for you."

There was relief in his face when I drew away, and also a spark of longing. Smiling at him, I held a finger to my lips and slipped back inside my quarters. Only then did I allow myself to crumble.

I have been spied upon.

The thought of unknown eyes peering into my bedchamber! I shall ensure my husband knows of the spyhole. I shall have him seal it before I return to

Unless he already knows. Knows and avails himself. Knows and

These quarters are dimly lit by moonlight and the remains of the fire. I have just spent the remainder of the night examining each and every inch of wall, removing every framed tapestry and painting — even rolling up the carpets. My hands spread themselves over every flat surface, including the backs of wardrobes, until, as dawn broke beyond my window, I felt satisfied that no similar spyholes looked upon my current habitations.

In here at least, I am on my own.

I am exhausted. My hands ache. From searching, and from writing all of this down lest I later doubt, and convince myself that it is a dream. I must sleep. I must not crumble any further.

. . .

It seemed I had barely closed my eyes when G— came bustling in with my breakfast tray, her round face aghast at the shambles that I have created.

"Are you ill, Majesty?" she asked. "Is this delirium?"

I managed to choke down the laughter that surged upwards. I was bored, I told her instead. There is nothing to do all day in these quarters and I wished to take a walk in the gardens. She was to tell my husband that I require fresh air, that my humours are disordered. That I might go mad if I am not able to see the sky.

G— looked very grave when she left. I believe that my wish may at last be granted.

I was brought a large sun-hat and a raggedy coat, as well as an old wooden cane. As we left my quarters, G— instructed me to stoop. "*Try to stoop,*" rather, as though I might be unable to accomplish such an outrageous feat of deception. No one must guess who I am, she insisted, offering her arm for me to which I was expected to cling. Assuming the manner of a creaky old crone, I shuffled by her side through the servant passages. Although we did not go through the kitchens, we passed near enough to hear the bustle of people within and catch the aroma of the ovens. My mouth watered.

It occurred to me then that I have never once set foot inside the palace kitchens, nor any kitchen at all since leaving my father's house. A part of me ached to see it. To plunge my fingers knuckle-deep in dough, to smell the rising bread. A foolish want, but still.

The Queen's Garden was quiet, as it usually is, and empty, with not even a solitary gardener in evidence. Vacated for my benefit, no doubt — or, more truly, for the benefit of the King and his precious secret. G— remained at the front gate. She had brought a little lacework with her and set herself upon a wooden bench. The woman's eyes must indeed be sharp for her age; her lacework is very fine and has not diminished in quality over the years. She made each of my daughters a handkerchief for their baptisms with their initials embroidered in cobalt blue — my husband's House colour. I realised that she must now be crafting a piece for ~~HER baby~~ my baby — *my baby* — I must say it again and again until it is true.

I left G— to her work and made my way to the middle of the garden where the hazel tree sulks, all stunted and sparse. There has been only a smattering of yellow flowers each spring and barely any nuts. Those that do grow each autumn have been small and stodgy, and bitter on the tongue.

I pressed my hand against the trunk and closed my eyes. I do not know what I expected; the tree has not spoken to me for years. Regardless, I felt better in her presence. Calmer. Stronger.

Less alone.

From behind me, there came a rustling sound and I turned in time to see a long, pink tail disappear around the side of the tree. I crawled after it and saw that a hole had been dug close to the trunk, between the roots. As I watched, a furry brown head peered out at me and squeaked once before vanishing again.

"I might have known you were behind them," I told the tree. "Run out of birds to do your bidding?" The tree was silent. Gathering my skirts, I sat down and leaned my back against the bark, in what I expect was a most *un*queenly fashion, and I thought about my daughters, away on their tour of the northern lands. I could not convince my husband to allow them to stay, although I would have dearly liked their company from time to time. But not even H—, who will soon be running her own household, can know the truth of our subterfuge.

Girls cannot help but gossip, my husband believes. For all their good intentions, they would tell someone, and that someone would tell someone and that is how forest fires begin. We cannot allow a single spark to fly free. I cannot deny that he is right. Women do gossip. Information is our currency, and our power. With what else do we have to barter in this world?

I must have dozed off at some point for G— had cause to wake me with an apologetic shake of my shoulder. The day was late and she had let time get away from her — she should have come for me well before now. Indeed, the shadows were long and my back spasmed as she helped me to my feet. There was a twig caught in my hair and G— pulled it gently free. She was about to toss the thing to the ground but I stopped her and she placed it upon my outstretched palm instead. I wanted to take a piece of the tree back with me to my rooms. It sits on the windowsill as I write this, thin and dry with a trio of small leaves at its tip.

We were almost out of the garden when I noticed HER. G— placed a cautioning hand on my wrist. She did not take hold — she would not have dared; not even her favour in my husband's household would have pardoned an attempt to physically restrain the Queen — but her voice was firm: "Please keep walking, Majesty. No good can come of this."

I paid no heed. I wanted once more to look upon SHE who has colonised my rightful chambers. I wanted to see HER face in the sunlight.

Moreover, I wanted HER to see mine.

For all my choleric fervour, I did not get within one hundred feet of HER before I froze. SHE was dressed in one of my favourite summer gowns, the one with the butter yellow trim and daffodils woven into the bodice. It had been altered to accommodate HER growing belly. The bonnet that SHE was wearing was unfamiliar, oversized as is the current fashion, but no doubt chosen to conceal HER visage from the casual observer — as was the netting that hung from its rim. SHE was flanked by HER trio of midwives and it was this that gave me pause. I could not let them see me — the risk was too great. G— was right. My husband was right. We have built too flimsy a screen behind which to hide; it would take but a breath to blow it asunder.

Still, my rage simmered and when G— caught up, I turned upon her with a hiss. How could the foolish old woman allow this to happen? How dare *she* be allowed in *my* garden? I was told that SHE was to be confined. Why was SHE not confined?

G— bowed her head. Oh! that I could have struck it from her shoulders!

"SHE is not a prisoner, Majesty. SHE takes the air each afternoon, for her health."

Was there a subtle emphasis in her speech? *SHE* is not prisoner ... as I am, or might be? I have played this over so many times since, I begin to doubt the veracity of my memory. Why, this very evening when G—

brought me supper, her face was as calm and equanimous as stone. My repast was meagre: a slice of bread and a sliver of cold smoked pork, with three fresh figs on the side. When I questioned it, G— frowned.

"You said you were of low appetite this evening, Majesty."

Had I said such a thing? I could not remember, but was not about to admit as much. I dismissed her, ate my paltry supper and remained unsatisfied. SHE will be given all the food she wants, I will warrant. SHE will wish for nothing.

I attempted to leave my quarters again tonight. My young, pretty guard stood to attention when I opened the door but took a step to block my path when I made to leave.

"I have orders to see you remain safe, M'lady."

He spoke nervously but the grip on his sabre was firm. I moved forward and again he blocked my way, this time coming close enough for his leg to brush against my skirts. His beardless face flushed. Please, he begged. It was not safe for me to walk the halls on my own. I bade him accompany me if that were the case but he responded that he must stay at his post, that I must — *must!* — stay in my quarters.

I smiled in my most charming fashion. "Then perhaps," I mused, "you might like to accompany me there."

He took a backward step, stammered "M'lady," in such a high-pitched voice I felt like strangling the poor whelp. Instead, I smiled and smiled some more. I was lonely, I told him, offering my hand for him to take. So lonely and in sore need of companionship.

He is very young, my pretty guard, full of speed with stamina yet to make a satisfactory appearance. But he is sweet as well and did all that I bade him with an endearing keenness. If it were not for the current circumstances, I might have groomed him for a lover. As matters stand now, I doubt that I shall see him again.

I feigned sleep until I heard his breathing deepen, then slipped from the bed. I intended to return to the Queen's Chambers or, more correctly, to the small alcove to spy upon HER and — although I scarce cared to admit it to myself — to make sure that SHE was sleeping alone.

I did not get that far.

A guard whom I recognised from my husband's private retinue, big and burly with a chestnut beard, almost walked into me as he rounded a corner.

"Majesty," he could not quite stop himself from blurting, his eyes wide. Quickly, the man collected himself. "M'lady," he said, more forcefully. "May I escort you back to your quarters? You appear lost."

It was not a question. Nor a choice.

Upon our return, a rat came scuttling down the hall towards us. The bearded seargent attempted to stamp the rodent underfoot but it was too quick for him. I buried a smile in the cuff of my gown.

We caught the young guard exiting my quarters, shirt agape and boots in hand. I noticed a fresh runnel of blood on his foot, as though from a small but ferocious bite. My escort raised an eyebrow at the boy, who muttered a story about checking my rooms for vermin, before sending him on his way. The man apologised for appointing me such insufficient protection. He would himself remain outside my door for the remainder of the night so that I should feel safe within. If there was anything further I required, I need only ask. There was no need for me to wander alone through the palace at night, he told me.

No need to wander at all, his sharp eyes underscored.

It has been more than a week since I have seen my pretty guard. An old soldier, grizzled and taciturn, has taken his place. My hope is that the lad has merely been banished, but I fear for his tongue, not to mention his other parts, as I have no doubt that my husband was informed of our transgression. The King commands absolute devotion from his personal guard; they hold all of his secrets, and keep none from him. I can trust not a man of them.

Neither do I trust G— with her flat eyes and mouth now set in a perpetual line. I am sure she must report to my husband and his advisors. I have not been permitted to leave my quarters since that afternoon in the garden. It is for my own protection, G— assures me — and, of course, for the protection of the Crown. If it were to become common knowledge, this plot to produce a legitimate heir, then we would all of us pay dearly. Without an heir, my husband's younger brother would petition to install his eldest son on the throne, a squirrelly weasel-faced boy and my husband's least favourite nephew, with himself as regent.

I know she speaks the truth. This does not ease the rub of it.

How much simpler things would be if a Queen would be permitted to rule in her own right. There would be no need for such subterfuge with two capable daughters waiting in the wings. Ah, but there we find the concern: *capable*. A woman could never rule with the same strength, the same cool measure and iron will that a man commands. Better for us to stand beside the throne, to whisper our influence in kingly ears who, if they are wise, will take our counsel into consideration. Certainly, I would not wish to be King, with the responsibility and wisdom that entails; I cannot imagine any woman who would. Leave it to the men. Let them rule the world as we manage our household affairs. We each leave footprints as befit the natural size and shape of our feet.

But I digress with such useless musings.

Let me instead record here that of which I am now resolved: if I am to be refused the freedom of walking out of doors, then no other shall be permitted the liberty of frequenting these quarters while I am in residence. G— has already been instructed to leave my meals in the ante-room. I will make my own fire and dress myself without her aid. Not that I have reason to dress, if all there is to do is stare out of the window, unpick my embroidery, and read my books until I am sick to death of the taste of their words in my mouth.

There is, however, a strange liberty to this existence. I am alone, unwatched and unremarked upon, with no appointments to keep nor petitioners to entertain. I feel almost like a child again, as I was before my mother died. My days belong to me alone; how grating that I am unable to do precisely what I want with them.

I have the rats for company at least. The large one with the silver streak down his back has mustered up a battalion of cohorts and they continue to bring me offerings from their travels. Tonight they brought me an ivory comb entwined with a single golden hair. I can guess to whom it belongs but not why the rats laid it at my feet. What is ~~my mother~~ the hazel tree trying to tell me? I burnt the hair in the fire, enjoying the acrid smell of its too-brief immolation.

One rodent, a small grey creature with aristocratic paws, is in the habit of fetching me little cakes. Such treats have never accompanied any of the meals that I have received from G— and I devour them with relish, content in the knowledge that one less delicacy will pass HER lips. Perhaps the rat has even crawled over the remainder of the cakes, gnawing at the edges and leaving pawprints in the frosting. I relish the notion that all the rest have been thrown away and I am the only one to taste them!

If only my new friends would refrain from nipping my feet to announce their nocturnal visitations. My toes are covered with wounds, some of which are healing less well than others. I asked G— to bring me a pair of fur slippers and she returned with a pair made from softest ermine. It is a relief to slide my poor, bleeding feet into them each day. I do not admonish the rats too harshly; they are my allies and cannot, after all, help their nature.

Last night I dreamed that my step-sister paid me another visit in her cloak and veil, which she did not remove as we strolled in the gardens. I thought at first that they were ~~the Queen's gardens~~ my gardens but, as we walked, I saw flowers that I did not recognise and heard strange bird-song among the trees. Before long, we were meandering through a hedge-maze, the walls of which soared higher than our heads. I do not remember much of what was said between us but I woke with an odd feeling of trepidation and longing.

Of course, I wonder now if there was not some magic to it, as M— indeed came to see me again this afternoon. She was veiled as before, and as in my dream, but her cloak this time was a drab brown. She reminded me of a house sparrow, flitting about from window to chair, refusing to sit still and take tea.

"Look at this place!" she burst out at one point, before admonishing me to allow G— to come in and clean from time to time. I reminded her that I have not forgotten how to clean for myself, and that I shall see to it when I feel the need. She wrinkled her nose at my clothes left in limp piles all over the floor, and at the dishes, which I had not yet returned to the ante-room for collection. I like to leave a portion for the rats to eat, by way of gratitude for their service.

When I asked her why she had come, the look she dared bestow upon me was so steeped in pity that I wanted to claw her eyes from her skull. G— was concerned for my health, M— said, making no attempt to hide her survey of my quarters. She pointed to the hazel twig that I keep propped up in an empty wine jug. Its leaves are still green, if wilted. But they have not fallen.

"What is that wretched thing?" she asked.

"My garden," I told her. "What garden I am allowed to have."

M— shook her head in disapproval. She told me that I have a beautiful garden in which I shall walk once again if only I am clever.

I glowered at her. I am not as stupid as she thinks. I have guessed her plans, I said: she will have her straw-haired slattern installed in my place, with the precious baby boy as bride price and M—'s mouth whispering constantly in her ear. But what did she hope to accomplish, I wanted to know. What did she think it would gain her in the long run?

My step-sister blanched. She has told me already, she said, she did not wish the girl to be here *at all*, let alone on the throne. She had wanted my help to remove her but now — and here she threw her arms in the air, gesturing at the disarray that surrounded us — she could see she was mistaken in her petition. What influence might a mad woman possibly possess?

"More than you," I snapped. Her jealousy was obvious, and pathetic. She has always been jealous of me, I reminded her; she has always wanted what was mine. "Careful how you step, sister. Should I desire it, I can take everything that is yours."

M— was furious. What more could I take, she demanded to know. Banished to an impoverished county with a husband who seems determined to throw every last copper he owns onto the card table. Forbidden by royal decree to see her own mother, for her own mother is forbidden to attend the court or visit the home of any noble family, including her own. Have I not had revenge enough?

"Go back to your household," I said. "I shall send your bitch to heel once she has whelped."

At that, M— flushed and raised a hand, but I took hold of her wrist before she could strike. My fingers dug into her soft flesh until tears sparked at her eyes.

"You would dare contemplate violence against your Queen?" After one final squeeze, I cast her wrist aside and watched with no small amount of satisfaction as she rubbed at her injury. "I could have you executed for that."

M— straightened and smoothed her skirts. "As I understand it, *M'lady*, you are not Queen. *Not while you live in these rooms.*"

I said nothing more but waited until the wretched woman took her leave and silence again settled in the room. Then I picked up the first item that came to hand — a small pewter goblet — and threw it against the wall. It made a somewhat satisfying clatter but I wanted more. A glass soon followed, then plates and a candlestick and anything else not fastened down. It was all *extremely* satisfying. Shortly afterward, as I sat slumped in a chair, examining a modest cut on my index finger, G— bustled into the room with mouth agape. Had she been spying on me? I told her to leave just as quickly, that I had not summoned her and had no wish for her presence.

G— made no reply, merely took my hand in hers and frowned. Then she retrieved a handkerchief from her apron and tied it around my finger, remarking on what a wonder it was that the whole palace had not been brought running at the ruckus.

Ignoring her, I demanded instead that I see my husband. Today.

The old woman looked quickly about the room. "Perhaps tomorrow, Majesty. The King is very busy with matters of court."

I told her again that I would see him today. She would bring him to me.

G— pursed her lips. I can picture that sour disapproval even now. How the crone galls me! She began to gather broken pieces of crockery in her apron and said she would draw me a bath, once this task was done.

"So you might drown me in it," I muttered.

The woman looked at me with such naked fear in her eyes that I knew I had caught her out. There *is* a plot against me and she must surely be a party to it. Have she and M— and the girl all conspired together? Have they planned, the three of them, to seduce the King and usurp my rightful place by his side? It seems clearer and clearer. If the Queen is mad — or dead — or both — then the King would be permitted to remarry ...

I refused a bath and forbade her to finish tidying or to bring me anything more until I have seen my husband.

He must be told what is happening.

He must be told of the conspiracy of these women against ~~me~~ us.

"Fetch my husband to me," were the last words I spoke to G— and I will speak no more, to her or to anyone, until I have seen him. I am sitting, by candlelight, writing this down before I forget too much of it. Outside my window the moon is nearly full. My husband has not visited today but I have a plan of my own. I will wait for the rats to come and then whisper into their ears. "Fetch my husband," I will instruct them. "His wife is in grave peril."

I have written a note for them to take. Once he knows how great my need, he will visit.

Unlike G—, the rats are loyal to me. They will tell him the truth.

They are the only living creatures I can trust.

It has been ~~three four~~ three days since G— attempted to clean my rooms. She has left food in the ante-room that only the rats have eaten. They have all lived but still I worry about poison.

My husband has not visited.

~~When I close my eyes, I can see him with her. Their bodies entwined. Her mouth open, his tongue on her throat. Majesty, he whispers, my Queen.~~

"Majesty," G— whispers in my ear. "Please, we must make you presentable if you are to see the King."

I push her away. Of course she wants me to be presentable. She does not wish for him to see what they are doing to me. It would mean her head.

I refuse to bathe. I refuse to let her brush my hair. I refuse to change into the new gown she has fetched. I refuse to surrender my ermine slippers, although they are stiff with blood.

Fetch me my husband.

Fetch me my husband.

He was here today, unless it was a dream. He held my hand but kept his distance on the edge of the bed. I told him of the conspiracy, of my fears of poisoned food, but he merely shook his head. His eyes were sad, and seemed somewhat — fearful? Of his wife? What terror can he have of me? When I moved to embrace him, he stood up, ~~nose wrinkling in distaste~~.

"Hush," he said. "You imagine too much. G— is your faithful servant; she would do nothing to harm you."

I asked him about M—, if he trusted her also, and he appeared puzzled. My step-sister has not visited for many moons, he told me. I was confusing my fearful dreams with the waking world.

Is he right? Did I conjure M— and her cruel visits only to torture myself? I remember her face so clearly. I remember what she said to me.

I wish I could be certain.

This morning, my head felt clearer and I allowed G— to draw me a bath. She boiled water in my fireplace and added lavender and rose petals. I asked her if my husband had visited yesterday.

"You know he did, Majesty."

And my step-sister, I further enquired. Has M— come these past moons as well, to sit with me in my prison? G— glanced towards the door and when she spoke again it was in a whisper. "You know this too, Majesty, though you be the only one who does. You and me and no other."

"Then you admit to conspiracy?" I retorted. "To placing a cuckoo in my nest?"

G— took a sharp breath. "Not a cuckoo, Majesty, but an innocent robin whose egg will be stolen from her." Her strong fingers worked to untangle my hair. Nothing more was said until she was done. Then, in a low voice, she inquired as to whether I would help them.

I made no reply. I need time to think on this, to figure the exact workings of the plot.

G— asked how I would feel if one of my daughters were taken away from me. If they were given to another to raise and never to know I was their mother. I can not imagine it. Never seeing H— or L— grow, never knowing them at all; even little S—, for all her difficult traits, never to have been her mother but knowing, always, that she was in the world, somewhere, and that I would never again speak to her, to them, my darling daughters — *NO!*

I *will* not imagine it.

Besides, this would not be the case. The girl would know at all times not only where HER son lived but that he was being given the best of all possible upbringings, infinitely better than any maidservant could dream to provide. SHE would see HER son become a Prince, and then a King. How petty a creature SHE must be to deny HER child such a glittering future in order to find solace for HERSELF. No, it is not the same.

If indeed, as I still suspect, SHE had not planned from the very start to beget a child with the vile purpose of holding it to ransom.

Either way, the girl is a pawn. Whether manipulated by M—, with her designs on my position, or by my husband to shore up ~~his own power~~ our power ... what then does it matter?

The child will be looked after. The child will become King.

No *worthy* mother could want for more.

I could not sleep, having been able to think of little else but the girl. My mind turns itself in circles, not knowing where to settle. SHE is a pawn; SHE is cunning. SHE wishes only to keep HER baby; SHE wishes to replace me. M— seeks to help her; M— seeks to have me dethroned. All things seems true. All things could just as easily be false.

This morning, I told G— that I wanted to see HER. I wished to speak to HER, I said, and to look HER in the eye while I did so.

G— was askance. It was impossible, she told me, an impossible thing that I asked. I could not be brought to HER chambers, nor SHE to mine. The risk of someone seeing us together was far too great.

I reminded her of that day in the gardens. I merely wished to speak with the girl directly; I grow weary of hearsay and whispers. I want to hear what SHE wishes from HER own lips. G— pursed her mouth in that familiar, sour way. Finally, after she had finished dressing my hair, she said that she would see what could be arranged.

Last night, I dreamed of walking in the gardens. The hazel tree was lush and heavy with nuts and, upon a branch low to the ground, there perched three white birds. They were not doves, nor any kind of birds I had ever seen. One by one, they sang to me in the voices of my daughters. I cannot now recall, in waking, the words of the songs, but they left me feeling sad and frightened.

I remember reaching out for the birds, wanting to take them into my arms and comfort them, but instead they took flight and circled away from me. Before she flew away, the third bird, the smallest one that I knew to be S—, regarded me with bead-black eyes and spoke words that I have also left behind in the land of dreams. I wish I could remember what she said because it seemed significant. But then, does not everything in dreams seem so?

Wait. I think — no, it is gone.

Gone as my three daughters, flying away into the clear blue sky, leaving me alone on the ground below. In the dream I could somehow see myself from their vantage, growing ever smaller as they soared higher. Smaller and smaller until I could not be seen at all.

G— left me by the hazel tree, which is, unlike the fruitful tree of my dream, as scrawny and sulky as ever. There was no birdsong and, on such an unseasonably warm day, I was glad of the meagre shade. It must have been a good hour, judging by the movement of the shadows, before I heard the whispered voices coming towards me. G—'s hoarse scratching underlying another's softer, higher-pitched tones. I had but a moment to gather my skirts about me and rise, before the pair of them came into sight.

The girl's belly was huge, jutting out like the prow of a galleon, HER dress floating sail-like behind HER. SHE hesitated when SHE saw me, so that G— had cause to nudge HER forward, her wizened lips murmuring words I could not quite hear. The old woman then turned her back on us, keeping a watchful eye on the path down which they had come.

When SHE was within two paces of where I stood, the girl stopped and sketched an awkward, ungainly curtsy. "Your Majesty," SHE said, keeping her gaze averted. "It is an honour and a blessing."

SHE has been schooled in courtly manners, at least!

I made no reply to begin with, merely stood and stared HER up and down, taking in HER yellow hair — so ornately tressed! — HER pale skin — smattered with freckles! — and HER tapered fingers that drummed softly, nervously, over HER swollen mid-section.

"You carry the future of the Crown," I told HER at last.

SHE swallowed and allowed that SHE did. HER eyes — green, as I had suspected — still refused to meet mine. I had expected a different attitude, truth be told, a smug contempt perhaps, or at the very least a naive and bubbling excitement. Not this pallid, craven child so frightened that SHE dared not even look upon me. What had my husband ever seen in HER, this whippet-girl so easily cowed? What does M— see in HER?

I reached out, took HER chin between my fingers and lifted it.

"Would you be Queen?" I asked her.

Eyes wide, the girl stammered a refusal. SHE had no wish to be Queen, SHE assured me, or a Lady or anything more than what SHE was. What SHE was soon to be — and then not.

I reminded her that HER son was to be King. Was that not a wonderful happenstance? Was SHE so selfish as to wish to deny him such a future in order to keep him to HER own lowly breast? My words called forth at last the spark I sought: a flash of defiance, or anger, or something close.

"He would not be *my* son, Your Majesty."

I released HER, suddenly, and SHE stumbled back a pace. A great honour has been bestowed upon HER, I reminded the girl, and SHE would be well rewarded for HER trouble. Besides, with many more children likely in HER future, this first would be soon forgotten. A stubbed toe, healed; a dropped hem, stitched.

HER reply was whispered so low that I could not catch it. Speak up, I told HER. SHE was not a mouse!

"Will you help, Your Majesty? I was told you might help."

"People will tell you many things," I said, "as suits their purpose. You must learn to hear the meaning beneath their words." I stared again at HER belly, resisting the urge to touch it, to feel its taut warmth beneath my palm. It surprised me, the sudden rush of longing that rippled through my body. I do want another child, I realised at that moment. Moreover, I want to *bear* another child, flesh of my flesh, blood of my blood. The scraps from another's table will taste of ashes. ~~But ashes are all I will ever have.~~

Irritated, I instructed the girl to take HER leave. Let HER play at Queen for a while longer, although SHE should not make HERSELF too comfortable. They are borrowed shoes SHE is wearing; they will never fit without pinching. I do not believe any longer that she is the conniving vixen I once thought HER to be. SHE seems too dim, too weak and muddled, for such a role.

No, M— is the clever one, and patient. I can see how cold her vengeance has grown.

I watched the girl waddle back to G— and take the arm that was offered. As the two of them departed, G— glanced over her shoulder at me. The afternoon shadows fell across her face so that I could not quite glean her full expression and, for that, she should think herself lucky. I suspect I would not like what I saw. It is bad enough that I was required to await her return, that I needed to be escorted to my quarters like a querulous child. As I leaned back against the hazel tree, there came a rustling above my head and several yellowing leaves fluttered down. Brushing them from my gown, I looked up to see a rat sitting on a spindly branch, its pink toes curled and clinging tight. The creature stared at me and twitched its whiskers.

"Be off with you," I snapped, flapping my hand at it. "You are not needed here."

The furry beast did not move, but simply sat beyond my reach and chittered disapprovingly. The hazel tree is indeed a pathetic thing: stilted and stubborn, and now infested with vermin! I told it that I would have it cut down when I am Queen once more, and at the time I even meant it. Perhaps I still do. I could plant a rose in its place, a robust and sturdy bush with an abundance of red and ~~fragrant~~ fragrant blooms. I shall have these cut and brought to my chambers so as to surround myself with their perfume and their beauty. ~~It is what I deserve.~~ It is what a Queen deserves.

G— has left just now, having had the temerity to question me about HER. She wants to know, now that I have spoken to the wretch, whether I will help her. Help them, M— and the girl both. And help myself to a sentence of treason into the bargain, no doubt! I cannot quite see the full tapestry they weave together, my step-sister and erstwhile matron, but I can feel my way around its edges.

Why does G— care, I wanted to know. Was she not loyal to the throne? Does she not see what a new prince and heir will achieve?

"I am loyal, Majesty," G— retorted, in a tone I did not care for at all. She was loyal to the throne and to our Lord God above us, she continued, and she trusted in one to do what's best for the other. This deception was not right, surely I must see that? Surely it must wound me?

Oh, how she looked at me then, her eyes brimming with pleading and rebuke. How dare she confront me so! Has she forgotten her place? Has she forgotten mine? I reminded her that I knew full well what it was to endure insults and injury and that she should not suppose I could not bear this current situation. That I could not make a small sacrifice for a brighter, more secure future.

"It is not your sacrifice, Majesty."

Those words still stain the air, even now, hours after G— first spoke them. That woman will sorely regret her liberties. ~~When I am Queen again, I shall~~ When my powers are restored, I shall see her banished.

I have laid out all the jewels my rats have brought me, and have polished each one, arranging and re-arranging them in the hope to scry their meaning. They are worth but a sliver of the Royal Treasury, but would represent a small fortune to, for example, an errant maidservant seeking a new and secret life. Surely this is not why the rats were sent! I have always trusted my mother's gifts but, at present, I cannot tell her intentions. Were these gifted to me as security, in case I am overthrown? In case my daughters are banished? ~~When the new prince is born~~

I wish I could see the whole of it. I wish I could know who I could trust. There is only so far in the future that can be seen; the thread of all possibilities disappears so quickly into the dark.

Help the girl go free and, yes, the threat of an interloper is removed. There will be no wedge to drive into my family. But there will also be no heir and down that path lies such uncertainty. My brother-in-law schemes even now, I am sure, hungry to put his son on the throne. If such an upheaval comes to pass, what then becomes of my daughters and myself?

I cannot lose what I have gained, not again, *not ever again*. I recall how G— ~~spoke to me~~ scolded me, as though she felt she had the liberty and the right. M— as well, with her scorn and her pride, rising above her station. "You are not Queen," she said, "not in these rooms."

They conspire; I know they do. They would have me play this role as liberator only to turn it against me, to turn my husband against me. ~~They would~~

I am so confused and the wine G— left with my supper has only addled my brain. I will think clearer on this in the morning.

I must think clearer.

I need to write down the dream from which I have just awoken. From which the *rats* woke me with their nibbling and gnawing. They are lined up at the end of my bed, the covers sloughed off in a tangle on the floor, and my toes are bleeding again. I have not slept long; the bedside candle is still an inch from guttering.

I do not wish to forget my dream.

There was my mother, or at least a woman I took to be my mother, for I have not been able to picture her face for many years. We were in the bedroom of my father's house, standing by her dresser (except it was *my* dresser, the one with the carved marble top; the Queen's dresser) as she pulled jewel after jewel from the drawers and passed them over to me.

This is for wisdom, she said, and this is for power, and this is for love, and this is for solace — and so on, and on — but each time she laid a jewel into my palm it changed form, becoming a dried leaf, or a pebble, or a bloated toad that croaked once and hopped from my hands. I could not hold on to any of the jewels and the woman who was my mother shook her head in reproof.

It is not my fault, I tried to tell her, but the words lodged in my throat and would not leave.

My feet hurt and when I looked down I saw that I was wearing gold slippers, shiny and too small, and they grew even smaller as I watched, welling with thick, dark blood. Again my mother shook her head.

You left me, I fought to say. You left me, and yet you will not leave me be.

The words were still in my mouth when I woke, bitter and cold.

The rats are all looking at me and I see now that they have ferreted out the pieces of jewellery I had hidden around my quarters. The large, silver-striped rat is sitting on the windowsill, squeaking at me. It holds something glittery in its paws.

I suppose I shall not be permitted to sleep again until I answer its summons.

Oh! It is done. It is over. Now I wait — how much I have waited these past moons; how patient I have been! — for my husband to attend me, as surely he must. I am his Queen and will need to be informed as to how the *situation* has been resolved. He will find me blameless in this, of that I am certain.

The grey light of dawn filters into these quarters and still no word. I tried to speak to the guard again, to at least see if he has returned, but the outer door remains locked. It has never been locked in all the time I have been here. I am a Queen, not a prisoner, as G— often told me.

G—. Where is she now?

~~I have done the right thing. I know that I have done the right thing.~~

I shall write down all that has happened here, while I am waiting. I need to keep my thoughts in a straight line, for I shall be asked about my role in this business.

I shall start ~~at the beginning~~ with the rats. I studiously ignored them while recording my dream, so fresh and vivid my recollection was, so significant it seemed to me upon waking. Although it is faded now and, even reading back upon my words, all import has vanished. All the while, however, they chittered and squeaked until finally I set aside my quill, heaved myself from the bed, and made my way over to the window where the silver-streaked rat waited. In its paws it clutched a large brooch, a cluster of rubies forming a flower at its centre.

It must have been well after midnight but, with the moon nearing her fullest, the courtyard below was illuminated well enough for me to spy three huddled figures scuttling across the cobblestones. They moved slowly — so as to be quiet, I presumed, but also because one of their number was clearly past the point of haste. They were right below me. If they had glanced skywards, they would likely have seen me at the window. Indeed, had I opened the casement, I might have called out to them in tones barely rising above a whisper. I might have taken the trinkets the rats had brought me and thrown them down, a rain of wealth and promise for a mother-to-be.

~~I might have done many things. And even now, as I wait alone with doubt gnawing at my stomach, I wonder if I have chosen ill. If I should have opened the window after all, if I should indeed have blessed the girl with~~

Had I such riches when I was young, what fortune would I have pursued? Would I have absconded from my father's house? Would I have forged my own bold way in the world? ~~But if I have *not* forged my own way in the world already, then what is it I have done?~~

Why did my mother not gift me with such a choice? Why was it only slippers and gowns and the hand of a prince to catch? Did she think such a situation would ensure my safety? Bring me happiness? Was she afraid for me? ~~I am afraid for myself.~~

I watched, motionless and mute, as the three figures reached the far side of the courtyard. Were there horses waiting beyond the walls? A carriage perhaps — for surely SHE could not ride in her condition, not even side-saddle. Who else did they enlist to their cause? My husband, I am sure, shall ferret out all *traitors*. ~~But why is it taking so long for him to send for me? Does he doubt my innocence? Does he believe I played a part in the conspiracy, rather than seeing to thwart it?~~

She stumbled at one point and, if I close my eyes, I can still summon to mind the picture of it. How she fell to one knee — or, no, rather how she *almost* fell, the other women grasping her arms before she touched the ground. How they helped her to her feet. I can see her hands cradling her belly — I imagine that they shook and she pressed them close to still them. Her hood had fallen back. Her yellow hair shone in the moonlight.

The silver-streaked rat nipped hard at my wrist. Enraged, I struck the creature so hard that it flew from the sill and landed with a small, pained squeak near the fireplace. I do not know where it has taken itself, nor where the other rats may be. ~~But I did see it limp away and was relieved. Relieved! That a rodent did not perish beneath my hand! What a soft, silly woman I have become!~~

I digress.

The grizzled old guard did not appear surprised when I opened the door to my quarters and stepped into the hall. Perhaps he had been anticipating an escape all these nights and felt himself at last rewarded! He moved immediately to block my path, but I shook my head and commanded him to fetch his superior.

"There are thieves in this house," I snapped when he began to make his refusal, "and that which is most precious to the Crown is being stolen away beneath our noses."

The guard stared at me, confused and clearly sceptical. He stated that he could not leave me. That my protection was his sole duty.

I held his gaze, my jaw tightening. I could not allow my wrath to come to the boil. I needed this man to *hear* me.

"Do as I request," I said, "or it will be your head on a pike come dawn. They leave by the West Gate."

Still he hesitated, so I lowered my head and stared instead at his well-polished boots.

"Upon my honour," I assured him, "I shall not leave these rooms while you are gone."

Then I stepped back into my ante-chamber.

After a moment, he closed the door gently behind me and I heard, for the first time, a key turning in the lock. The tumblers fell, as heavy as bones, and then came the echo of the guard's footfalls as he marched swiftly down the hall.

When I returned to my bedchamber, the rats were gone, leaving their trinkets scattered about the floor. I picked them up, one by one, and returned them to the drawers where I kept them, hidden beneath shawls and gloves and petticoats. ~~I might need them one day~~. They might still be needed one day.

I donned my robe and pinned up my hair as best I could before taking my place at the window once more. I expected the women to be brought back the same way they had fled and wished *this* time to tap upon the glass to draw their attention. I wished for them to see me. *I wished them to know.*

I am Queen. *I shall always be Queen.*

But they have not been brought back, at least not across the little courtyard beneath my quarters, and I grow weary of waiting. Once I am returned to my rightful place, I will destroy this journal. Burn it to ash. It is too dangerous to be left intact. Until then, I shall keep it safe to show my husband. These honest pages *prove* that I am *blameless*. That I took no part in M—'s conspiracy. It will not be long, I am certain. He will send for me soon.

The room is quiet; there is not even the squeak or scuttle of a rat to keep me company. For the first time, the walls feel too close about me.

I shall write no more until I am free.

~~It is late morning and still no one has come to~~

~~No. No.~~

My promise I will keep: I shall write no more *until I am free*.

BRAID

Winter makes me think of the tower. Even now, after all this time. Trapped here in the valley for these months of snow and ice. Unable to pack up and leave at will, no matter how much my spirit chafes at being made still. There's a world waiting past those spiny mountain ridges and I ache to move within it.

Gryff likes the winter. His restless years are winding down, he says, and he looks forward to laying his bones in the same place each night. For many nights. He looks forward to evenings in the village mead hall. To the drinking and telling of tales, tall and not so tall. We're safe here, he tells me, we've always been safe here. Would it be so dull to settle for a time, to spend a year or three watching the seasons change in this little valley?

Watching our great-grandson grow?

He still wishes for it to be a boy, Willa's baby. I'm certain it's a girl; she's carrying so high. Willa thinks so too. She wants to call her Chance. I've said nothing, though it weighs badly on me. Willa's headstrong, like her mother was — is, like her mother is. If I take against it, the name will stick faster than flyrot. The child, she thinks, was seeded by the spice trader from the south; the timing lends itself to him at least. She always speaks of the man fondly. His thighs, long and taut. His kind eyes. But theirs was no more than a summer cleaving, as bright and as brief as the courtship of fireflies.

I hope she has his sweet brown eyes, Willa has said more than once. I hope her heart is kind.

The dark bay mare whickers as I near the stables, water bucket in hand. She'll drop her own baby come spring, a foal we've promised to Boorma. We've camped in the yard beside her home for several winters and she's always vouchsafed us to the village circle. I want to do this for her. I want the dark bay mare to stay fat and happy. I want the foal to be born healthy. Strong. Steady on its hooves.

The bucket barely fills the water trough a quarter way. The mare has been thirsty overnight; I'll need to bring more from the well, or else send Boorma's son. He's young and strong and can carry a full bucket in each hand. I fork fresh hay into her feed bin. She pushes at me to get past, her big head knocking me off kilter. My feet slip in the semi-frozen mud and I snatch a handful of mane to keep from falling. The mare pays me no mind. If I break my leg, I tell her, you will starve to death. It's not true. No one in the village would allow a good broodmare to starve, especially not one with a belly full of legs.

A flash of unseasonal colour catches my eye and I turn, almost falling again when I spot the bird perched on the railing outside. It's about the size of a hill pigeon but with plumage the colour of precious jewels. Sapphires, emeralds and rubies, all a-gleam in the weak morning sun. I haven't seen its like since I was a girl.

Silvery stitches run the length of its breast. Not ordinary twine or thread, I see as I move closer, but a thin strand of hair. Deep in my bones, I know that hair was once a bright, burnished auburn and that it curled in waves down to wide and comfortable hips. I can hear laughter, throaty and warm. I can see narrowed eyes, wet with anger and hurt.

The bird allows me to pick it up and turn it over onto its back. Its stitches pull loose with a tug, and that beautiful blue breast opens.

Inside, the creature is hollow and black. But not empty.

The ring is just as I remember it. That thick silver band. That huge, smooth-polished moonstone. Deceptively plain, unlike the woman who used to wear it. My stomach tightens; the cup of warmed goat's milk I had for breakfast curdles within me. She always wore this ring. Always.

She wouldn't have taken it off while there was still breath in her body. Or only when there was breath just enough.

The bird now hangs limp in my hand. The silver hair has turned dull and brittle, its magic spent.

Picking up the bucket, I drop the feathered corpse into it then run a slow, shaky hand over the mare's belly. Good girl, I tell her, good little mother. The steps I take back to camp are equally slow, equally shaky. Beneath the cap Willa knitted for me, my scalp crawls. Wisps of greying hair escape and catch in my mouth. I've kept my hair cropped short for more than three decades, much to Gryff's sorrow. I see the disappointment in his eyes each time I take up the shears. Long hair is trouble, I tell him. You of all men should appreciate that.

At the door to our yurt, I pause, heart racing despite my steady pace. As long as I don't see, as long as I don't *know*, the world can remain unchanged. But what kind of fool would I be to make such a wish? I spit onto the ground. Rub it into the muddy snow, the toe of my boot moving widdershins, and mutter a blessing.

Inside, Willa is still sitting by the stove, still at her knitting. She looks up as I come in, a smile faltering on her lips. Mother Zel? she asks. What's wrong? At the sound of my name, the thick golden braid coiled in her lap stirs and slides noiselessly to the floor. It covers the distance between us in less time than it takes for me to draw a single deep breath and curls itself about my ankles. I drop the bucket and gather it into my arms, pressing my face into that warm, silken hair. The braid smells as it always has: of springtime and sunshine and safety. A half-strangled sob escapes my tightening throat.

Mother Zel? Willa asks again. Her voice trembles.

Gothel is dead, I tell her. Dead or so near it makes no matter.

I hug the braid close. Coiled about my waist and shoulders, it squeezes gently in return. My knees weaken and I sink to a crouch. How I feared to find it changed, reduced to something as lifeless and spent as those stitches I pulled from the bird. It came from Gothel's magic, after all. How long can it survive her death? In my worry, I've forgotten to close the door and now a chill wind sneaks across the threshold. My granddaughter heaves herself from her chair. I'll fetch Boorma, she tells me.

I nod. Tell her to find Gryff. Please.

She sidles past, her rounded belly brushing my shoulder. She pauses for a moment, her breath catching as she stares no doubt at the contents of the bucket, before pushing the door shut behind her. It's quiet in the yurt, and still. The braid nudges the hollow of my throat, presses against my cheek. I know, I whisper, I know.

People know the tales about Mother Gothel, or think they do. Some grew from my own words, my own past relayed to the wise woman who first took pity on me, windblown and pregnant, soon after my exile all those years ago. Her joints beginning to creak with age, she allowed me a straw-filled mattress and what food she could spare in return for feeding her goats and collecting the eggs from her motley flock of chickens each morning. It made for a rude change from the tower, but the smell of feathers and warm shell comforts me to this day. In the evenings, I told her about Gothel, about her wild, wondrous garden and the tower in which my most recent years were spent, about my impossibly long hair and the iron shears that had cropped it from my skull.

Gothel is a witch, the wise woman told me. And I should know.

She calls herself an enchantress, I said.

The wise woman shrugged. Witch, enchantress, healer, crone. Names only matter to those what wield them as weapons, girlie. Rest of us prefer plain-speaking to fancy talk.

I told her about my prince as well. At the time, I had no idea what had happened to him but feared the worst. If Gothel could turn on me so savagely, shear the hair in which she had taken such pride, send me with a blink to this strange and desolate land, what would she have done to him next he came calling? Worrying kept me awake most nights, at least until the twins were born and my days became filled to exhaustion. Chance, I named the girl, and the boy was Will. Both had dark brown hair and big green eyes so like their father's it made me weep.

Don't fret on him, the wise woman told me. He'll have found some other lass to woo by now. A princess, most like, or some fine lady, if he's what you say he is.

But he hadn't, and he wasn't.

The twins were only a moon off their second birthday, the day Gryff dragged his blinded self to our door. It was your singing, he told me. Your sweet voice drew me here sure as the north star.

Which might have been part of the truth, but wasn't the whole. It was the braid, my braid, that led him to me. He told me about climbing the tower that final time and how his eagerness for our time together was dashed by Gothel's triumphant sneer. He told me about the rose bushes below and how they took his eyes as greedily as a child plucks fruit from a pudding. I remembered the rose bushes and their perfume that drifted to my window on warm, windswept afternoons. I remembered their sharp and wicked thorns.

Mother Gothel pushed you? I asked.

Gryff hesitated. I fell, he said. I was shocked to see her and I slipped. She didn't touch me.

I loved him for that small honesty, when so easily he could have lied. I love him for it still.

He had wandered for less than a week, or so he figured, before the braid found him. He knew it was mine. It smelled like me and, besides, who else in the world had ever hair long enough to cover the whole of his body on those frostbitten nights when temperatures plummeted to freezing? The braid nudged him and nuzzled him and kept him moving when he felt like crawling into a hole, covering himself with dirt, and coughing his last. It nosed out fresh water in unexpected crevices and found wild berries and mushrooms which he ate in greedy handfuls. Day after footsore day, he followed the braid until they came at last upon the wise woman's cottage. When he heard me singing a song he remembered from the tower, he could barely breathe for joy.

I know the tales they tell about my tears. How they spilled with love and wonder onto my prince's face and made whole his poor, damaged eyes. I did weep over him, that's true enough. We wept together, the two of us, but it was my braid that worked the magic. It curled itself around us, brushing against our cheeks and mingling our tears. Then it flicked itself across Gryff's eyes, once and once again, and his lids fluttered open and his brilliant green irises stared, astonished, into my own.

I thought I would never see you again, he croaked. I thought I would never see.

My dear prince, I said, come meet your children.

Gryff wasn't a prince, of course, mine or anyone else's. On the night of our reunion, as our fingers explored bodies grown unfamiliar and strange, he told me the truth. Not a prince but the third son of a bankrupt lord. There was no throne awaiting him, no inheritance and certainly no line of fine ladies jostling for a ring.

You asked if I were a prince, sweet Zel, that first day I came to the tower.

And you said that you were.

It felt like a game, or a dream. The tower felt like a place for dreams.

Not for me, Gryff.

Then we fell in love, he said, and it was too late. I didn't know how to tell you. He rested his head on my shoulder. His hair was damp and smelled of lavender from the bath I'd given him earlier. Do you still love me, he asked, even if I have no kingdom to offer?

I kissed his brow. I kissed each of his eyes in turn. It was never a kingdom I wanted, I said. And then I kissed his mouth, deeply, hungrily, as a princess never would.

It might have been the wise woman who planted the seeds, spreading stories of my healing powers to further her own standing, but I have cultivated them mercilessly. Though I've only one tenth of Gothel's power, I'm a quick learner and reputation makes up for a lot. No one knows about my braid, and the magic contained within its strands, save a handful of trusted souls. In all my life, I've only used it twice. Once, when Will burned for three nights straight with marsh fever and the second, years later, to save my daughter's life. She's never thanked me for that, nor forgiven me.

Boorma believes that our lives are fated to unfurl as they will. Just because we can't see the path ahead of us, she says, doesn't mean there isn't a path. Take your steps and trust where your feet lead you. I don't agree, a stand which has given rise to many a gentle argument over the years. I think that we make our path as we go, and that each and every footfall could have so easily landed at a different angle, skewed our direction, turned us completely about. Sometimes, I look back at all the steps I've taken and a deep longing churns my stomach. In my head a voice whispers, if only. If only. The voice sounds like Gothel's. Or it sounds like my daughter's. If only.

If only I had turned away from the pearl house that awful summer when the world tilted slantwise. If only I had galloped back to the hillside where my family was making camp. If only we had all packed up and left. That step. That moment. That choice. But what would be lost to make it anew? Willa, most certainly, and the baby with her — and there it begins and ends. I will not play this game. If only. If only. It doesn't matter, none of it. Our paths may not be fixed but, once forged, they're irrevocable.

Mind your steps instead, I tell Boorma, and know when to stop walking in the first place.

Our own advice, of course, is always the hardest to follow.

Not a month passes that I don't think of that summer, the last that Boorma travelled with us, the last my family would spend unbroken. I'd been so eager to see Heggu before dusk I left Gryff and the twins to unload the wagon and set up our shelters. Boorma was already nursing her new baby and she raised one arm as I trotted away, calling out for me to pass on her good wishes to Heggu. The chestnut gelding was sulky, resenting the extra length to his day while our other two horses were happily grazing in their hobbles, and I dug my heels hard into his sides. By the time we reached Heggu's little cottage by the lake, the beastly nag was tossing his head so violently that my hands were chafed from reining him in.

It was the first sign, but I failed to heed it.

Cursing, I slid from his back and yanked him over to the tether-line. It looked ill-maintained, the overhead rope mossy and close to fraying. I tied the chestnut gelding to an end-post instead. I should have thought more about the state of the line, and how odd it was that no horse seemed to have been tied to it for months, but I was tired and cranky and looking forward to Heggu's lavender tea. It was the sight of her door that first gave me pause. This early in summer, it should have been decorated by a garland of wildflowers, strung on horsehair with a pearl or two hidden among the petals. Or, at the very least, a bushel of dried lakeweed offered in expectation of the oyster harvest. The bare wood troubled me, as did the rusty, unadorned nail. I pushed open the door.

The cottage was empty, and had been for some time. Instead of the aroma of woodsmoke and cooking grease, the place smelled musty and close. The round glass window — a particular point of pride for Heggu — was half-obscured by cobwebs. It hadn't been cleaned in months. But there was no sign of abandonment, nor ransacking. Whatever had happened, Heggu had found time to pack up her most personal belongings before she left. Most of the drawers in her wooden cabinet were barren, but the secret compartment at the back held a small cotton bag. Pearl dust, by the weight and chalky smell of it, the very thing I came to trade with her each summer.

Blessed by three, I muttered, dropping the bag into my pocket. Thank you, Heggu.

It was only when I turned to go did I notice what else she'd left for me. On the back of the door hung an ornate sigil, woven from dried plains-grass and the weed that grew near her oyster beds. She'd woven it herself over many months and had taken the time one summer to tell me the meaning of it. Not the whole meaning — some knowledge was meant for only Heggu herself — but enough. It was the story of her life, and the places she had lived over the years, and the lessons she had learnt. Except now it was the wrong way around, the hook stuck rudely through a piece of weave on its lowest arc rather than the loop she had fashioned to hang it from.

The world, Heggu's world, had been turned upside down.

I couldn't leave it like that. But as soon as my fingers touched the sigil there was a spark, like the small shocks that come from brushing long hair on a dry summer day, and a whisper that I heard more in my head than my ears.

run

Clutching Heggu's sigil to my chest — silent now and still, no more than dead grass — I fled the cottage. But it was too late to run any farther.

Waiting outside were four men on horses, one of them holding my chestnut gelding by its rope. I recognised three of them from the nearby village. The fourth man was thin and tall, even for sitting on his mount, with a narrow face and eyes that seemed like they could be kind when they wanted to be. One of the others, a man I knew as Jacoby, shifted in his saddle. His wife had been pregnant last summer and sick more mornings than not. I'd given her a tincture, told her to roll a pearl under her tongue when she needed to be on her feet. She would've had the baby by now. A son, or so I'd reckoned at the time.

That's her, Jacoby said, lifting his chin. That's the witch.

By the time the door to the yurt opens again, I've gathered myself together. There's a pot of water coming to boil on the stove and I'm sitting in my chair, cutting up root vegetables on a board in my lap. The braid is curled around my feet and ankles. It stirs as Willa comes in then settles itself again. Willa asks how I am. I tell her that I'm almost done with the turnips but that we need more sweet potato for the soup. Her smile is weak and worried. She glances into the bucket left by the door.

In here, I say, kicking a heel against the basket under my chair.

With some effort, Willa stoops to pick up the bird. My chair wobbles as she uses the back of it to pull herself upright again. How strange, she says, turning the bird over in her hands. Its head lolls like that of any dead thing. She tidies the colourful feathers. Ventures tentative fingers inside the cavity of its breast. So smooth, she says, and clean as cloth. She waggles unblooded fingers at me. How's it done?

That's beyond my ken, I say. It's Gothel's working.

Like your braid.

Like my braid.

The ring is in my apron pocket. Willa doesn't need to know about it. I keep chopping turnips until Boorma and Gryff arrive, breathing hard and brimming with questions. Boorma is keen to see the hollowed bird; Gryff refuses to touch it. He places a hand on my shoulder and gets down on one shaky knee. It's over, he says to me, isn't it? I don't look at him, not even when he puts his hand over mine, stilling the knife's work. Zel? It's over? She's dead?

I nod and he presses his cheek against the back of my hand. His whiskers are rough and scratchy. When he looks up again his eyes are wet. She'll come back now, he says and the hope in his voice hurts to hear. Gryff has always believed that Gothel had something to do with our daughter's leaving, that she wove a spell from afar to draw yet another girl to her tower. Nothing I've said in the past has convinced him otherwise. Nothing I say now would make a difference. I turn my hand to rub at his beard.

Gothel's death sits between us, and always will.

She's gone. She's gone and I'll never see her again. I'll never have the chance to scoop the forgiveness from my heart and offer it to her. I'll never know if she forgave me. There should have been more time. How can there be no more time?

A sob breaks in my throat. Gryff squeezes my hand and tells me that all will be well. We can stop looking over our shoulders now, he says. Gothel can do nothing more to hurt us.

My grief is a foreign thing, sharp and murky all at once. I haven't the first idea how to explain it — to my husband or to myself. Around my ankles, the braid tightens gently. I rest my head on Gryff's shoulder and let my tears run their course.

Despite what the stories say, Gothel didn't steal me.

The woman who carried me in her belly, who eventually birthed me 'neath the light of a near-full moon, was young and unmarried. It's true that she stole from Gothel's garden and that Gothel caught her. It's true that a bargain was struck, but not the one that people gossip on.

When Gothel spied the woman, barely older than Willa is now, plucking parsley in desperate handfuls for the third night in a row, she knew what was what. But it was too far late for the herb to have done her any good and, besides, the silly thing was eating it. Gothel had laughed when she'd told me that, but it wasn't a cruel laugh. Incredulous, indulgent even, but not cruel. Half-right can be worse than wrong, she'd said. Remember that.

Gothel might still have been able to help the young woman, then in her fourth moon and me not yet quickened within, but the risk was high. Instead, she told her to eat her fill of parsley — and furnished her as well with fresh eggs and salted pork and, when the cravings came, a basket of oranges that cost Gothel a small fortune in trade. In return, should the fates deem it proper, the woman was to bear the babe to term and Gothel would take care of matters then.

Don't think your mother didn't want you, Gothel often told me. She didn't know you, my darling. It was a baby she was so desperate to rid herself of, the notion of a baby and all that came after — and that's not the same as ridding herself of you. But you're *my* daughter, Rapunzel, as much as if you spilled from my own loins. Never doubt it.

Gothel had no desire for me to think myself unwanted and I never did. Not before my exile, at least.

Why she took me for herself, I'll never truly know. Maybe she didn't either.

Gryff insists that I'm naive, willfully blind even, where it concerns Gothel. I was a child, after all, and I only knew what Gothel wanted me to know. What mother would readily surrender her baby once it was born? The wise woman who'd sheltered me agreed. Unnatural, she said, a mother's love runs deepest of all — you've felt it yourself, girl. And I had, of course I had. The twins were my moon and my sun and I would have killed anyone who tried to take them from me.

I would have died for them.

But for all her faults, and the terrible things she has done, Gothel never once lied to me. I'm certain of that. Nor did she ever cast my birth mother as a villain. Neither strumpet nor slattern nor heartless wretch, simply a young woman with a burden too big to carry by herself. And this I know as well: not every woman yearns to be a mother, not even all those who already are. I've seen this for myself and make no judgement on them.

On most of them, in any case.

The men escorted me back to the village in silence, leading my chestnut gelding by his rein rope. I kept my hands in my lap, knotted into fists, and stopped asking questions after the first ones went unheeded. The narrow-faced man had simply instructed me to accompany them. The village circle required my presence, he'd said. I would not be harmed, he'd said. At that, Jacoby's face had tightened, his lips rolling to a thin line.

There were four of them. Tall men and broad.

I'd clenched my teeth and allowed them to take me.

The village was quiet. Laari, who normally greeted me with an excited grin before launching into a report of all that had happened since my previous visit, stood at the front of her cottage with water bucket in hand. She dropped her gaze as we passed, taking a sudden interest in the fraying hem of her apron. Nor would anyone else meet my eye, though several men exchanged nods with my captors. A woman whose name escaped me turned her shoulder away, hurriedly draping a corner of her shawl over the baby she held.

My heart beat hard against my ribs. This was not the village I knew. There was a brittleness to the air now. The tension of a breath held for too long.

On the outskirts, near where the trees grew thick and their branches darkened the ground, stood three small round huts. They were fashioned from rough-hewn timber and their roofs were neatly thatched. The doors of two of the huts yawned open; the third's was held closed by a heavy wooden crossbar. There were no windows that I could see.

If you would, the narrow-faced man said. He gestured towards the nearest hut.

I thought the village circle wished to see me? I asked, not moving from my horse.

The narrow-faced man shook his head. I did not not say that. He gestured once again.

Four men, tall and broad.

I dismounted. Strode into the hut with my chin held high. Behind me, the door creaked shut. Its crossbar fell into place with a thunk. I closed my eyes, letting my sight adjust to the windowless dark, as the sound of hoof-beats receded into the distance. There was a mound of straw on one side of the hut — half gone to mould, by the smell — and an empty pot on the other. The last weak light of the evening filtered through the gaps between the timbers. I was glad for the season; in winter, the hut would freeze its luckless inhabitant to the marrow. I pushed at the door. It held fast. I hadn't really expected otherwise.

Resting my back against the wall, I took the small bag of pearl dust from my pocket. The weight of it in my palm was a comfort. The men had taken Heggu's sigil from me back at her cottage. Stamped it into the dirt and spat. Jacoby had made a sign of warding with his fingers. They hadn't searched my pockets, though. Hadn't seemed inclined to touch me at all.

What's happened here, Heggu? I muttered.

Night settled and the hut fell near to blackness. Would Gryff be worried when I didn't return, or would he assume I'd lingered late at the pearl house, drinking plum wine till my head was too muddled to ride back to camp? It wouldn't have been the first time I'd shared Heggu's bed; he likely wouldn't begin to fret until morning. At least I could rely on my chestnut gelding being cared for. Whatever fault the village had found with me, a good horse was too valuable a creature to be mistreated.

Choosing a spot away from the mouldy straw, I sat myself down to think.

Though I don't remember nodding off, I awakened with a start, all senses alert. A rough, rustling noise came from outside, followed by the scrape of wood on wood. I held my breath. More rustling, more scraping, and then the heavy thud of the crossbar hitting the ground. The door inched open, admitting a weak stream of moonlight, as my braid came snaking into the hut.

I could have wept, the relief was so great.

The braid wrapped itself around my waist and shoulders, nuzzled at the hollow of my throat. It quivered and hummed, as though each and every hair vibrated in the pleasure of finding me. I squeezed it tight. Pressed that golden, glossy hair to my mouth and whispered thanks, before disentangling myself from its coils and getting to my feet.

Scarce a dozen paces into the open, I paused. Turned to look at the other hut, the one with its door still closed and latched. The back of my neck itched. The braid bumped against my ankles, urging me forward. Hold a moment, I told it and marched across to the hut's door. The wood was rough beneath my knuckles. Who's in there, I asked, and rapped again.

There was a shuffling and then the sound of breathing, soft and close.

Who is it, I asked again. Speak if you wish to be free.

A sob, choked swiftly down. Zel? Is it you, Zel?

I lifted the crossbar and dropped it to the dirt, then pulled the door open. Meena, Jacoby's wife, was on her knees, her eyes hollowed and haunted. Come, I said, gesturing to the night outside. She shook her head, ground her lips hard together in a way that made me wince. Taking a deep breath, I leaned close. What is it, Meena? Why have they put you here?

The woman grasped my hands in both of hers. Bony fingers dug into my flesh, as she tried to pull me to my knees before her. We must be penitent, she said. We must show how penitent we are, and if we are penitent, if we are penitent, if we are penitent, we can walk again in the light.

It took many precious minutes to work the story loose.

Meena's baby had been born without breath. A boy, her first boy, he'd lain still and blue in her arms as she sobbed over his tiny body. Jacoby had been distraught at first, then withdrawn and distant. Only later, after Keeper Dorn had come to counsel him, did she find anger in her husband's eyes. Anger and disgust and something worse. I didn't know this Keeper Dorn but soon placed him as the narrow-faced man who'd led the party back at the pearl house. He'd come to the village at the end of the previous summer, Meena told me, bringing with him small items of trade and a recipe for a thick, fermented drink that several of the men took to sharing late at night. He brought words with him too, seductive and new, and a way of seeing the world by which some in the village began to abide.

They said it was because of me he died, Meena whispered.

I squeezed her hand. They're wrong. Some babies aren't for this world — that's the truth of it.

Shoulders slumped, the woman bowed her head. I told them it wasn't nothing, Zel, I told them. Just for the sickness, I told them, and nothing you hadn't given me before. My girls were all born, weren't they? Strong girls, pretty girls. I miss them, Zel, I miss them, I miss them — oh, we must be penitent.

It was Jacoby who'd brought the bottle of tonic to Keeper Dorn, along with the charm that Heggu had woven for Meena from dried lakeweed and which he'd found beneath his wife's pillow. Rough words had been slung from mouth to mouth. Witchcraft. Evil. Murder. When they'd gone to fetch Heggu, they'd found only her empty cottage.

The sacred balance was tilted out of true, Keeper Dorn had explained. The weight needed to be made up. On his instruction, the penitent huts had been built. With Meena locked in hers since late winter, I marvelled aloud that she hadn't frozen to death.

It's not *my* death that will balance things, she replied.

That's right, I said and tried to pull her to her feet. But a stubborn strength lingered in her wasted frame and she struggled against me, eventually falling limp and boneless to the ground. I begged her to leave with me. We could walk to my family's camp by dawn and be away from this place. She laughed at that, a harsh and empty sound that brought the taste of fear to my tongue.

They will have your family by now, Zel. Like they have mine. We must be penitent, penitent, penitent.

Stomach churning, I backed out of the hut. The pitiful woman pulled the door shut behind me but I refused to replace the crossbar, despite her pleas for me to do so. Instead, I returned to my own hut and sat cross-legged in the centre of the floor. My braid slid from the shadows and wove about me, nudging at my feet, my hips, growing more urgent with each passing moment. But as much as I wanted to believe otherwise, I knew that Meena was right. The village had known of our arrival. Another party of men would have been sent to collect Gryff and the twins and poor Boorma as well, most like, with her babe. A party larger than what came to fetch me — and armed, no doubt.

What would happen to my family once I was discovered gone?

And what did I suppose to do with my freedom?

I wasn't Heggu, solitary and self-sufficient. I could not run. I would not leave my children.

The braid wound itself around my shoulders and I hugged it close. Go, I whispered, keep yourself safe from sight; you will know when I need you again. After one final squeeze, it uncoiled and slipped from the hut with barely a sound. I left the door open. The sky was cloudless and, with the moon having travelled close to setting, the stars were bountiful. On their light, I made a solemn vow. Protection. Vengeance. Sacrifice.

As needs demanded. The decision to stay was heavy on my chest, its uncertainty a suffocation.

(What if Meena was wrong?)

She wasn't.

(But what if?)

I shook my head and sat, straight-backed and silent, waiting for the new day to break and bring to bear what it would.

The moon is scarce more than a sliver and my breath frosts in the darkness. I don't need light to recognise Boorma's heavy tread as she approaches. Too cold to be out here, she says. Passes me a bowl of warm, spiced wine.

I won't sleep well tonight, I tell her.

She stands beside me, leaning against the goat pen, and we take turns sipping from the bowl. The animals are all huddled together, sharing their heat. A brown she-goat had gotten to her feet when I'd first arrived, bleating softly as she trotted over to greet me. Disappointed by my failure to bring food, she's settled back down with the rest of the flock now. Goats are pragmatic creatures. Sensible. I doubt they waste time dwelling on the past.

Boorma wants to know where we'll be going come spring, and I tell her that we haven't decided yet, Gryff and me. She knows he's reluctant and I suspect she'd rather we stayed in the valley as well. Her son, Maator, is clearly fond of Willa and my granddaughter's shown no sign of rebuffing him.

Not into the west, Boorma says.

I grit my teeth. Shake my head. There've been many tales passed around the mead hall this winter. The Keepers of the Balance are spreading their ways and their words through the foothills out west. We'll travel east, if we travel anywhere. Swing down to the south. There are trades we can make along those routes, and women who'll welcome my visits. I'll not go where Keepers tread, not so long as any I love in this world draw breath.

A sudden shiver rumbles through me. Wine splashes onto my gloved hand and Boorma takes the bowl, swallows what remains. Let's get your bones to bed, she says, before they freeze. We link arms and shuffle back to my yurt. Willa will already be chasing sleep and Gryff, I suspect, still tarrying at the mead hall. Smoke curls listlessly through the stovepipe; I'll need to stoke the fire with more dung before bedding down. Boorma gives me a rough hug then turns to leave.

I reach out and grab her by the sleeve. I thought I would see Gothel again, I say. I thought she would come find me.

Boorma touches my cheek, wipes at my tears with her glove.

I loved her, I say. I wanted her to know that.

She was your mother, Boorma tells me. She knew.

But I hated Gothel as well. Cursed her many times after being banished to the tower, though I had no skill in the practice and my muddling about with stolen hairs and furious words wrought no discernible effect. I cursed her to be struck down with boils and warts. I cursed her beloved garden to wither and die. I cursed her to fall from the tower as she climbed. The last, of course, committed without much thought for the consequences on my own imprisoned self.

There was a time one autumn when she didn't visit for more than a week. After five days my food was all but gone, though my water jug continued to replenish itself as usual. My only sanity was the brightly coloured bird that fluttered onto my windowsill each morning, bearing sprigs of berries or bushels of nuts or, once, a thin crust of bread. I was terrified that my curses had worked, that Gothel was dead and I would be trapped in the tower until I followed her at last to the grave.

When Gothel did finally return, I barely waited for her to climb into the room before exploding. I yelled at her, struck out with fists that she caught before their blows could land. Gently, she held me to her breast, pinning my arms to my sides until my rage abated.

You left me, I choked through my tears and snot. You abandoned me.

I would never abandon you, my darling. Did not my little friend come to visit? Did she not bring sustenance and sing my heartsong to you when I could not?

Gothel never told me where she had been, only that a matter of urgency had kept her away. It happened several more times over the years and each time my guts curdled with an anxious dread. I hated her for making me feel like that. I hated myself for the relief that swept my soul when she came back. For the meekness with which I lay my head in her lap while she unbraided my hair and combed the golden strands until they crackled and glowed. Occasionally, she took a pair of silver scissors from her pocket and snipped one or two to take with her when she left. Only Gothel could do that; not a single hair ever left my scalp without her permission.

I hated her, and I loved her, and I wanted to believe her when she said it was for my own protection that I was confined to the tower. The world was dangerous for girls my age, she said. There was magic in the flow of our blood, magic which would lure the danger close, and until I was a woman, until I was grown into my powers and had the cunning to know how to wield them, the tower would keep me safe.

Oh Gothel, you taught me so much and yet so little.

You taught me magic and herblore, but not the workings of my own body.

You taught me love, but said nothing of the intoxication of another's mouth on my own, another's hands on my skin, another's flesh pressed hot into mine.

You taught me how to watch the world from above, rather than walk within it.

But as much as Gryff would have me judge you, I refuse. Our twins — the grandchildren you never got to see, to hold, to know — our children who were raised on open plains and the backs of wagons, who rode a horse as soon as they could keep their balance, who slept with a starlit sky unfurled above them as often as they did tented roofs — oh, for all that freedom, would they have not been *safer* in a high, round room built from unyielding stone?

And might they not be with us now?

Keeper Dorn came to see me while the sun was still rising over the treeline. The two burly men who flanked him were clearly uneasy to see the hut with its door wide open. Even more so to find their captive unfled. Their leader revealed nothing, that narrow face calm and still. The three of them stopped a few paces away. Dorn nodded to me. When he spoke, his voice bore the gentle tones parents use when speaking to young children. You are what they say, then?

I'm not a witch, I told him.

Dorn tilted his head, his gaze travelling the length of my body. I did not move a single finger beneath his scrutiny, though my heart beat faster and my stomach clenched upon itself.

You gave Brother Jacoby's wife a witch's potion last summer, Dorn said.

I gave her a tonic, for the illness a pregnancy can bring.

Brother Jacoby's son was blue-born.

The one did not cause the other.

Dorn stared at me a moment longer before stepping in close, his movement so sudden and so fast that I cried out in surprise. He reached for a lock of my hair and gave it a light tug. Women should not wear their hair so short, he said. It is not balanced.

With that he turned and left, followed by one of the men. The other closed the door to the hut, repugnance twisting his face. I heard the crossbar fall and the creak of timber as he leaned his weight against the wall outside. I was not to be left alone again.

Almost three hours passed, to judge by the play of shadows along the ground, before I heard footsteps approach once more. Deep male voices muttered among themselves. Someone cursed. Then the crossbar was lifted and the door flung open. This time the men had chains — an expensive trade to have made — and I instinctively stepped back as they stepped inside.

She's afeared of the iron, like the Keeper said.

Bind her quick. Don't let her catch your eye.

There was no point in struggling. They wound a loop around my waist, threaded the ends of the chain through cuffs that were somewhat too large for my wrists. I squeezed my hands into fists to hide how easily I might be able to slip free. The men did not notice. One of them made a sign of warding and spat at my feet. The circle is waiting, he said.

I was led to the centre of the village, an open area where harvest fires were lit and marriages celebrated. And where the village circle met.

There were no women among those gathered, which was strange. Discomforting. Sweat trickled down my back and I longed to scratch at it. They should think themselves lucky, these men, these cowards who do not deserve the name of men, that I am no witch. That I could not curse them.

Then I spied Gryff. Kneeling off to the side, hands bound with rope, face bloody and bruised. Our eyes met and he made to rise, but the broad-chested man standing behind him pushed him back down. The man carried a cudgel. Gryff lowered his head. His shoulders slumped. I had never seen him look so defeated. A sour taste coated my mouth and I swallowed hard, stumbling as one of my escorts pushed me forward to where Keeper Dorn was waiting. His narrow face seemed softened. There was an almost peaceful quality to his eyes, an upwards quirk to his lips.

For a moment, I felt hopeful. For a moment, all might still be well with the world.

Dorn lifted a hand to hush the murmur of the crowd. We serve the balance, he told them. In turn, the balance serves us. We are here to see it righted.

But when he turned to me, his gaze bore the chill of midwinter. Zel of the Tower, your actions have caused imbalance. A father has lost a son. This is a grave circumstance.

I glanced at Gryff. He wasn't looking at me. He wasn't looking at anyone.

Where are my children? I asked Dorn, hating the quaver in my voice.

Someone shoved me roughly from behind and I fell forward, chains clinking as I reached out to catch myself. But my restraints were drawn too short. I hit the ground hard, one shoulder rolling under me. There was a single cry from the crowd, quickly bitten off. It might have been Gryff. Dorn stepped forward and pulled to my feet. He admonished the man who pushed me, reminding him of the need to keep the balance, however difficult. Our female companion and her baby had been permitted to wait at our camp, Dorn told me, along with my daughter. They'd had no part in what had happened; they were not needed in the village. It was best they stayed away.

I could not breathe for all that was not said. Gryff still would not meet my eye. Others were only too keen to stare, their faces sharp and smug.

And my son, I croaked. Where is Will?

It wasn't anything that could be rightly called a smile, the thin, pallid thing that stretched Dorn's mouth so taut. A father lost a son, he reminded me. A boy-child was killed. It was an imbalance.

It was only when two men grabbed me by the arms that I realised I'd launched myself at the Keeper. Then kill *me*, I yelled at him, at the two who held me, at all those gathered around us. You believe I'm guilty of this sin, then avenge yourself on me. My son has done nothing; he is innocent. *He is innocent.*

The two men wrestled me to my knees. One of them snatched a fistful of my hair and pulled my head so far back I thought my neck would snap. Dorn stared down at me with a kind of pity. This isn't about sin, Zel of the Tower, or vengeance — the balance is all that concerns us. If it is not kept, then we walk in darkness as beasts.

I tried to speak once more, to beg again for my son's life, but Dorn held up his hand.

You do not understand, he said. This is not a trial. This is a witnessing.

It's difficult to remember all that happened next, and in what precise order. The door to a nearby cottage opened and Jacoby marched out, a sneer of triumph on his face. After him came two men, one I recognised as Laari's husband, transporting between them a limp, unmoving shape wrapped in a blanket. Will was only fourteen, and as slight as his sister. One man could have carried his body with little effort. They put him down, not ungently. Laari's husband, bending to tidy a corner of the blanket, flashed me a glance. His eyes were glossed with tears.

Rage and grief burst within me. I battled free and half-ran, half-crawled over to my son. Vaguely, I was aware of shouting around me and a harsh, broken bellow that a part of me knew to be Gryff's. But all I could think of was Will. I uncovered his face, his beautiful, perfect face which was still beautiful, still perfect, for all its terrible, irrevocable stillness. My son, I whispered, my darling, my boy.

I remember my throat closing over, my lungs seizing on airless space.

I remember the numbing, roaring silence filling my ears.

Most of all, I remember the agonised shriek that pulled me back to the world.

Dorn was lying on his back, a dark puddle seeping into the dirt from his side. Gryff was on the ground mere paces away, face down and struggling against the knees that dug into his back, keeping him from rising. And, inexplicably, there was Chance, right in the middle of the whole mess. A man had her about the waist, her arms pinned to her sides. She was twisting to free herself, kicking at anyone who got near. I called her name. Staggered to my feet.

Then I saw the knife fall from my daughter's hand.

What had she done, my Chance? My girl, so bright and bold. And whose death would serve balance this vengeful deed? Her own? Her father's? My mind cleared. My thoughts narrowed to a sure and certain focus.

I ran towards Dorn. Still on the ground, he'd propped himself up on elbow and hip to better see the wound. His face was pale. Jacoby blocked my path with a raised fist.

Let me pass, I said. If you want him to live.

Dorn called for Jacoby to stand aside which, after a small argument, he did. Should the Keeper die, he muttered as I pushed past, I'll throttle you myself.

The wound was long but shallow, a slash more than a stab, and it was bleeding profusely. Clean edges, at least. Easy enough to stitch together. Gently, I prodded at the surrounding flesh. Dorn hissed. It burns, he said. It burns as fire does. Sweat ran down his face; his eyes were more red than white. I peered closer and my heart sank. Inside the wound, the tissue was tinged the subtle silver of winterfrost. I knew of only one thing that would cause such a symptom.

Later, my daughter would tell me how she waited until dark, waited until Boorma had finally worried herself to sleep, to sneak from the camp. Before she left, she took the small bottle of viper's wine from my healer's box and used it to coat the blade of her knife. She'd hidden all night in the village, tucked behind someone's woodbox, not knowing what had happened to her family but hopeful that morning would furnish her with answers. And a clear path. But the first she saw of her brother was when his body was delivered to the circle. She never stopped blaming herself, no matter how I tried to reason with her. If only she'd searched for him. If only she'd found him. If only they'd escaped. If only, if only — my daughter is expert at that game.

Viper's wine is useful in so many ways. A drop mixed in various tinctures and teas can help with troubled sleep, or stopped-up bowels, or twinges in the heart; alone and without dilution, it's a deadly poison. An open wound exposed to viper's wine will turn brittle and waste, the flesh will break down, the body will eat itself alive. It is the slowest of tortures.

I swivelled to see Chance now crouched on the ground, one man twisting her arms cruelly behind her back. Blood rushed to my cheeks. Fingernails dug into my palm. It took all that was left of my will not to run to my daughter, not to scratch out the eyes of her captor and trample them into the dirt. Chance met my gaze; a ghost of a smile tripped across her mouth. Pale, frightened and yet — triumphant.

I turned back to Dorn, to the circle of men crowded around us. He needs to be out of the sun, I told them. Dorn quieted the resulting growls with a wave of his hand. Listen to her, he said. The mother can balance the daughter's work. I've no idea if he really believed such a thing but he must have realised he'd suffered no ordinary injury. As the men lifted him, the Keeper groaned and clamped a sweat-slicked hand around my arm. The daughter will be held forfeit, he said, loud enough for all to hear. The father as well.

Dorn's home was little bigger than the penitent huts, and windowless. As the Keeper was lowered onto his bed pallet, Jacoby pushed me up against the wall. You're all going to die, he whispered, his breath hot in my ear. But I will make sure to give your witch-daughter a fine send-off.

I dug my nails so hard into my palm, they drew blood.

Once all the men had left, all but Jacoby who took up a position beside the door, the Keeper rolled his yellowing eyes towards me. How long, he asked. I told him that I wasn't sure. Until dawn perhaps, or perhaps sooner, but if I could retrieve some ingredients from camp then —

There'll be none of your witchcraft here, Jacoby interrupted.

Will it help, Dorn asked?

Perhaps, I said. He knew I was lying. With the viper's wine spreading through his body, there was nothing I could do apart from administering opium to quell the pain — and even that would only work for so long. In truth, I'd wanted the time to think. There must be a trade that would vouchsafe the lives of my daughter and my husband, some bargain I could strike. But it needed to be done while Dorn still drew breath enough to command it. Once he was dead ... I cast a surreptitious glance towards Jacoby. The man's eyes were flat and dark. His hand clenched and unclenched around the cudgel he carried.

At least he was in here, with me, and not standing guard over my daughter.

The day wore on. Water was brought for me to wash the wound, and vinegar too. Needle and thread were fetched, my chains unshackled and, more for appearances sake than anything else, I stitched the wound closed. The bleeding stopped but the spread of silver was visible under his skin. Beautiful, in its own terrible way. I wiped Dorn's face with a sodden rag and squeezed drops into his mouth whenever he seemed lucid enough to swallow. Fire, he kept murmuring, my blood is aflame. I kept hoping for another man to relieve Jacoby of his watch, someone like Laari's husband perhaps, a man more open to reason, or even compassion, but all who came to the door were sent away.

We were to keep vigil alone then, Jacoby and me. I sat in my chair at Dorn's side. He remained in his place by the door. We didn't look at each other.

As night fell, I began to hum softly. It was a bedtime song I used to sing to the twins when they were very young. It hurt to remember how Will would try to sing along, giggling and making up his own words. Jacoby, slumped now on the floor, growled for me to shut up, but Dorn reached out and clasped my hand in his.

See, I said to Jacoby, it is a comfort to him.

He said nothing more. I continued to hum, low and lilting, spying sidelong at my guard in the candlelight. After a while, the man's head drooped to his chest. His breathing deepened. I hummed on, waiting, waiting. Finally, there came a feather-light brush of hair against my ankle. I looked down and my lullaby faltered. Jacoby snuffled loudly in his sleep, just once, before I forced myself to pick up the tune.

My braid had found a way into the Keeper's hut. Only, not as my braid.

Through every slim crack or knothole, loose stands of hair slipped in through the walls and curved their golden, glowing path across the floor. Tears pricked at my eyes. For if this was the *only* way my braid could enter without notice, it meant there was no escape to be made. Men must be keeping too close and wakeful a watch outside, even at this late hour.

Hairs curled around my fingers, my wrist, wound right up to my throat. More of them converged to make a spiral in my lap, quivering as I stroked them. I stared at the needle I'd left on the small table beside the bed. At the coarse thread I'd used to close up Dorn's side. It might be too late. It was probably too late. And yet.

Bending close to the wound, I sawed one of the stitches back and forth between my teeth until at last it snapped, then carefully picked the rest free. The stench was terrible. Sour and acrid, not the smell of rotting flesh so much as bitter greens left to drown in a sodden field. Still humming, I gathered a handful of loose hairs and rolled them together as I would stuffing for a rag doll. Then I held apart the edges of the wound and pushed the bundle inside.

Dorn gasped and arched his back but did not appear to waken.

Neither did Jacoby, over at his post by the door.

It took three attempts to thread a single hair through the needle, my hands shook so much. But finally I managed it and, by the flickering candlelight, I stitched Dorn up again. His skin rippled, or the flesh beneath it did, and grew so hot I could feel the fever from where I sat. Please, I whispered, oh please. I wiped the cool, wet cloth over his face and chest. Steam hissed into the air. The Keeper arched his back again, tossed himself from side to side so vigorously he would have fallen from his pallet had I not thrown my body over his.

Jacoby startled from sleep, scrambled to his feet. What happens here, he demanded. Is this death come to claim me? He spoke the last too eagerly, or so it seemed.

No, I snapped. This is death taking her leave of you.

By break of dawn, the Keeper was able to sit up and drink from a bowl of mutton broth while several of the village circle gathered to examine him. The wound was healing to a reddish, puckered line that itched, he said, but no longer burned. His skin was still clammy to the touch, but cool, and a healthy flush of colour was returning to his face. There was no sign of the thin golden hair I'd stitched into his side, nor of any else left inside the hut.

She spelled you, Jacoby insisted. It was witchcraft and no good can come of it.

The balance has been kept, Dorn replied. But there was a fearful new light in his eyes when he looked at me, and he would not hold my gaze for long. Fetch her people, he told the circle. They are no longer forfeit.

As long as I might live, I shall never again see anything as beautiful as my daughter's face that morning as she was led into the centre of the village where I'd been made to wait. Grubby and red-eyed, her long brown hair tangled and snarled, but alive, oh blessed by three, my darling Chance, *alive*. Gryff walked by her side, one arm tight around her shoulders. His face appeared neutral but I could see the tightness in his jaw from where I stood and I knew the small vein in his temple would be throbbing fit to burst.

Jacoby dug his fingers into my arm one last time before letting me go. Witch, he hissed, shoving me forward. Though weak with hunger and trepidation, I forced myself to keep to a steady walk, first one foot and then the other, chin jutted high. The men of the village pressed closed, watching. Some, like Jacoby, wore murderous scowls; others seemed merely fearful. I was put in mind of the packs of half-wild dogs that roam the outskirts of the larger townships in the south, seldom a danger unless you were foolish enough to run from them, or tempt them with uncovered meat, raw and dripping.

Or if you had the misfortune to be a child. Isolated and vulnerable.

When I reached my daughter, I stooped to hug her but she stiffened in my arms, her shoulders sharp and stubborn. Gryff took hold of my hand and brought it to his lips. His eyes were hollow. My love, I said to him, we must go while we can. Please.

Dorn escorted us from the village himself, followed by Jacoby and a dozen or so men. All the cottage doors we passed were shut; the few windows curtained and blind. I imagined all the women locked behind those door, children pressed into their skirts. Forbidden to look upon the witch in their midst lest they become likewise corrupted. Lest they be banished to the penitent hut along with Jacoby's poor wife. I kept hold of Chance's hand. Squeezed it so tight that a small, plaintive sound escaped her throat. Hush, I said. I loosened my grip but did not let go. I thought I would never let go of her again.

At last we came to the tether-line, where my chestnut gelding waited, tossing his head and fretting over the terrible burden that had been roped across his saddle. Gryff stopped in his tracks. I could hear his teeth grinding together at the sight of that motionless, blanket-wrapped form. He half-turned and I stepped in front of him, keeping myself between my husband and Dorn. Grabbing his chin with my free hand, I forced him to look at me. To see me.

You cannot, I whispered. We still have one child — would you leave your daughter fatherless?

His eyes gleamed. His face was flushed. It would take so very little to spark him.

You will leave this village and its lands, Dorn said. We will not suffer you here again.

Behind him, Jacoby raised his voice. *She* should not be allowed to leave. My son is murdered.

Dorn nodded towards the tether-line. The balance has been righted, Brother Jacoby. Would you set it off its kilter once again?

She should be made penitent, Jacoby retorted, pointing at me. Around him, other men began to mutter words of assent.

I pushed my daughter behind me, felt Gryff move forward. Blood rushed through my ears. Get Chance away from here, I whispered. Protect her.

Gryff's hand gripped my shoulder. I wanted to sink beneath its strength. No, Zel, he muttered, his breath warm in my hair. I will protect you both.

Brothers! Dorn raised his hand. She is not a member of our village; the penitence is not hers to take. One by one, he turned to look at the men. Held their gaze until they dropped it. Seeing the battle lost, Jacoby swore and kicked viciously at the ground. I do not doubt it was my face he imagined crushed beneath his boot.

Alone, Dorn took us the remaining distance to the tetherline. He untied the chestnut gelding's rein-rope and handed it to Gryff. Pack up your camp with haste, he said, glancing up at the noonday sky. It will be best if you are far from here once it is night. There are some who find a brutal freedom in the darkness.

The twins had been close, inseparable, indivisible. The death of her brother was a wound Chance carried always. Worse than viper's wine, and even slower to wend its way through her veins. He was my heart, Mama, she screamed at me once. They cut out my heart and you did nothing. Worse than nothing — you *saved* the man who murdered him.

Perhaps I should have told her what I actually did afterwards. If I had, she might have found some solace in it. If I had, she might still be here with us, with Willa. I wasn't ashamed — I'm *still* not ashamed — but neither was I proud. The comfort that vengeance offers is a hollow one; I did not want to teach my daughter otherwise.

My hair had found its way back to the camp before we did, scruffy and dishevelled, but braided together once more. Boorma was overcome to see us, ecstatic and then distraught, and we all wept together as we packed up our belongings and loaded the wagon. Will, we would farewell the next day, with many miles between us and the village where his death had come for him. A grave dug beneath an ancient tree. His body nestled within the roots.

(Earth take you, my child, my son. Earth take you, and goddess keep you.)

That first night, while Gryff kept a jaw-tight watch, I undid my braid and brushed that wave of golden hair until it shone. Then I plaited it tightly together again, smooth and glossy and sleek, and hugged it close. Go, I told it, go and finish this.

It was several days before the braid found us again. I gathered the warm, sluggish weight of it into my arms and felt no different. Not better, not worse. The stone that had been pressed against my chest since my son's death remained solid, immovable; for the first time, I found myself thinking of Jacoby with something other than loathing.

We wintered deep in the south that year, deep in our grief. Strange stories followed in our tracks, were traded in the mead hall and grew ever taller in the telling. A village out east where all the menfolk had died in a single night. Strangled, or so it looked, with several of them chafed red about the throat — but how could such a thing be done? It was a plague, people said, or a punishment. It was the women who did it and made up fancies to cover themselves. It was a a lie, made up to scare credulous children.

Do you think them all dead, Gryff asked me late one night, his voice lowered and hoarse.

I looked over at Chance, curled into a ball on her sleeping pad.

Would you weep for them if they were, I asked my husband. He didn't answer, just pulled me close and kissed the back of my neck. I relaxed into his embrace, ran my hands over his skin. It had been a long time. His body felt different. Sharper in some places, softer in others. Wordless, breath hot between our mouths, we moved together. Found ourselves, each other.

We never again spoke of the village, or the vengeance my braid had wrought there.

The following spring, Boorma told us she would be staying in the valley. She'd cleaved to a local horse breeder, a good man whose eyes brightened with adoration whenever their gaze lit upon her. He loved both of her children as well, and said he would teach Maator how to bring young horses to the saddle, and how to keep a breedline strong.

Chance never found her balance.

She drifted along with us, stoic and mostly silent. There were many she took a tumble with, once she came into her womanhood, but none to whom she cleaved. Not even for a season. When her bloods stopped, she couldn't say for certain who sowed the seeds. Couldn't say, or maybe just wouldn't. As her belly rounded, a light returned to her eyes. A certain hopefulness, sometimes even joy. I hadn't seen her look that way for many years. Not since that awful summer. Not since Will. And I allowed myself to hope as well. That Chance was returning to us. That this small new life would bring her back.

What a fool I was to think it.

. . .

There'll be no snow today. The sky is a pale, sparrow-egg blue and stretches cloudless and clear across the valley. Gryff has gone to tend to the dark bay mare. Willa is still in bed, snoring gently. The bigger her belly gets, the more trouble she has getting to sleep at night and we don't like to rouse her too early in the morning. There'll be enough of that when the baby comes.

The baby. My great-granddaughter. My daughter's granddaughter.

I thought I could do it, Chance told me. Willa, scarcely eight moons old, lay settled in her arms. But this is too big, Mama. I look at her and I see him, I feel his death all over again. I love her so much, Mama, but the love, it claws me up inside and I can't ... *I can't.*

I didn't listen, I didn't *hear*, and a week later she packed herself a travel-sack.

Don't think you can crawl back here, I snapped when she came to say goodbye. We'll raise your daughter, your father and me, of course we will. But if you walk away now, Chancey-girl — if you abandon this child of yours like she's an old toy you've grown tired of playing with — then don't dare call yourself her mother.

All these years later and those words, the last I ever spoke to my daughter, hook fresh in my heart. I'd been furious, frightened and half-sick with the shock of it, but by the time I'd calmed down she was gone. My Chance is clever and, moreover, as stubborn as I am. If she doesn't want to be found, she won't be — not by any common means, at least.

In my hands, the brightly coloured bird is limp. I smooth its plumage with my thumb and turn it over so that the cavity in its breast falls open. The space is small but there's room enough to hold what I need.

A long, thin plait made from three strands of golden hair, wound to a neat coil.

Petals from a white tulip, dried and pressed. I would have preferred a fresh bloom but it's not the season. Chance knows her herblore; she will understand the meaning.

And my words, my whispered plea: *forgive me, daughter; you never left my heart.*

The braid stirs sluggishly at my feet. There's silver winding through the gold now, more and more with each passing hour. I tug at the end of a single strand, still brassy-bright, and it comes loose willingly, threads itself through the needle with swift and eager speed. It's but the work of a dozen stitches to sew up the bird and, as I tie the last one off, the creature begins to flutter in my hand. Its eyes are bright onyx jewels.

I set it upright, watch as it flits to the back of my chair and begins to preen.

Reaching down, I run my hand over the braid. It's almost wholly silver now and makes only the slightest response to my touch. I want to offer thanks but my throat closes on the words. They are not enough, they are not nearly enough. Still, I try to believe that what Boorma says is true: Gothel was my mother, and she will know. Wherever she is, she will know.

As soon as I open the door, the bird finds its wings. It makes a swooping circle of the yurt then darts past me, trilling joyfully. I watch it fly, a speck of colour against all that the limitless blue, until it's gone too far for my old eyes to follow. In her bed, Willa stirs. Who's there, Mother Zel?

I close the door against the cold. A messenger, I tell her. Go back to sleep.

I can't, she groans. The little one's turning somersaults.

That's a good sign, I say. She'll be healthy and strong. She'll ride before she can walk.

Smiling, Willa beckons me over. I sit on the edge of the bed, my hand pressed to her belly, and laugh as a tiny foot kicks at my palm.

Can we stay on this spring, Willa asks. Just for the spring? Boorma says we'd be welcome.

I recognise her mother in the shy, hopeful way she tilts her head. Her mother as a young girl, before the terrible summer that quelled the light in her eyes for good.

Just for the spring, I tell her. Willa grins and I feel the baby within her kick once more.

BY THE MOON'S GOOD GRACE

It be all I can do to keep still in me bed, waiting in the dark for the snoring to start up on the other side of the curtain, that snuffling death-rattle of his I been hearing most of me life, and when it does come I gotta wait some more till I be sure me Mam be sleeping sound as well. She been giving me the side-eye since we come back damp and wretched from the woods, me stepfather carrying his story the way he sees fit to show it and me with me mouth pinned shut, not knowing what to do with the words even if I could lay tongue to the right ones. Not me story to tell, he says, not me place to bring such frightful tidings to me own Mam, specially when I don't see the proper shape of them.

I can still feel where his fingers dug into me arms, shaking sense into me; the bruises'll bloom with first light.

Waiting, waiting, while the crimson thread knotted round me breastbone thickens and twists, becomes a cord, becomes a rope, becomes a cable like them what pull Old Yag's punt across the river, and so it drags on me, tugging till I can't bear it one breath more and throw off the blankets. Quiet, mindful of the creak and tattle of the floorboards, I make me way to the door and grab me cloak from its hanging hook. So soft, this fine woollen weave me Granmama must've bartered more'n a few good hens over, more again to have it dyed red, red as a castle rose, and her stitching be finer still.

The thirteenth moon of your thirteenth year, my girl; a milestone to be well marked.

Me eyes prickle and I rub at them, angry and sad and scared all at once, but I push the whole mess down, throw the hood over me head and slip from the cottage into the night.

Full-bellied Moon shines the way but I don't need her, don't need nothing but me own bare feet that know this winding woodland path better'n any paved or cart-runnelled road, me feet and the pull of the thread that draws me on sure as any compass. Running till the breath catches cold in me throat, ducking each low branch and leaping over roots that hump and thrust from the dirt, running till me toe catches on some unseen thing, some stone or twig that sends me sprawling. I break the fall with me hands, palms scraping raw along the ground but better that than another bump on the head, and I roll panting onto me back to see I've landed in the same little clearing where I seen the wolf this afternoon.

Where it seen me.

Those sharp amber eyes fixing on mine as it stepped from the trees, paw by careful paw. I were frozen, breathless, but outta wonder more'n fear, standing motionless as it circled towards me, muzzling the air. Were it the basket in me hand that caught its nose, the cloth-wrapped salted pork tucked in beside the apple scrumpy and fresh-baked bread? If I tossed the meat to the ground for toothsome jaws to chomp over, would I be allowed to go on me way?

The wolf come so close I might've touched it, might've bent and run me fingers through that thick grey pelt to feel the softness of its fur, the heat of its skin. Me own skin itched with the longing of it.

As it stared at me, yellow eyes clever like no beast's should have a right to be, a trembling welled up inside me, a great shivery warmth that filled me chest and belly and legs, and I swear that when that hot, pink tongue licked over the back of me hand it be like Goddess Moon herself reached down through the clouds to touch me. Me knees buckled and I crumpled to the ground like poor wooden Judy with her strings cut off.

The wolf growled.

I lowered the hood of me cloak and lifted up me face, thinking that this weren't no bad kind of death if it be the time for it. But the beast stared past me, back into the forest the way I'd come with me Mam's last words an echo in me ears — *straight to Granmama's, you mind me; this ain't no day for flower-plucking.* Thunder rumbled in that pale throat and its hackles spiked stiffer'n any tomcat's. Then, just as sudden as it showed itself, the wolf turned and loped off into the trees. The forest round me kept still, kept hushed, like it be holding its breath but I didn't stay to see what it might be expecting. Only gathered up me cloak like I be doing now and scrambled to me feet, bidding me traitor legs to come to their senses.

Wolf-clearing or no, this ain't where I meant to be stopping tonight. The thread, it keeps on tugging and atugging, and I got no answer but to let it run me all the way to me Granmama's house. Even then, hunched over with me hands braced on me knees, trying not to retch up me dinner amid all the huffing and apuffing, I still feel the pull of it. Only when I find me way down to the old mill pond does it let up some, does it let me stop and fall down beside the water which be still and smooth as a Lord's window pane.

Now I know why I been led here.

Stop your shrieking, girl, he yelled at me this afternoon, axe dripping blood onto the floorboards. *It were nought but a damned wolf about to have your throat out, and you standing there mouth open like a bullfrog catching flies. Now hush up and lend me a hand.*

He wouldn't listen. Wouldn't stop to hear about Granmama, or what happened — what I *thought* had happened — before he busted through the door all fury and fright. And me not able to find the proper words neither, so he just kept yelling at me to shut me gob and help him, and when I didn't — when I *couldn't* — he pushed me away. Pushed me hard. Me foot slipped in something, maybe the blood, most likely the blood, and I remember falling with me fingers grabbing at the air, and I remember nothing else.

Till he be shaking me and slapping at me cheeks. His clothes were wet. The wolf be gone, the floorboards smeared pink in his hurry to clean up. *You say nothing to your Mam,* he told me. *You know how she be about the bloody wolves, she'd have me hide as quick as spit.*

But Granmama —

Your Granmama ain't come back yet; Lord know where she's taken herself off to.

The wolf —

You think your Mam wants to hear your lunatic ravings? That wolf ain't touched your Granmama, I cut open its belly meself. All you gotta tell her, it be stalking you and I come by and scared it off. You hear me? His face all scrunched up and ugly with anger, maybe a little bit of fear as well, so I just nodded and let him help me stand. I felt woozy and when I touched the back of me head, I found me a swelling and some crusted blood. It come away in dry black crumbs under me fingernails.

His own hands were clean. Freshly scrubbed.

The Moon throws her reflection onto the surface of the pond, so clear and perfect it might be her own twin sister rising in greeting. I take off me cloak and fold it neatly on the grass. Me white cotton nightgown be torn now, dirty round the hem, and I can hear me Mam already, sighing and tutting as she tells me to fetch her sewing basket. I take it off as well, place it on top of the cloak. Me skin prickles with gooseflesh and I rub at me arms, teeth chattering.

The crimson thread tugs, gently.

Water, cold as snowmelt, laps at me ankles, calves, thighs. Before long me foot bumps against something solid, something soft, and I reach down with both hands, shivering as the water splashes round me. I grab a chunk of fur, wet and thick, and pull. The body barely budges, so I crouch down to brace meself then pull even harder, grunting through me clenched teeth as I try to drag it back to the shore. It takes a good long time and clumps of fur keep coming away in me hands, dumping me on me arse more than once. Each time I swear a bit louder, then find me a new grip and keep on going.

It be only in the shallows, with the wolf lolling on its back and those pale front legs bent awkward in the air, that I see all the rocks stuffed into her belly. I swear again, thinking that the Moon, she might've told me. The Moon, or her water-logged sister, now broken into so many silvery splinters.

Nothing for it but to kneel down, reach me way into the beast and roll out stone after stone. Most of them be slippery with moss and slide easily enough in me hands. There be a couple caught stubborn 'neath her ribs and the dull crack of bone makes me wince as I wrench them free. Emptied out, it still be a strain, but there be enough useless weight gone now for me to pull her up outta the water and on to the grass.

"You a heavy bitch," I tell the dead wolf, then I lay me weary self down beside her and stare at the Moon.

I don't remember even closing me eyes, but I must've done cause the next thing I know I be waking up to a warm tongue licking at me cheek. I let out a cry and roll away, scrabble to me knees to find meself face to furry face with the same yellow-eyed beast from the woods this afternoon.

Me teeth be all achatter from the cold and me skin be prickled as a plucked hen's.

The wolf tilts its head to one side. If it had lips, it might be smiling.

"Wh-what you after?" I ask, getting to me feet proper. Beside me, the dead wolf I dragged outta the pond lies still. Its hollowed belly gapes in the moonlight and I swallow, feeling sick to see it.

The other wolf, the wolf with the too-clever eyes, nuzzles at me hand. It takes me wrist in its mouth, all gentle like a mother cat moving her kittens, and tugs. Fangs press into me skin but don't break it. The wolf tugs again, then lets me go. It trots a few paces away towards me Granmama's house before stopping to look back over its shoulder, head cocked. Its eyes glitter in the moonlight. I grab me cloak from where I left it near the edge of the water and wrap it round me shoulders, the wool soft and warm on me shivery skin. Then I bundle me tattered nightgown up close to me chest and run after the wolf.

By the time I reach the front door, the beast has lifted the latch with its too-clever paws and slipped inside.

Behind me, there come a spat of barking noises, ratchety as an old sinner's cough. I turn round and see maybe seven or eight big grey wolves all jostling and asnuffling round the dead one down by the mill pond. One of them nudges the body with its nose, licks at lifeless jowls that won't ever lick back. Another sits on its haunches and shows its silvery throat to the moon. That howl be full of hurt and helplessness. It sinks into me bones. Into me blood. Me heart beats with it.

Wiping at me eyes, I push into me Granmama's house and shut the door on the night and all its wolves.

Excepting one.

Which I do me best to ignore as I busy meself lighting a fire in the grate. I still be chilled from me swim and me hands shake as I shape the kindling. Sneaking a sidelong glance, I see the wolf sniffing over the stain on the floor. It makes a kind of whine, a kind of growl, and scratches at the wooden boards. The fire takes and I use the bellows to build the flames till they big enough to keep spitting and acrackling on their own. Then I sit back and pull me cloak tighter round meself, pull the hood up over me head. Outside, another howl splits the night. If I be still, if I hold me breath, I can feel the echo of its song in me heart.

The too-clever wolf finds the basket I left behind on the sideboard this afternoon. The hunk of salted pork disappears between its jaws in three quick bites. Now it looks to me, amber eyes bright, and for a moment I wonder if it means to fill its belly with girl flesh after all. If it maybe just wanted me all warmed up first.

"Do what you gonna do," I says. "Only do it quick."

But the wolf just closes its eyes and dips its head and then —

And then —

Smarter folks'n me might find the proper words for how it happens, but they not here to see it.

The arch and crack of a furry spine, the stretch and pull of slender legs.

Paws spreading and splaying into feet and into hands, ten fingers and ten toes all neatly nailed if you pay no mind to the dirt and grit lodged under them.

That long snout pushing back somehow, pushing in, the whole head bulging and breaking and putting itself back together in ways that seems like it gotta *hurt*, but the wolf, it makes no sound at all, even as fur melts away to skin like frost meeting the winter sun.

In me mind, I see me Granmama again. *Don't be frightened, my girl,* she says this afternoon, *you watch now, and you see.* I remember how her dressing gown puddled to the floor. I remember how I screamed at the shock of it.

Me face burns with shame.

Maybe now I *should* look away, but the only naked woman I ever glimpsed before be me Mam with her soft curves and dimples, belly all skin and wrinkles after me baby brother come wailing into the world, and the woman squatting here before me be a different creature. Her legs be hairy and lean and muscled and I can see the rise and judder of her ribs with each panting breath. Her shoulder blades stick out like stunted wings and, between them, a line of coarse dark hair grows right down the middle of her back to disappear into the crack of her arse. She smells like sweat and earth and something else besides. Something musky and wolfish that sticks in me throat and makes me cough.

The woman looks up. Pushes the tangle of long, brown hair outta her eyes and makes her mouth into a shape kinda like a smile, kinda like a snarl. Maybe she outta practice.

"Don't be scared," she says. Her voice be rough, like tearing cotton. Maybe she outta practice with that as well.

"What there be to scare me?" I ask, bold as I can. "You lost those nasty old fangs of yours."

The woman blinks. Then she throws back her head and laughs, a great howling bellow that makes me shiver, makes me flinch. A sudden yearning bubbles up inside me, a feeling like seeing some fine court lady in pearls and a pretty dress and wondering how me own self might look in such a getup, or watching the miller's oldest son heave round sacks of flour at market and thinking how it might be to lick the fresh dusting of white from his cheeks.

I want to laugh like the wolf-woman laughs. I want to howl down a blessing from the Moon.

Instead, I pull me cloak tighter round me shoulders and stick out me chin like me stepfather does when he gets mean and no nonsense. "Granmama were like you," I says. "Weren't she?"

"No." The woman runs a flattened palm over the stain on the floor, slow and gentle. She lifts her hand to her face and sniffs, then licks at her fingers with a bright pink tongue. When she looks back at me, her eyes be all aglitter. "*I* were like *her*." She makes a gruff, throaty sound, not really a growl, not really a sob, as she pushes herself to her feet. Her first couple of steps towards the fire be wobbly as me baby brother's but she soon rights herself. "Been a while since I went on two legs." Where her thighs meet, the hair be dark as the rest of her legs, dark as me Mam's down there as well, but thicker. A corkscrewed tangle of black curls that spread and spike almost up to her belly button.

I turn back to the flames; me face can't get no hotter.

The woman kneels, then tips back me hood and runs a hand through me hair. It still be damp from the mill pond but she be gentle, like me Mam would be. Each time her fingers snag on a knot she stops to work it loose. "You and me have talking to do, Little Red," the woman says in that rough, scratchy voice of hers. "You need to tell me about your Granmama, about what happened here. You need to speak for her, what can't speak for herself no more."

Me stomach clenches. Bile scrapes at the back of me throat. I don't want to remember what happened today. What I seen, or thought I seen. (What I *know* I seen.) Better to keep that all squashed down hard inside me guts so it blackens and rots like cabbage left in the ground and I don't need to think on it no more. Just turn it and till it and seed it over fresh.

"Who *you* be?" I says, jerking free from those gentle hands as I twist round to face her. "Who you be to be pawing at me and asking for me Granmama's story like you got some kinda right to it?"

The woman sits back on her heels. "I gotta right to it," she says, quiet and careful. "Your Granmama were me *mother*, Little Red. I got more right to her story than any soul you care to name."

I don't believe her at first, or I don't wanna believe her. The weight of it be too heavy to hold, too hard to carry. Me Mam had a sister, that be true. A sister who went away before I were even born, who skipped off with some fella what made wicked eyes at her and promised her the whole of the Moon, or so me Mam says. She don't talk too much about it. When she does, her face gets all sorrowful and less *solid* somehow, like you might break it with a breath.

I never wanted a sister, if that be what loving one gets you.

But now I peer at the woman real close, and she pulls that dark mess of hair outta her face, and there be that same quirk in the corner of her mouth that me Mam gets when she be worried about an eggbound hen, or whether the flour might stretch to a last loaf of bread, and I try to picture this woman being plumper in the cheeks, rounder all over like me Mam, and I think maybe I can see it.

"So you me aunt?" I says.

The woman nods. "That I am."

"And you a wolf, too? And me Granmama were a wolf?"

"Not for always, but there were some moons she ran with us." She smiles. "Some *months* even."

And in that smile, me Mam and me Granmama both be shining bright, and me tears start spurting before I can stop them. "She ch-changed," I says. "Needed to sh-show me, she says." The woman reaches out, squeezes me shoulder and the words, they spill from me like beads poured from a pouch. I tell her everything I can remember, not in any kind of order but just as it comes into me head, one big jumble for her to gather up and winnow as she please.

"This axe-man, he be your mother's husband?" she asks after I can speak no more. Her voice has lost its rougher edges; her tongue be steel-tipped.

"He don't mean to kill Granmama; he took her for a wolf — an ordinary wolf, I mean."

Her nostrils flare. "But he did mean to kill this *ordinary wolf*?"

"It were gonna eat me, he thought." Guilt makes a hard, cold lump in me throat; it hurts to swallow round. "Were me own useless screaming that brung him here."

The woman stares at me, head tilted to the side. I can only match her gaze for a moment. "That fire of yours be dying," she says at last, pushing herself up from the floor. "You ain't got the touch for flamework." She rolls her shoulders and rubs at her arms. Her skin be goosepimpled, her nipples chilled to hard, brown nubs. "I forget how it be to be furless."

I poke at the half-burned logs, not really expecting them to catch. Me stomach turns queasy and sullen, like I been gorging on apples filched too early in the season, and me eyes itch from crying. Rocking back and forth, wishing I could wind it all backwards, wind meself right back to this morning and start on over. I wouldn't scream this time, wouldn't say nothing or do nothing but kneel down and wrap me arms round me Granmama's neck and press me face to her soft, wolfish fur.

"Must have big ears, your mother's husband. To have heard you all the way through them woods."

I wipe me nose and look up. The woman has put on me Granmama's nightdress, the one with tiny yellow and blue flowers embroidered round the collar. It stretches across those broad shoulders right enough, but then hangs too big and billowy, missing me Granmama's bosom and hips to shape it proper.

"Ever get to wondering why he be snuffling round so close?" The woman climbs into me Granmama's bed and pulls the blankets up to her sharp and pointed chin. "Why he be following on your heels, Little Red?"

I lay the poker aside and hunker down into me cloak, trying not to think on how he been looking at me different this past year. Sneaky glances out the sides of his eyes when he supposes I ain't paying him much mind. Me chest ain't nothing like me Mam's yet, or me Granmama's, but it ain't dead flat no more neither. And he been looking. A shudder runs up me spine. With the fire down to embers, the house be getting cold.

"You meaning to sit there all night like some poor senseless cub left out in the snow?" The woman lifts one side of the bedclothes. "Plenty room for your scrawny behind."

I half expect her to take me in her long, strong arms and cuddle me, the way me Mam used to do when I be sick or fever-ridden, or when I woke up in the night from dreams I didn't wanna remember. Or maybe it be more of a wish, cause when she rolls over instead, her back curving away in a bony arc, I feel so sad and hollow I nearly start crying all over again.

"What those wolves be doing?" I ask after a time. "Down where I pulled Granmama from the pond?"

"Won't be there no more," she says. "They'll have taken her, those what can make themselves hands for hauling. Rest of the pack be guarding their passage."

"Where to?"

"We got our own ways to farewell the dead. Our own places to honour them."

I think on the little churchyard in our village and the vicar with his black robes. Me Mam's never had much patience for preaching or church learning and he frowns at us whenever we cross paths at market or along the road. She just smiles and nods and sometimes, if her arms ain't full of sewing or vegetables or me baby brother, she even curtsies. *Always be polite to that man*, she tells me. *Ain't nothing in that fat little book of his'll teach you more'n what me or your Granmama can, but he thinks it gives him power. Let him think it, him and other men like him, and you go on your way knowing better.*

"Shouldn't you be there?" I whisper. "With the other wolves, saying goodbye to your Mam?"

"I should," the woman says. "Yet here I be with you, Little Red."

"That ain't me name," I tell her.

"Maybe it be your wolf name," she says.

I take a careful breath then inch across the bed till I be pressed tight against her back, the two of us snug as roosting hens. She makes a soft sort of growling sound but don't move or shove me away, and so I risk laying me arm across her hip. Her rich, earthy scent be strange and strong, but it don't hide the smell of rosewater from me Granmama's nightdress, not wholly, and so I sniff deep and deeper still, pulling the both of them into me, me Granmama and me new gruff aunt whose words catch in me heart like a fishhook.

Maybe it be your wolf name.

We be about halfway home when me aunt stops sudden and grabs me by the arm. She sticks her nose in the air and sniffs hard, then closes her eyes and keeps very still, like she be trying to catch some faint or distant noise. All I can hear be the birds squawking out their morning songs, and I be about to walk on when she drags me off the path and behind a thatch of prickle-bush.

"Do not move," she whispers. "Do not speak."

Frightened, I do as I be told.

After only a moment or two, there come the sounds of footsteps, the strides long and sure. Peering through the dense leaves, I see enough to know him, that axe swinging sharp in his hand as he heads back the way we come. Back towards me Granmama's house. I hold me breath and look down. Me aunt be clutching me hand tight and I notice a smear of jam on the cuff of her sleeve. Strawberry or raspberry or maybe even boysenberry — she were up with the sun, opening every jar of preserves in the larder and spreading them thick on chunks of bread from the loaf me Mam baked.

I forget the marvel of such food; wolves have no tongue for sweet.

If we hadn't left when we did —

If I weren't so keen to get home to me Mam who must be worried near outta her wits —

If we still be there, scoffing down jam and trying to find some smock and kirtle that fit me aunt better'n old flour sacks, while the front door burst open and he come storming in —

I bite down on me lip, not wanting to think on it.

"That him?" me aunt asks after he be far outta earshot. "That your mother's husband?"

I nod, and she makes a low growling noise then pulls me to me feet. We move quicker now, not stopping for breath till we reach the cottage and find me Mam out front with me baby brother stuck on her hip, tipping out breakfast scraps for the chickens. She sees us too and her face come over all changeable, like she be surprised and angry and excited all at once and don't know what she should be feeling most.

Then she drops the scrap bucket and marches across the yard. "Take him," she says, thrusting me brother into me arms. "Now get inside and keep your ears to yourself."

I start to explain, start to apologise, but she just roars at me to *get your arse inside right now*, and so I go as fast as I can manage it, what with a newly squawling brat trying to kick and wriggle his way free of me grip. I don't think I ever seen me Mam furious enough to be trembling.

I plop me brother down in his cradle and scout round for the bit of leather he likes to gnaw on, but me Mam probably has it in her apron pocket. No matter, even I can tell it ain't his teeth that be bothering him this moment. "Shhh," I says, finding his rag dolly stuffed down the side of the bedding. "Shhh," I says again, waving it in his face. "She weren't yelling at you; it be me she mad at."

I leave the dolly on his chest and scurry over to the window for a peek. They both still out there in the front yard, me Mam with her back to the cottage so I can't see her face, and me aunt stooped a little, her hands moving in a quick, urgent language all their own. No one be yelling no more, excepting me baby brother who don't seem to have no use for his dolly today, so I can't hear a word of it through the window. But I keep watching as me aunt reaches out for me Mam and me Mam shrugs off her touch like it belongs to some beggar woman, as fingers point and heads shake with anger and then with sorrow, as me Mam finally steps forward and sags into me aunt's chest and their arms wrap round each other's waists and they both crumple to the ground like they got not a single leg bone between them.

Me aunt looks up over the hitch and shake of me Mam's shoulders, looks up and stares me straight in the eye, and all of a sudden I feel like a thief caught with some treasure I ain't got no right to be holding.

I lurch away from the window and go back to me baby brother. I waggle his dolly about and pull me face into silly shapes and blow farting noises through me lips till he starts to giggle. He reaches out with his pudgy little hands and I let him grab me finger. I even let him suck on it a little. "You not too bad," I tell him, tickling his tummy with me other hand. "For a stinky little goblin."

We be sitting like there that when the cottage door opens and me Mam and me aunt come in, both of them with eyes swollen from crying.

"Boil some water, Little Red," me aunt says. "Strong talking gonna need strong tea."

Me aunt drips four slow spoonfuls of honey into her cup and stirs it counterclockwise. "Our family always been wolves, long back as can we remember. We always been wolves and we always been secret, till time come it needful to tell. This secret be the most important one you ever gonna keep."

I fasten an imaginary button over me mouth. "I won't tell a soul, I promise."

"This ain't no game," me aunt snarls. "Swear it on your life, swear it on your *mother's* life — for it might come to that, up to the end."

Startled tears prick at me eyes. Me Mam reaches across the table to lay a hand over her sister's. "Don't scare the girl, Rachel. She been through enough already." She turns back to me and her face be so kind I just wanna curl up in her lap and have her stroke me hair, like she used to do when I be littler. "But you need to understand," she says. "You never talk to no one about this who ain't wolf. No matter if you think they your best friend in the whole world, or if they even more to you than that, you don't say a word, mind me?"

"Then why *she* telling *us*?" Me voice be too loud, but that be the only way to stop it breaking. "We ain't no wolves to carry her secrets for her."

Me aunt snorts, her cup clattering onto its saucer. "You told me this child be bright."

"Bright as the Moon," me Mam says with a glare. Then she takes me hand in hers and I feel the roughness of her skin and the hard little calluses from all her sewing, and I want time to stop and whatever be coming to stop with it. But time pays no mind to such useless prayers as mine, and me Mam, she keeps on talking.

"I *am* a wolf," she says. "Like me sister and me own mam, though I ain't worn the fur since long before you be born. And you a wolf too, me girl, and now you come to the age for changing and for choosing what kinda wolf you gonna be. There be fur and there be skin and there be those what live betwixt, like your Granmama kept herself. There no wrong way to be a wolf, mind me, but no easy way neither."

Me aunt takes me by the chin, lifts me face so there ain't nothing to do but look her dead in the eye. "You search inside yourself and think on how you been feeling since your bloods come, the itch of being stuck all the time in your own skin, your jaw aching like it want nothing more'n to rip and to rend. Think on how you felt last night, seeing the Moon swollen up in the sky, hearing your kin howling for her comfort, and you know me and your Mam be speaking the truth."

She lets me go and I slump back into me chair. Under the table, me toes curl and clench. "How I come to be a wolf then, if I don't get bit by one?"

"Peasant superstition!" Me aunt's laugh be bitter as old ale.

"You a wolf because you born a wolf," me Mam says, and sighs. "Rachel, we doing this all wrong."

"You expect us to do it right? Were our mother kept all the stories, this be her job."

"Well, she not here no more!" She thumps her fist on the table. In his crib, me baby brother starts crying again. "Goddess preserve us," me Mam mutters, getting up to soothe him. She brings him back in her arms and unfastens her bodice, pushes a nipple into his grizzly mouth till he latches on and begins to suck like her milk gonna dry up any moment.

"Be Jacob a wolf too?" I ask.

"No," me Mam says. "This little tyke be just a boy, through and through. He gonna grow up a man and never know nothing of wolves save to stay outta their way."

"Like his father?" me aunt says, low and dangerous.

"You let that alone," me Mam snaps. "That ain't for right now." Her voice sounds strained, tired, but there be steel running through it. I keep perfectly still, fingernails digging welts into me palms as the two of them glower at each other across the table. Cause I see it now, the wolf curled up inside me Mam all these years, hibernating behind her plump cheeks and pretty smile. I see it sleeping, and I don't want it to stir.

"Well then," me aunt says finally. "We start over. We start at the beginning."

And so she explains again, about our family, about the wolves and their secrets. Me Mam chips in now and then, to add a bit more or to put the words another way when she sees me getting confused, but mostly she just sits, nursing me baby brother and letting me aunt shape the story to her own way of telling. I learn how most wolves, once they get to changing, run in fur near all their lives, how they make families with wolves of the woods — them that won't never know skin — and how they be treated no different by their natural brethren, never hunted down or driven away, never shunned or scorned or had violence done to them for what they happen to be. I learn how if a she-wolf gets herself with cub while running in fur, then those cubs will always be natural wolves no matter the father, and how if she likewise be skin-walking and find herself a man, then her children be just the same as him, like me own brother who ain't never gonna feel the howl of wolf-blood in his veins.

And how if she change her shape while her belly be heavy, then there won't be no cubs, nor baby neither.

Only when two wolves lay together in their skins, do a moon-baby get conceived, and only if the she-wolf keep herself a woman all those months of growing, do a new beast get born what will come to know both worlds as well, or as little, as it wishes.

"Wolves like us," me aunt says, "they be rare."

I turn to me Mam. "Then me Pa, he be a wolf too? Like you?"

She always told me he were a hunter. She told me he got stuck out in a blizzard the very first winter after I be born, that he caught chill and died. Now she nods. "A wolf what couldn't bear to walk on two legs from moon to moon, a wolf what went back to run in the woods."

A sharp pain stabs between me ribs. "He didn't wanna be me Pa?"

"He didn't wanna be a *man*," me Mam says. "There be a world of difference in those two things, though you too young to see it. He did love you, girl, and he might've stayed if I pressed him to it, but it would've been a misery to us both. I never took to the fur so much; he were a lost thing without it."

"But might he still be living?" I ask. "And might I meet him, as a wolf?"

Me Mam looks to me aunt, who shakes her head. "He don't run in our woods no more, not for years, nor any we keep treaty with. Might be dead, might be living, but you ain't ever likely to find out, Little Red."

I don't know why I feel so sunk. I ain't had a father growing up and this only means I still ain't got one, and there should be no difference in it, and yet, and yet. Seems it be one thing to think me Pa dead all me life, and another to know he shot off and left me behind. I wonder if he ever come back some moonlit nights to take a peek through the window at me sleeping, furless face.

If he ever wishes he could wind back time and make his choice over again.

"You go with Rachel tonight," me Mam says, and I jolt forward, realising she been talking a whole bunch more besides. "She might not have all your Granmama's stories down perfect, but she got more'n enough to guide you through your change."

"Tonight?"

"The last rising of the full Moon," me aunt says, sounding impatient. "You gonna run with me and mine this month, we see how you take to four paws."

It all be rushing on me so fast, I ain't got no way to keep up. "But Mam, I thought *you* would —"

"It been so long, I probably forgot how to change *meself*, let alone show you how to go about it."

"Don't listen to your mother," me aunt says. "Once you learn the trick of it, ain't nothing you ever gonna leave aside — no matter how motheaten and raggedy your fur be getting."

"Maybe so," me Mam says with a frown that don't quite manage to hide the smile underneath it. "But I can't be leaving our little Jacob behind now, can I?"

As I look at me baby brother, asleep on her breast with his golden curls all aglow in the sun, there come this great hot seething from deep in me guts, a rolling and a roiling heat like I never know before. If not for him, we could all three of us leave this stupid shack, me Mam and me aunt and me; we could wear our finest fur and moon-sharp fangs and chase each other's tails through the trees. If not for this mewling brat, this pathetic creature so soft and pink and helpless I could rip open its belly with less effort than it be to —

Me aunt slaps me cheek and I round on her, snarling —

And she slaps me again, harder, and then she has me by the jaw, her fingers digging into me flesh like they not gonna stop till they find bone. "Never," she growls. "Jacob may not be wolf, but he still your brother and we never turn on kin. *Never.* You bare teeth at that child again, you gonna have more'n a slap or two coming for you."

She lets me go and I can't help it, I start sobbing worse'n me baby brother ever done in his life. And I try to tell me Mam how sorry I am, how I didn't mean it, how I don't even know where it sprung from, that murderous heat so sudden and fierce, but she just shushes me and squeezes me hand. "You go with Rachel," she says. "This be your change coming on you, and it ain't good for none us to be holding it back longer'n we already done. You can be any kinda wolf you choose but you need to learn the ways of it first, and me sister be your best teacher for that."

I nod, staring down at the tabletop. I don't wanna look at me aunt, don't want her to see the shame in me eyes, don't wanna face the disappointment in hers. "Now then, Little Red," she says, ruffling me hair. "Wolves don't sulk, we —"

As she turns her head towards the cottage door, I hear it, the tread of boots up the front path, their heavy scrape on the stoop. Then the door opens and me stepfather come inside, axe still in hand, mouth falling open with no small measure of surprise.

"How long you been here?" he shouts at me. "I been out in the woods all morning, searching. Your Mam worried herself sick when she see your empty bed."

Before I can find a lie to pin to me tongue, me Mam pushes herself up from her chair. "Only thing I worry about now, Stefan, be your great hullaballoo waking your son, just as I coax him to sleeping." She makes her careful way over to the crib to lay me baby brother down, touching her husband's cheek as she passes. "Girl took herself off for a early walk, but she home now, and safe, and that be all that matters."

He stares at me, eyes all dark and narrow as they take in the nightgown I still be wearing, before turning his sneer on me aunt. "And who might this fine lady be, gracing our humble home with her presence so unexpected?"

"You ain't never met me sister, Rachel," me Mam says, hurrying back to stand by his side. Me aunt got a face on her like she ready to open his throat with her teeth.

"Your sister," he says. "Rachel." He put his arm round me Mam's waist.

"She gonna take our girl off our hands for a bit. Give us some time to ourselves."

"Who gonna help you round here then, you and the wee one?"

Me Mam laughs, slaps him gentle on the shoulder. "She only be gone for a month; I been on me own with a babe longer'n that before your grumpy self even come into the picture. Now sit and I'll put your lunch out."

He grunts and slips his arm from her waist, hefts his axe in both hands. "Ain't got time for sitting, what with half the day gone chasing after girls what never been lost in the first place." And so, while me Mam rushes about fixing bread and meat and his favourite red onion relish, putting it all in a sack along with a bottle of scrumpy, he just stands there, running a thumbnail over his blade and glancing up every now and then at me aunt who don't offer up even a single word by way of conversation.

Only after he leaves, does she get to her feet and stalk over to me Mam. "You'll keep that man in your house, knowing the blood he got on his hands?"

"It be *his* house and, I told you, this ain't the time for talking on it."

Me aunt don't say nothing to that, but the muscles in her jaw tighten and twitch like it be all they can do to keep her mouth shut. Me Mam, she quiet now too but when I go over and take her hand, she lace her fingers through mine so hard it hurts.

"Wolves never turn on kin," I says to me aunt, me voice sounding stronger'n I feel.

She tilts her head, her lips twisting to a grim smile before she turns her back on the both of us. "You just make sure'n get to your Granmama's by sundown, Little Red," she says, pausing at the cottage door. "Us *wolves*, we got business with the Moon tonight."

I wrap both hands round the mug of water me aunt gives me and gulp the whole of it down in three hard swallows.

"Gonna be thirsty after," she says. "Specially the first time. Your mother, she don't tell you nothing about this?"

I shrug. "She says, better I come here with an empty head than one full of second-best shadows."

"Me sister still got *some* wolf-sense left to her, then."

It be cold in me Granmama's house without the fire burning, so even though me aunt strips down to her goosepimpled skin, she lets me keep me cloak draped over me bare shoulders, long as the hood be down and collar unbuttoned so me wolf self be able to slip out under it. Anything else just gonna tangle or tear the seams, she tells me, and me Mam got better to do with her days than stitch up after me.

"This gonna come natural, I promise." Me aunt crouches on the floor beside me. "You made for this, Little Red; you be wolf as much as you be woman." She smiles. "Now, you tell it back to me, the story of the Moon, in words of your own so I know you got it fixed in your noggin."

"Long as the Moon be full," I says, "she let us choose our shape, be it fur or skin. And time, that don't matter none, only that day-shifting be harder, so for now I best to call on her when she riding through the sky, not when she moving down under the earth. Which means three nights each month and, later, when I be better at the ways of me changing, the two days between them, and that be all."

"Cause what gonna happen when the Moon starts to wane?"

"Whatever shape I be, fur or skin, that be the shape I keep till her belly swell up round again."

Her long fingers ruffle me hair. "Good little wolf. Now we ready."

At that, me throat cinches tight, and I croak out the one question I been too scared to ask till now. "Will it hurt?"

"Not enough to make trouble," me aunts says, and then she tells me to shut me eyes and think again on how it be last night, running barefoot through the woods, not knowing where I be headed, or even why, but running all the same, cause there be something dragging on me, something calling on me, and *the crimson thread*, I whisper, and *yes*, she whisper back, *find it, it belong to you*, and so I think on that, and remember the tug of it on me ribcage, and I reach into meself and there be the thread already laying over me palms, sliding through me fingers, the Moon thrumming through it and thrumming through me, and I pull on it and let it pull on me and feel the loose and stretch of me limbs

as the crimson knot unravels

and me body unravels

and rebuilds

and knows itself a Wolf.

. . .

Wolf got no words for being wolf, they useless as cloth and knife when we got fur and fang to keep us warm, keep us fed. Wolf live in the sight and sound of the world, thick in the smell of it. Our tongue be for tasting blood of the hare, flesh of the deer. For licking up the mouth of other wolf, to show we be of the pack and honour it.

I honour me aunt and I honour her mate, for they be top wolf.

Her mate what give me a rabbit, let me tear open the soft fur so the guts steam on the snow, so I know I be of the pack and always welcome.

Wolf time be hunting and sleeping and wrestling with the cubs of me aunt and the other cubs of the pack. It be feasting when we run down our prey and hunger when none be found. It be nosing out scents and knowing what passed here, and when, and if it come back or go on its way. It be casting our howl to the wind and catching some other song thrown back from over the woods.

Wolf watch the men work, watch them stalk with their gun and lay their trap, too lazy to hunt with tooth and claw of their own. Wolf watch and wolf see, and wolf slip back into the trees quiet as the shadow.

Man never know what wolf know, that always be the way of it.

Heart beating, blood rushing, breath frosting.

Earth below to feed us. Moon above to bless us.

And now the Moon grow big again, me aunt nuzzles me snout and nips me haunch. I turn me shoulder, cause I be wolf, and won't be girl not ever again, but she growl and snap and fix me with her yellow eye to remind me of the promise I make.

And a great shame come over me, worse'n not sharing a kill, and I follow me aunt with tail tucked tight all the way back to the den of me Granmama.

Where be the woman-scent of me own Mam, come and gone this very day, and the crimson thread, it tug on me, and me aunt growls again, her clever paw on the latch, and she push us inside before the unravelling truly begin.

. . .

Panting and sore, I roll over to find me aunt still in her wolf shape. Though it be dark inside, and I ain't got the sight no more for nighttime, there be enough moonlight shining in the windows to get by. "You ain't changing?" I ask me aunt and she cocks her head in that way I come to understand means it be a stupid question below her dignity to answer. I get to me feet, rub me bare arms. Sweat be turning to frost on me skin, and I feel more naked than ever in me life.

I feel like me fur been stolen from me.

Me aunt makes a sharp, rough bark — *look here; look close* — and I see me cloak folded up neat on the table and, sitting beside it, a basket.

Me useless girl-nose has lost the scent of me Mam, but I know this be her handiwork. There be bread and eggs already boiled in their shells, thick slices of smoked pork, and scrumpy that I gulp straight from its little jug once me aunt turns her nose up at it. Under the cloak, a fresh-washed smock I be quick to throw on, as well as a kirtle and the woollen tights I tore on the fence nail, climbing over when I should've gone round, darned so fine I can barely see the stitches.

I picture me Mam trekking all the way out here in the snow, me baby brother hitched on one hip maybe, just so there be fresh food and warm clothes waiting for when I be done with me change, and I remember how I nearly didn't come back this night at all, how me aunt had to snarl and take me by the scruff, how I didn't spare me Mam no mind when I be wolf.

I think on these things, and they settle in me stomach like stones.

Me aunt, she pads across to the door, nudges it open with her snout.

"Don't leave," I beg. "I ain't ready for you to leave."

She looks back at me and makes a sound something like a bark, something like a whine, before loping off into the night. This ain't goodbye for good, I know that — we be kin, and I always be welcome to run in her pack, whether it be the very next moon, or any number from now — but she be *wolf*, not some tame hound to slaver at me furless heels, and I should know better'n to ask it.

Not one of us be more important'n any other, and me aunt always gonna put the needs of her pack first.

That be the way of it with wolves.

Shivering, I close the door. I be exhausted, tired down to me very bones as me Mam would say it, but if I gonna rest here then I need to light a fire, get some heat into this empty house before the winter chill seeps right into me chest, right into me heart. The cloak me Granmama made be no match for this kinda cold, and I ain't got me cousins to curl up with no more, ain't got their thick wolfish pelts to nuzzle into, let alone a pelt of me own.

Twice, me clumsy fingers drop the tinderbox before I get a spark to take and coax some hopeful flames to dancing, but then, as I push more twigs in between the bigger logs, there come a sly creaking from behind and I swivel round to see the door swinging open once again.

"Thought wild beasts be scared of fire," me stepfather says. He holds his axe in his right hand; the blade glimmers as he steps towards me.

I scrabble to me feet, almost tripping on the hem of me smock. "You got no place to be here," I tell him, edging sideways and trying to get the table between us.

"Saw me the strangest thing while I be out there in the night, waiting and watching. Two wolves come into this house, but only one wolf leave. And now you be here, all on your own." He moves to his left and I dodge in the other direction, but he only be feinting and he grabs me by the arm as I hurtle past, throws me so hard against the wall, me breath gets knocked from me lungs. "Little wolf-girl," he says, pressing himself to me, pushing the head of his axe up under me chin. "That what you be?"

Me eyes blur with tears, and me heart beats so fast I think it gonna burst itself right through me ribcage, but I ain't got it in me to change again so soon, not so drained as I be right now, and so terrified. I bare me teeth at him instead; it be all I can do.

He laughs, a nastier sound as ever I heard. "Think you scare me, little wolf-girl? Already sent one of your kind on her sinful way, reckon I can deal with the grand-pup she made." Lowering the axe, he takes a step back then punches me full in the guts. I slide down the wall to the floor, feeling like I'm gonna vomit. "Not hard to puzzle out, your Granmama gone after I kill that wolf right here in her house, then you off with that filthy woman, night o'the full moon. Your mama always been so protective of the wolves and no wonder, her own mama being one, for how long only the good Lord be knowing, and now her daughter. What I gonna find, little wolf-girl, I slit open your belly? Rabbit fur, chicken feathers? Bones of little children snatched from their beds?"

I start to crawl towards the open door, but he kicks me twice in the side and so I just lie where I be, matching his hateful sneer with a glare of me own.

"Your mama too soft, sending you away with them monsters rather'n do right by her people." His axe swings like a pendulum, counting off the seconds left to me. "But you ain't gonna pollute me family no more, not you nor any like you. Come morning I gonna round up some good men, and we gonna clean them woods of wolves. Have ourselves a righteous burning. But first, I gotta clean me own house."

He spits in me face, his disgust slipping slimy as frogspawn down me cheek and over me lips, but I ain't about to look away. If he gonna kill me, he gonna do it with me eyes full upon him. For I still be *wolf*, and ain't no man foul as this gonna make me cower.

The axe lifts, and time swells, and I suck me last breath from the Moon-blessed world —

— as barrelling through the door there come a great growling fury what knocks me stepfather to the ground like he be nothing more'n a scarecrow. Powerful jaws snap the bones in his wrist even as he tries to swing the axe, and his screaming barely starts before it trickles to gasping and gurgling from a throat torn crimson by sharp and bloody fangs.

This wolf be a stranger to me. It not of me aunt's pack and so, when it starts towards me, I shake me head and plead to be left alone. "You got more'n enough meat already," I tell it.

But then it looks at me, then *she* looks at me, and those pale blue eyes shine so fierce and sorrowful that I flush with shame not to have seen straight off, not to have known. She licks the tears from me cheeks with her pink wolf tongue, and I put me arms round her neck and bury me face in her fur and breathe her in deep as I can.

She smells like wolf, and she smells like me Mam, and there ain't no telling where one nor the other begins.

.   .   .

The Moon be set and the sun not far off rising by the time we done with the cleaning and tidying away.

"Jacob gonna wake before we get home, we don't hurry," me Mam says, pulling on me Granmama's winter boots. "He be frightened half to death, no one be there for him." Still, she spares a moment to frown at her fingernails, even though she already scrubbed them twice, and makes me check her face again.

"Ain't not a speck left on you," I promise. "You washed it all clean."

"Maybe one day, that be the truth of it," she mutters, hustling the both of us outta the house.

There still be patches of blood on the snow where we dragged his body, where it lay before the wolves come slinking outta the woods to carry it off. I ain't ever gonna forget the deep, mournful sound of me Mam's howl as she called to her kin, or the way me aunt yelped and bounded about her, excited as cub in its first spring to find her sister wearing the fur at last. But me Mam, she just turned tail back into Granmama's house and by the time I followed her, she already be woman again.

I kick at the biggest stain, hoping to bury it 'neath cleaner snow, but it just spreads itself bigger and me Mam yells at me to keep up. "Little bit of blood don't matter none," she says. "Ain't no one gonna find any piece o' that man, once they be done with him." Her face be tight and hard, her lips pressed to a trembling white line, like she be furious but trying not to show it. I seen her make that face before, when me stepfather come home stinking of ale, or when some fine lady dream up a fault in her stitching and wanna pay less than be promised.

"Sorry, Mam," I says, me voice wheedling with worry. "I ain't meant for him to find out I be wolf."

And then me Mam, she stops dead in her tracks and turns round, grabs me shoulders with both hands like she means to shake the teeth from me head. "You don't apologise for this," she says. "You don't apologise for what you be, not ever. That man were gonna take your life, girl, just as he took me own Mam's and would've taken mine, he ever found out, no matter that I be the mother of his child, no matter that I loved him." Her words break, and her breath billows in frosty plumes. "Maybe I *still* love him, and maybe I be loving him till the end of me sorry days, for in many ways he were a fine man, and better women than me been known to blind themself to what lie black and rotten under a man's finery. But that be *my* burden to carry, not yours. Not ever yours."

She hugs me close and the crimson thread thickens and tugs, the pull of it gentle as me Mam's hands, and I know it be knotted as tight round her breastbone as it be knotted round mine, that it binds me to her now and always, as it always has done, and there be nothing in the world what could ever see it severed.

Far off in the hills, there come a howl, long and yodelling. Me aunt's maybe, or maybe one of her pack, and I yearn to throw back me head, open me mouth and call back an answer full-throated.

"Would you still love me if I be wolf," I ask me Mam. "If I never be nothing else?"

She smiles, all wistful and strange. "Wolf be simple, don't it? Wolf be an arrow, shooting from where you be to where you *want* to be, without the muddle of a woman's heart to skew the path. Sometimes, wolf be what we need most." She pulls up me hood, presses a kiss to me brow. "Skin or fur, daughter, you be me kin, and I love you for it. By the Moon's good grace, that be nothing you ever need doubt."

Then she takes me hand and we run together, me with me red cloak and her wrapped in me Granmama's forest green, and I feel them all threaded through me, me Mam and me Granmama both, and me aunt as well, those clever yellow eyes watching the wane and wax of Moon, watching and waiting for the night I come to run for a time with her.

WINTERBLOOM

Some nights, entwined together in the spice-scented darkness of our bedroom, my husband sighs and strokes the soft curve of my throat and says:

Sometimes, I wish I were still the Beast.

I run my hand over his skin, so smooth and sweat-slick, curl my fingers through the coarse hair that too sparsely covers his chest, and remember the velvet warmth of the pelt that once clothed him from snout to claw-sheathed paw. Then I say:

I'm glad you are not.

Time cannot be spun backwards; curses cannot be respelled. There is no profit but melancholy in yearning for what has passed, and so I will never admit to my husband that I often share in his wish.

I love the man I have married, but it was the Beast that I fell for first.

My sisters have all but finished their latest bloom. Grace has scattered her bright pink petals all over the drive, while Patience hoards hers close, those once-crimson flowers shrivelling brown and resentful among her thorns. I always wear soft leather gloves for pruning; Patience, in particular, seems to go out of her way to draw blood. For the first two years, I dared not touch them at all, imagining such savagery akin to the shearing of fingers and toes, but my husband persuaded me otherwise.

They are rose bushes now, love. Treat them as you would any other.

Indeed, they looked so miserable after a while, their canes knotting and twisting like unkempt hair, their last yellowing leaves hanging listless through winter. Grace sent forth a blushing profusion from the start, but I didn't know the colour of Patience until her third summer when two dark buds finally emerged, sullen and haughty, and then took more than a month to unfurl.

My eldest sister cultivates spite like fine wine.

Nail parings and hair, I tell myself now, snipping off the deadheads and thinning the canes. I don't know if that's precisely true, but both look healthier these days and bloom from late spring until the first winter frost. It's more than most of the roses in the gardens can manage, although the two Chinese bushes my husband brought me from his Parisian sojourn last year are constantly in flower during the warmer months. Quite the little wonders, especially as one of them is yellow! I intend to cross them this season with several of my more stalwart roses to see if their abundance might be drawn across, if not their most unusual hue.

A thorn stabs through my glove, piercing the tender web between finger and thumb, and I draw a pained breath. Stretched out nearby, Jules lifts his wolfish head and whines. After reassuring the hound, I peel down the leather cuff and suck at blood beading from my newest wound. "Patience," I scold my sister. "Will you never yield?"

"It seems highly unlikely."

The voice is light and lilting and comes from over my left shoulder. Startled, I turn to find a tall, beautiful woman standing outside the front gate, her turquoise silk robe patterned all over with golden flowers and trim to match, the panniers beneath more ostentatious than any I'd seen even in Paris. Her hair is piled high atop her head, and she holds a parasol even higher, keeping the touch of the sun from her painted face.

No — not paint. Her skin is bare but unnaturally smooth and pale, tinged the same silvery blue I sometimes glimpse on my husband's body when moonlight spills through our window on cloudless nights. Only this woman seems to glow from within, as though she has swallowed a handful of stars — or is about to birth one.

I've seen such a complexion before.

"You're fey." I step back, the shears lifted before me. There is some comfort in their iron blades, though I fear that is little more than superstition. Jules is by my side now, a suspicious growl rumbling deep in his throat.

"Oh, sweet puppy-dog." The woman smiles and extends her arm through the railings of the gate. "Shall we be friends?"

Jules rushes forward and I open my mouth to shout a warning, but his tongue is already licking her palm, his shaggy tail wagging in welcome. Apart from my husband, he's never greeted anyone with such enthusiasm before. My stomach tightens. I'm alone here, deserted even by my loyal hound. The shears tremble in my hand.

"May I enter your home?" Still smiling, the woman scratches Jules behind the ear. Her eyes are the bright, brilliant green of winter moss.

"Do I have the power to prevent you?"

"No," she says and — *shimmers* — and in a blink she's standing right before me. "But I thought it awfully rude not to at least ask first." Jules dances about her skirts, staining the silk with his dusty paws. The woman frowns and plumps at her ludicrously widened hips. "Is it all too much? I wanted to make a favourable impression."

Suddenly, I'm all too aware of the shabby day dress I'm wearing, the loosened stays beneath, and my slippers, muddy and scuffed from the gardens. My hair, I'm certain, looks as though a passing bird might choose to nest in it. "Who — who are you?"

"I'm Peregrine," the woman announces with a flourish.

"I don't ..."

"Peregrine," she repeats, quirking her lips. "Your husband's favourite sister."

The shears fall from my grasp and land, point first, in the ground between us.

My husband doesn't speak of his family. He's never known anything about his father, other than the man was human, and on his mother's side … well. You don't talk about the Fay behind their backs if you value your health and good fortune. We've had scant to do with any of them since the wedding, although every day I'm reminded that we build our lives on fey largesse.

The meals that manifest on our table.

The beds that make themselves each morning.

The clothes that return, freshly laundered, to our closets.

Only the gardens are left for me to maintain, a concession for which I am grateful. On our third anniversary, my husband commissioned a lavish conservatory so that I might tend to my favourite plants no matter the season, and each summer he returns from Paris with at least one new rose bush to further my collection. There's not a drop of magic in a single leaf or petal, only the hard work of my decidedly mortal hands.

"This is delightful," says Peregrine, sipping her rosehip tea. By some strange and subtle means, her attire has become less flamboyant, and she sits comfortably in the parlour chair across from me.

"The hips are mine," I tell her, hoping she hasn't noticed the thin rind of garden grime beneath my fingernails. Hers are a pale pink and clean as the day she was born. "I mean, from my roses."

"Not …" She raises an eyebrow.

"Oh no, my sisters might be full of flowers but they never produce any hips." Almost never. I force a smile. "The insects don't seem to care for their pollen."

"Bees are highly suspicious creatures." She glances about the room, taking in the tapestries on the walls, the small marble busts of composers my husband admires, and the vase of fresh-cut flowers I'd filled only that morning. Her face is still as a winter pond, her judgement beyond ken.

I clear my throat. "Did you plan on staying for long?"

Peregrine raises *both* her eyebrows.

"It's only that your visit is unexpected." My words are rushed, tumbling over one another in their haste to correct any prior offence. "Your brother won't be home for more than a month, and the guest chambers aren't prepared, and — and I don't even know if we still have the guest chambers, it's been so long since anyone came to stay." I offer a small shrug. "This house is fond of rearranging itself."

Flapping a dismissive hand, the woman leans back in her chair. "You must miss him, when he's away."

"The house is quiet without his music, and still. But I have Jules" — the hound, stretched beneath the window, thumps his tail on the carpet at the mention of his name — "and I spend most of my days out in the gardens or my conservatory. At night though ... it's an odd thing. We often sit together and read in the evening, speaking no more than a dozen words to one another, so why should it make any difference for me to sit in here on my own with a book? And yet, it does. It does."

Peregrine smiles. "He leaves a shadow behind, and it makes for poor company."

"It sometimes feels that way, yes."

"Why don't you travel with him? Be at his side while he performs."

"Hardly at his side." But I smile, genuinely this time. "His piano provides the music of my winter and my spring. I hear his compositions before anyone else; I have no need to sit among the crowd and applaud, and he needs me there even less."

The first two times I did accompany my husband to Paris, I tell her, we barely found any hours together, so occupied was he with rehearsals and recitals and society suppers where I felt as welcome as an unwashed milkmaid. The tours are always scheduled during summer months as well, when my roses here are in their prime and I was miserable with missing them. We would fight over the silliest things; he would sulk and I would leave to wander the Tuileries Garden alone, admiring the well-kept grounds and impressive statuary, but feeling the wrench of our argument like a bone lodged in my throat.

"We love each other better if we spend our summers apart," I finish, "and our reunions are all the sweeter."

Peregrine settles her teacup neatly in its saucer before placing them both on the little round table beside her chair. "Well now, sister-in-law, I would very much like to behold this marvellous garden of yours."

The bearded irises have long since finished, and I've been more lax than I would like in removing the shrivelled remains of their flowers, but many of the lilies are in extravagant bloom as we walk along the path towards the conservatory. Peregrine pauses on several occasions to admire them. Some she cups in her hand, bending to inhale their fragrance; others, she gently rubs between finger and thumb. Once or twice, she stops to whisper into the trumpet-shaped flowers but her words are soft and garbled and I cannot catch their meaning.

"They're very content," she tells me, beaming. "You take good care of them."

Once we're inside the conservatory, her green eyes widen and she twirls on the spot, demanding to be introduced to all the roses in turn.

"There are orchids as well," I say. "Although they aren't in bloom just now."

I escort her through the rows of planters, giving Peregrine the name of each rose along with its history, and before each she sketches a shallow but respectful curtsy. This year's seedlings I leave for last. Most have a flower or two and I take great delight in detailing their parentage, explaining which two bushes I chose to bring together, and why, and whether the pairing has been successful. I'll transplant the weaker specimens to the gardens in late autumn, keeping the more promising inside for future hybrid experiments.

"Clever little bee," Peregrine says. "Flitting about, spreading pollen hither and thither. What magnificence you have wrought."

My cheeks warm. "Let me show you my favourite."

In the far corner of the conservatory, tucked behind its showier cousins, is a bush sporting several pale pink roses. The colour is common enough, their size not out of the ordinary, but the deep red thorns that bristle the length of each cane are long and curved, sharp as kitten teeth, and gathered so close there's scarcely a space to grip. Pruning will be a hazardous endeavour.

"What a savage she is." Peregrine's tone is one of admiration.

"I've been selecting for fragrance." I motion her forward and she bends, sniffs delicately at the closest bloom. Her lashes flutter and she sways, a small mew of surprise parting her lips. "Heady, isn't it?"

Her fingers brush the petals and she tests the point of a thorn, gently, against her thumb. It scratches an even whiter mark along her pale skin. When she speaks, her voice barely rises above a whisper and her words remain unintelligible, though I find myself leaning in close to listen.

"Is that the language of flowers?" I ask, only half in jest.

She straightens. "It is the language of the Fay. But plants fathom it well, as do many wild things."

I chuckle. "These roses of mine are hardly wild, cossetted as they are."

"Are they not?" Her expression is unreadable, her gaze unwavering. "My dear bee, you should never mistake cossetted for *tamed*."

Why is she here, I want to ask again, if not to visit with her brother? Is there a test I'm meant to pass, some esoteric examination that will find me lacking — or is this a kind of game, or sport, and what will happen if I lose? My husband has told me many stories of fey caprice and cruelty, however incidental the latter may be. *They seldom entertain notions of consequence, and you slight them at your peril; your sisters know this too well.* I've no desire to spend the rest of my life as a statue, or a rosebush, or worse.

Peregrine touches my wrist. Her skin is warm, surprisingly so. I don't know why I expected the chill of morning glass. "May I take a rose?"

I swallow, hard. It's the question my father should have asked, all those years ago, the single act of unsought permission that swung the needle of fate's compass so irrevocably in my direction. She *must* know this.

"Do you mock me?"

The woman frowns. "It is not my intention."

I find my shears and snip one of the pink roses from the bush, taking care to leave all thorns behind. Peregrine tucks it into her bodice, lowering her chin to breathe in the fragrance once more. When she lifts her head, those green eyes seem brighter, sharper than ever. "Be at ease," she says. "I am not a trap to be tiptoed around."

"Forgive me." I busy myself trimming dead leaves, all too conscious of her scrutiny. My chest is tight. "It's rare we have guests, let alone ones such as yourself. If I have caused any offence—"

"Please." She covers my hand with her own, stilling my work. "Will you cease to think of me as a guest? I would very much prefer to be your friend." There's a softness to her features now and, unless I imagine it, a hopeful curve to her smile. Though what she would want from such a friendship, I cannot guess.

"I was planning to gather some pollen today," I tell her. "Would you like to help?"

"Oh, yes." Her smile broadens to a grin. "We shall be bees together!"

The deliberate crossing of two roses is no delicate matter.

First, decide which bush shall set the seed. This is the mother rose and you should select her for the large and sturdy hips she already produces. Choose, but leave her be for now. The remaining of the pair shall be father, providing the pollen. Find a bud, not yet opened but not still so tightly closed you cannot tear the petals away. Remove them all, petals and sepals both, revealing the fine stalked anthers within. Carefully pluck these into a cup or bowl. The pollen is hoarded inside, so allow them to sit for a full turn of the sun to dry. Only then will they shed their precious yellow dust.

The father's role is finished now. Come evening, it is the mother's turn.

Again, begin with a bud. Tear off her petals and sepals, and this time strip away the anthers as well, making sure to hold them clear. Self-pollination is not desired. She should sit this way, naked and vulnerable, overnight. Her stigmas, all that remain, will grow sticky, desperate and receptive. With all her finery and perfume stolen, neither bee nor bug will care to visit, and she knows this.

You will be her only chance for motherhood.

Next day, shake the anthers to release the pollen. A wealth of gold should coat the bottom of the cup. Press a fingertip into the dust and brush it over the mother's exposed stigmas. Be gentle; after all that fearful expectation, it needs only the barest touch for the pollen to cling. Do this three or four times more over the next two days until the pollen is exhausted. Even then, despite your efforts, fertilisation is not always assured. Tie a ribbon with a paper tag around the stalk — it will take many weeks for a hip to form, and you do not want to forget the parentage. It is a pretty sight at the end. So many curled and colourful ribbons, so much flagged potential.

Now wait.

Watch the hips as they form and swell and blush. When they are the colour of sunrise, they are ripe and ready to harvest. Snip them from the bush and, with a sharp blade, remove the top and tail. Slice the hip in half, carefully. Sometimes there are only three or four seeds, sometimes up to a dozen or more. Small and brown, the fruits of all your labour. Be pleased. You are almost there.

Set them in soil, one seed per pot. They will need to endure the winter, to feel the cold biting at their cosy isolation, in order for life to spark. Leave the pots outside for at least two frosts. Let death lace the topsoil. The best seeds will rise to the challenge; the weaker will surrender and pass — you don't want those anyway.

Now wait some more.

Come spring, the successful seedlings will push their green and stubborn selves out of the earth. Greedy for sunlight, they will be eager to show off their finery and, within weeks, the buds will come. New and unique roses, seen by no one else before, brought to life by your own two hands. There is a miracle in that. Amid the viciousness.

And, although I will admit to being tempted once or twice, it is not a process to which I could ever submit my sisters.

Peregrine takes up just three replacement cards, discards and declares her points in triumph. She wins first and last trick as well, and all but two of those in between. It's the third game of Piquet we've played, and she has beaten me decisively each time. She must be cheating, but I can hardly level so blunt an accusation.

"What luck you are having," I say instead. "Each card you draw seems of benefit."

She stares at me, confused. "Isn't that the point? To draw beneficial cards?"

"Yes, but ... they should come by chance."

"Oh." Her long fingers blur as she shuffles the deck. "I did think it was rather a dull game, Bee." She deals us each another hand. "How's that?"

I flip my cards around to show her. A huitième in hearts; a quatorze of aces. "Did you simply deflect your luck to me?"

She grins. "There's little else I can do. It clings to me like gossamer."

"Can you try? There's little amusement in cards otherwise."

We play several more rounds and Peregrine tries, she honestly does, but the risk of losing chafes at her like stale sheets in summer and she cannot mask her displeasure. Nor does she understand the appeal of winning against the odds, when the odds are so easily within her power to control. Finally, when I manage to win both the declared points and the majority of tricks, she hurls her cards with such vigour that the corner of one lodges neatly in a hunting tapestry across the room, right where the boar's heart would be. Jules lifts his head and whines.

"It makes no sense," Peregrine snaps. "It's the same as with the roses."

"I thought you loved the roses."

"But all that work! All that time waiting and watching and not even knowing whether the flower will be the colour you want, or whether there will be a flower at all. You want a yellow rose? A blue one?" She waves her hand, that narrow wrist swivelling. "I can conjure such a thing in a blink."

"I don't wish for a magic rose," I tell her. "There is satisfaction in the work, a pleasure in anticipation. And also … if I could conjure precisely what I wanted, then I would only ever get just that."

"How terrible, to always get what you want."

"But it is. Because sometimes you can't even imagine wanting a thing until it's right there in front of you, blooming and beautiful and utterly unexpected."

Peregrine leans back in her chair. "You are rather enamoured of chance, Bee. But then so are all your people; your lives are governed by it."

"The Fay do not believe in chance?"

Her laughter is a bladed weapon, sharpening on a whetstone. "Of course we do. Chance is the very substance of wagers, and the Fay love nothing more. But it isn't ours to wield. On my side of the veil, everything is *exactement*, just so. Wild chance is a dangerous beast; you cannot predict the paths it will forge."

I reach down to scratch Jules behind the ear. Pushing his heavy head against my hand, the hound makes a low grunt of pleasure deep in his throat. My husband presented him to me as a birthday gift, several years ago. Then only a pup, I could carry him as easily in my arms as I might a babe. Although it wasn't a dog that I'd yearned for, I now can't imagine my home without him.

"Good boy," I murmur. His tail thumps.

"Shall we play once more?" Peregrine asks, shuffling with a motion too swift to follow. She never rose to retrieve her flung cards, but they will have returned to the deck all the same. How quickly I have become used to her ways.

"Is there a game you would prefer to Piquet?"

"None that I could teach you, dear Bee." Her fingers flash as she deals the cards. "And none, I'm sure, you would wish to learn."

My husband can no longer recall the music that rolled through his rough and shadowed mind as a beast. *I'm merely chasing echoes*, he tells me, his voice thin with loss. *The notes, the cadences, the melodies — they are dust in my ears.*

He was a promising composer before his *retreat*, as those in the world refer to it, bright and ambitious, the youthful swagger of his work still in minor need of refinement, but now ... oh now. Often, he brings his notices home and reads from them of an evening, those ardent words others have sought fit to bestow. How his music moves gentlemen to tears, and ladies to swoon. How it fills all manner of hearts with such profound and sorrowful joy they can scarcely bear for it to end. And how, on at least one memorable occasion, a listener attested to the opening sonata forcing a crack so deep in his soul he feared he might never again be whole — only to feel the wound miraculously healed by the majesty of the final movement. Although the scar, he wrote, would surely burn eternal within him.

Such praise always brings a flush to my husband's cheek, and grief to his eyes. *If they could only hear what I once heard. The music at which I can now only hint.*

And if you were the Beast again, my love? What then?

He stares at his hands, at their smooth skin and neatly manicured nails. *I could not play it, nor transcribe the notes.* His sigh is hollow and worn; he has turned this ground many times before. *Sometimes I fear it was but a balm, an illusion concocted to soothe. If I could hear it now, might it be nothing more than a simple child's rhyme? Or merely a discordant mess? What can a beast really know of music, after all?*

My fingers lace easily through his. I press my ear to his chest and listen to the slow rhythm of his heart. *As much as he can know of love, surely?*

Though now a man, my husband is still more than strong enough to lift me in his arms, to lower me to the bearskin rug before the fire. His tongue is no longer coarse, but it knows well the places that please me and is skilled at seeking them out. He plays me as he would his fine piano, with gentleness and force in equal measure, with desire tuned to perfect pitch — and with love.

Sometimes, I can sense the Beast rippling beneath my husband's skin.

Sometimes, it is enough.

It takes another week to summon the courage to ask Peregrine about the curse visited upon my sisters. You do not seek favours of the Fay lightly. We stroll to the front gate, Jules at our heels, and she considers both rose bushes in turn.

"She has a miserly scent," Peregrine says, wrinkling her nose.

Patience shudders, her dark green leaves rustling. It might be a stray breeze is the cause, but I imagine a haughty squaring of shoulders, as she so often did when we were girls. Of the three of us, my eldest sister was the most ill-named.

Still. "That's hardly her fault."

"Is it not?"

Grace has only two pink roses fully open, though there are plenty of buds coming through. She never stops, spring through early autumn;

her eagerness is exhausting. Peregrine sniffs at the nearest flower and, smiling, runs a careful index finger along the cane. The thorns are small and widely spaced, providing no danger of accidental snagging, and the perfume Grace exhales is as delicate as wedding lace.

"She plays her cards close, this one." Peregrine plucks a petal and lays it on her tongue. After a moment, she swallows.

The action is slightly shocking to me, but I can't pinpoint why. "Is there anything you can do for them?"

"You are doing enough, Bee. They seem well."

"I mean, can you restore them?"

The woman sighs. "It made them statues, yes? The original spell?"

I will never forget their empty, blank-eyed gaze as they stood on either side of the gate, staring not so much at one another but through. Pleased with her work, my soon to be mother-in-law turned with a gracious smile to receive my expected, effusive appreciation, only to find me in tears. *But they were dreadful to you*, she said, her tone hovering dangerously between confusion and pique. *Let them think long upon their malicious and envious hearts and repent should they wish a return to their former selves.* Malicious they may have been, and envious no doubt, but they were — they are — still my sisters, and I'm not too proud to admit that I begged. On my knees, with the bare-faced stranger who was so recently my Beast pleading my case in tandem. *Mother, see not ingratitude but instead behold my bride's capacity for love — even for such wretched creatures as these.* Despite growing fearful of her wrath, I persisted, asking that she consider it a wedding boon: restore my sisters to life; it was all I would ever wish.

"A most generous bargain," Peregrine says. "If somewhat short-sighted."

"I was careless with my words. She gave them life but not their true selves."

"It was perhaps all she could do."

"It was her spell. Surely she could uncast it if she wanted."

"My mother is impulsive, Bee, but seldom petty."

My mother. It comes near to a surprise to hear her use the phrase. She is my husband's sister, but until this precise moment, I had not forged a conscious link between Peregrine and the tall, imperious woman who officiated at my wedding all those years ago. Hastily, I think back, hoping I've said nothing to which a daughter may take offence.

"Here." Peregrine holds out her hand. In her palm sits a small, white stone of the kind that line the sides of the drive. "Throw this as far as you can."

The stone is warm in my grasp. I recall what my husband has said about the Fay over the years, all the reasons he has given for wanting to live on this side of the veil and to never cross paths with his family again. *You cannot trust them, my love. They play with lives as boys do with toy soldiers, and care just as little for their loss.* Will my mistake be to throw the stone, or to let it drop?

Peregrine nods her encouragement. Her eyes are brighter than ever.

I throw the stone. Hard.

"Now stop it," she whispers as the thing arcs away from us.

"What? I —" The stone lands with a soft thud on the lawn, several metres distant. Jules ambles over to investigate. "How could I have stopped it? You ask the impossible."

"But you threw it. I saw you throw it."

"That doesn't mean I can call it back like a trained dog."

Peregrine smiles, but her lips hold no joy in their curves. "Magic works much the same. It follows its own rules and they cannot be broken. Sometimes bent, if you're strong enough, but never broken." She picks another petal from Grace's rose and rubs it between finger and thumb. "You knew not what you asked, Bee. It would have taxed my mother greatly, forcing such a deviation from the path. But even she must allow the spell to run its course, just as your stone finished its natural flight."

"So my sisters ..."

"Need repent of their envious ways." She pops the petal into her mouth, chews a couple of times before spitting it out again. "Bitter, for all its soft and sweet appearance. This one shall be a rose some while yet."

Jules has returned, disappointed. He barks, rough and throaty, and Peregrine laughs. With a neat swivel of her wrist she produces a short stick, curved just so, and tosses it in the same direction as my stone. It flies, turning end for end, much further than it should by any natural rights, and the hound bolts after it like gunshot.

"Tea?" she asks, offering her arm.

I link my elbow through hers. We walk in slow silence back along the drive, each winnowing our own thoughts. Peregrine looks over her shoulder, just the once. Whether it's a parting nod to my sisters, or simply to check that Jules is following, stick wedged happily between his jaws, I cannot tell. Beneath her breath, she hums a vague and unfamiliar tune.

"Is that fey music?"

Startled, Peregrine slides me a brief, sidelong glance before shaking her head. "It's an old song. I doubt you would know it." She says nothing more for the remainder of our walk, but simply stares straight ahead, her features calmly rebuffing all scrutiny.

Still, the strange tune has caught my ear and burrowed deep. I suspect I shall be humming it myself by nightfall.

Four summers ago, Grace brought forth a single rosehip, one hopeful nub hidden amid the dozens of dried and barren pistils. It was, and would be, the only time either of my sisters had done so and I warned myself against undue expectation. But the hip stuck firm and grew swollen, blushing a bright orange as the early autumn winds crisped the air. I pruned back only a few of her canes and tied a protective gauze netting around the hip, lest some passing bird mistake it for a juicy berry.

Each morning and evening I paid a visit to Grace, chatting idly as I snipped away dead leaves and inspected her foliage for aphids — an unnecessary precaution; pests have always avoided my sisters as much as pollinators.

Except, of course, in this one happy instance.

I always made sure to include Patience in my conversation, but it was Grace I fussed over, remarking upon how healthy she was looking, how beautiful her flowers had been that summer, how plump and burnished her rosehip was becoming. As the season drew to a close, I became confident enough to muse on how many seeds might nestle within, and where to plant out the bushes when the time came.

Perhaps along the drive, evenly spaced on both sides. They would be Grace's seedlings, but it would be cruel to leave Patience standing by herself.

Would they flower like Grace, sending forth a profusion of flagrant pink?

Or had some adventurous bee brought pollen from afar?

I was getting ahead of myself, I knew that; too much could still go wrong. The seeds might succumb to winter's bluster and chill, too fearful to germinate. Or the seedlings themselves might be feeble, unable to be planted anywhere outdoors. What would I do with such weaklings? Certainly not mulch them, as with my more common failures. Keep them in pots? Bring them out to visit with Grace when the weather was mild?

I shook my head of such thoughts and allowed my excitement to blossom.

You're like a giddy aunt, my husband remarked.

I suppose that's what I am, I replied with a grin. *Or will be.*

Finally, I awoke one morning to find a thin layer of frost thrown over the gardens.

It's time, I told Grace, the snips steady in my hand.

Cushioned in its gauze, I carried the hip to the conservatory where my work table awaited, along with several nursery pots filled with rich, moist soil. Her progeny would have the very best chance. As the tip of the paring knife touched the smooth red skin, I hesitated. Closed my eyes for a moment and took a deep breath. *Be plentiful.* Less than a prayer, not quite a wish. Then I sliced the fruit in two.

At first, I didn't understand. The rind was thin and brittle for such a swollen vessel, the flesh that clung to it meagre. I set the knife aside and dug into the pulp with my fingertips, searching frantically for the seeds but finding only the short, fibrous hairs that should have surrounded them, keeping them warm and safe. They coated my skin, their touch as light as scorn. Later, I would realise that one had worked its crafty way beneath my fingernail; the irritation did not ease for days.

But the hip before me was barren, yielding not a single seed.

I wept then, hot and unexpected tears that seeped down my cheeks unchecked as I sieved through the pulpy mess on my table a second time, then a third. Nothing, nothing. Wiping my face with my sleeve, I surveyed the ruin. It is strange to think upon it now, but at the time, the loss felt close to unbearable. With shaking hands, I scooped it all together, gathered it gently into the gauze and tucked the dismal package into my apron.

Three days passed before I could bring myself to tell Grace.

I buried the remains in the soil beneath, digging until I could nestle them between her roots. It was a risk, breaking the ground already near frozen, but I bedded Grace down with plenty of straw, and Patience as well.

Roses cannot speak, nor shed a tear. But the next summer Grace produced not a single bud, only a mournful robe of thick, green leaves I did not dare to prune until the spring. It seemed too unwelcome an intrusion. Patience, I noted, arrayed herself in such bountiful crimson finery as I had never seen before, nor have I since. They are my sisters, and I love them still, but they have passed well beyond my understanding.

Perhaps I have passed beyond theirs as well.

The weather has grown unseasonably cool, and Peregrine is wearing a cloak made of feathers. Entirely of feathers, as far as I can tell, with nary a stitch in sight. They are brightly coloured and shine with iridescent splendour whenever the sun sneaks a glance from behind the dreary, grey-bellied clouds.

"The rain at least will be welcome," I mutter, yanking out weeds from the carnation beds. "If it rains, after all this bluster."

"Oh, it will." Peregrine sounds certain.

The next weed comes up with an earthworm tangled in its roots, fat and wriggling. I free the creature with a tine of my gardening fork and drop it back into the soil, covering it over with a sweep of my hand.

"Such kindness, for even the lowliest worm," Peregrine says. "I can see why my brother fell in love with you."

"Worms are useful. I'm not so kind to aphids or thrip."

She chuckles, returning her attention to the slim volume of poetry she found in the library. "Then I shall make sure to keep myself of use to you, Bee."

I wonder, though not aloud, what use she deems herself to have been already.

But no, that isn't fair. As my trepidation eased, I've looked forward to seeing Peregrine at the breakfast table each morning. She does not rise as early as I do, and so I carry out my morning rounds in thoughtful solitude, greeting the flowers and noting tasks to which to return later. By the time I'm hanging up my hat, she is waiting with hot chocolate and a wealth of sweet pastries — daily luxuries I've come to enjoy. Likewise, I appreciate her easy companionship throughout the day. She seems happy to read beneath the shade of a tree while I tend to the gardens, or else cavort with a newly rambunctious Jules, and she shows keen interest in my cross-breeding experiments with the roses. In the evenings, and occasionally late into the night, we sit and talk, books discarded in our laps as she asks about my life, or else offers wild tales of her travels on either side of the veil. Hearts beloved and broken, wagers won and lost, slippers worn out from dancing followed by days slept away in a blink.

How bored you must be, stuck here with a little country mouse.

Mice are never boring, dear Bee, and they make the finest of friends.

The house will feel smaller when Peregrine leaves, as she eventually must.

I pull several more weeds, shaking the soil back into the garden. "May I ask you something, Peregrine? About magic."

"You may ask. Though I may not be able to answer."

"The spell laid upon my husband, what do you know of its effects?"

"It turned him into a fearsome beast, did it not?" She smiles. "A glamour which did not dissuade your true-sighted heart from loving the man beneath."

"My heart was dissuaded for a time."

"But not for too long. Or else we wouldn't be here."

"Could it be yet unfinished?"

Peregrine takes a sharp breath. "What has my brother told you?"

Very little, I admit. Cursed for some small slight by a woman deep in his past. Years lost to bitter loneliness and despair until my father stumbled upon the estate that fateful winter night, and dared to steal a rose. My husband does not like to speak of his life before, except in sketches, lightly drawn and quickly discarded, and of the particulars of the spell that ensnared him — never.

"Then I cannot tell you more," she says. "It's not my place."

"But, do you think it over and done with? Or might there be some magic lingering still?"

"What are you asking, Bee?"

My throat is too dry to swallow. I thrust my fingers deep into the dirt, searching out the roots of a particularly mendacious weed. "We haven't been blessed with children, though we would both dearly like them. I've wondered of late if that's part of the curse, if it continues to this day. Or else, if perhaps it ... broke something. And if so, might it not be fixed by magic as well?"

"Oh, Bee." Peregrine is beside me now, her feathered cloak rustling as it drags along the grass. "You don't know."

The problem is not due to the spell, she explains in low and gentle tones, nor to any kind of *worked* magic, but only that I am not of the Fay and so am unable to bear a fey child. No human woman could or ever has; our bodies are not strong enough — or perhaps it's that they are too strong-willed and simply refuse the burden. How run my courses? Strange and unpredictable?

I nod, thinking of the lapses that come from time to time, a moon or more without bleeding and hope caught in my ribs like a gaffer's hook; then of the thick and clotted mess that comes after. My vision blurs.

Peregrine takes my hands from the earth and peels away my gloves. Her skin is warm as she laces her fingers through mine. "You may occasionally conceive, but I'm afraid you will never carry."

"He — he is only half-fey," I whisper. "Does that make no difference?"

"Your kind have such a mathematical way of looking at the world. My brother is fey, with no parts in need of counting, nor discounting, no matter how earthly his father may have been. Your husband is fey, your child would be fey, and your body — your body will not countenance it."

When the tears at last subside, she pats my cheeks with a lace-trimmed handkerchief and tucks a stray curl of hair back in place. A desultory rain begins to fall as Peregrine helps me to my feet. The day has grown cold, and dim.

"Does he know?" I ask on the way back to the house. "Has he known all this time?"

"Perhaps not. My brother was young when the spell was cast and has wanted nothing to do with the Fay ever since. He knows little of his heritage, or our ways."

"I don't think he would deceive me like that. He would not be so cruel."

Peregrine squeezes my hand. I'd barely noticed her taking it. "No," she agrees. "He has not an ounce of cruelty in him. Not for you."

Sometimes, I dream of my belly grown swollen and red as a rosehip. I caress the taut, glossy skin and it splits beneath my hands, spilling forth a mass of short, spiked fibres that feel nothing like the hair of a newborn babe. I dig, reaching inside myself, searching for seeds I know I shall not find. I always awake with a jolt, my throat dry and voiceless, my fingers clutching sweat-damp sheets.

When my husband is home, I curl against his shoulder and breathe in his warm, sharp scent until I can sleep again. If he rouses, he'll stroke my hair and whisper that he loves me, that he will always love me, and I believe him.

Sometimes, I can even believe this is enough.

In summer, alone in a bed grown impossibly vast, I press my face into the pillow and allow the tears to run their reproachful course.

These past few weeks, with Peregrine here, I have not dreamed at all.

Unlike cards or games played with dice, draughts contains not a single element of chance, and we often play a round or two after lunch. Peregrine keeps a tally and so far I hold the lead. She seems less bothered when she does not win, as long as she isn't being forced to curb her luck. I'm setting up the board for a second game when Jules jumps from his customary place beneath the table and trots over to the windows, ears pricked.

Only seconds later, we hear it: the urgent clatter of hoofbeats coming up the drive.

"It must be my husband," I say, rising from the table. "The gates would not admit another soul."

"Another *human* soul," Peregrine corrects.

As if in confirmation Jules lets loose a joyful bark and runs from the parlour, heading no doubt for the entrance foyer. My own delight is threaded with concern: why is he home so early in the season? Where is his carriage? Why did he not send word? But no, he must be well if he can ride a horse at such a gallop!

Peregrine remains in her seat, hands clasped tight together. Though I would not have thought it possible, her complexion is even whiter than usual.

"Are you coming?" I ask.

She shakes her head. "Don't tell him I'm here. I haven't — I haven't prepared."

Though unsure of her meaning, I do not linger but instead hurry through the house, skirts gathered in my hands. Jules is already at the front door, sitting with his tail at a furious wag. The big brass handle turns and my husband marches in, face flushed with exertion and brow deeply furrowed.

It's odd, the minor jolt upon first laying eyes upon him again after he returns from a lengthy sojourn. He doesn't seem as tall as I remember, or no, merely not as *large* somehow, not filling quite the amount of space I expect. His features, too, take a moment to slide into place, to become *present* rather than drawn from memory's unreliable store. Then his arms are around me, his breath warm against my neck, and his scent, his unmistakeable scent — and, oh! Here he is. My husband, home.

"Are you well, Beauty?" he asks, pulling out of our embrace. His anxious eyes search my own, briefly, before lifting over my shoulder. "Are all things well here?"

"Of course they are." Jules is jumping at us, whining for attention, but I tell him to sit and be good. "What troubles you, my love? Did some misfortune occur in Paris to send you home so soon?"

And now he looks at me properly, with such close and careful scrutiny that the blood rushes hot to my cheeks. "There is no misfortune, Beauty, save what has inveigled itself into this house. Tell me, please, where is my sister?"

Before I can think of how to respond, Peregrine's voice sounds from behind me.

"Here I am, brother."

She stands a few paces down the hall, having changed from her usual regalia into garments of a strange and ethereal fashion with which I'm wholly unfamiliar. Keeping to her favoured hues of turquoise and gold, the dress is little more than a shift, worn loose yet still hinting at the shape of her body beneath, and from her shoulders spiral ribbons of silk in a weave so sparse as to be almost transparent. Her pale arms are bare, as are her feet and ankles, and I do not think those fine blue veins are painted on.

I look away, unnerved by her new and open vulnerability.

My husband, however, is already marching towards her, his face furious, more bestial than I've ever seen it. "How dare you pollute my home with your presence!" Clutching Peregrine by the arm, he pulls her towards the front door. Jules barks in confusion until my husband roars at him for silence and the hound skulks away, tail between his legs. He jerks his sister forward once again. "You are leaving, now, and will never bring yourself before me again."

"Stop it," I say, reaching for his wrist. "Let her go."

He swats my hand aside, dragging his sister on despite her plaintive cries, and a sharp, sudden anger knifes through me.

"Let her go," I shout again, launching myself to land with both palms flat against his chest. Though I'm smaller and no match for his strength, I gather enough momentum that he staggers, surprised, and releases his grip. Peregrine's arm is bright pink where he held her. She rubs at her skin, moving to a safe distance.

My husband stares at me, confusion and hurt in his eyes. "What has she told you that you've taken her side so readily?"

"I've taken no one's side," I snap. "Peregrine, are you harmed?"

"Peregrine?" he laughs. "Is that the name she gave you?"

His sister squares her shoulders. Her gaze is severe, and chilling. "It's the only name I have now, brother. Having lost my own."

"Better a name than years."

"How can you still count yourself the loser?" She tilts her chin towards me. "Would you give up all you've gained to have a handful of time returned to your pocket? I knew you were a dullard, brother; I did not take you for such a fool."

Exasperated, I step between them. "Stop it, both of you."

"Beauty, please, this argument doesn't concern you."

"You are my husband and she is my friend; I think it concerns me very much."

"Your friend?" He snorts, shaking his head. "My love, she is the one who cursed me. It's because of her I suffered so long as the Beast."

Shocked, I turned to Peregrine. "All this time, you did not say?"

"It was not a curse!" she says, more to her brother than me. "It was a *wager*, which he freely entered into — and which he *won*."

"Why are you here?" my husband retorts. "Behind my back, a fox in the henhouse."

Peregrine takes a deep breath, then softens. "I wish you to release my name."

He crosses his arms. "Never."

"Brother, please. It has been long enough."

"One thousand winters will not be long enough. Now leave, *Peregrine*."

Desperate, his sister looks to me. "Bee ..."

"You — you lied to me."

"I did not lie." Her green eyes gloss with unspilled tears. "It was not my story to tell if he had not, but I never *lied*."

My throat tightens, and I cannot precisely remember all that she has told me, or all that I have asked. We've talked so much these past few weeks, of so many things, but surely no mention even once that it was *her* spell that wrought the Beast, and broke him, that it is *her* curse that has squatted toadlike beneath our marriage all these years, a poisonous creature over which we both tiptoe, wary of its rousing —

surely *that* is deception of the highest order. All else washes to insignificance.

I step closer to my husband and tell Peregrine that she needs to leave.

For the span of several heartbeats, all is silent. Heavy. Still.

"I will go," Peregrine replies at last. At the door, she turns. Her eyes lock with mine and my breath catches. "I *am* your friend, Bee, as much as I am his sister. That remains unchanged, and unchangeable." A thin ghost of a smile haunts her lips.

Stay, I want to call as she swings the door open. *Please stay*. But I say nothing, merely stand with my husband's arm around my waist as his sister slips outside and draws the solid, irrevocable wood closed behind her.

"How did you know she was here?" I ask later, hovering in the doorway of the music room. There's a loose chip of paint on the jamb — a most unusual happenstance for this house — and I slide my fingernail beneath it.

Seated at the piano, my husband lifts his hands from the keys. He's been playing for hours, frenetic melodies fuelled by anger and sorrow both — though the former has been most often in ascendance. Now, with light growing dim, he swivels to face me.

"I saw her in the mirror," he says.

It takes me a moment to understand. "Our mirror?"

"What other?"

Though I haven't laid eyes on it for years, I can still picture the humble wooden frame, carved with roses, and can easily recall the warmth of the handle within my grasp. I only used its magic once, scrying forth an image of my dying Beast prone among the rosebushes, his once luxurious mane grown matted and dull, that mighty chest moving with but the shallowest of breaths. I have no desire to look upon its glass again.

"You took it with you to Paris?"

"I always take it when we are apart," he says. "I like to see your face from time to time, when the loneliness presses too close. I thought you knew."

My skin itches, as though I am right now being observed. "I did not know."

"I'm sorry, my love. I will not use it, if it bothers you."

Does it bother me? I don't know that either. I thrust my fingernail until the paint-chip detaches and falls to the carpet. It will doubtless be gone in the morning, the doorjamb restored. There are words lodged in my throat, pushing upwards. I've no idea what they might be, and right now I don't want to find out.

"I shall leave you to your music," I say instead. Piano notes follow me from the room, slow and hungry as winter bees.

It *was* a wager, he confesses that night, the two of us lying side by side in our bed. In his youth he was too reckless with the hearts of others, one of which belonged to a girl whose name, he is now ashamed to admit, he cannot remember. But for some likewise forgotten cause, his sister was fond of the lass and took umbrage over her abandonment. *It is the fey in you that wins them*, she sneered, *you would be nothing without that gloss.* And so the bet was laid: his feyness set aside, his own intrinsic nature stripped bare and left to fend for itself; in such a state he would remain if he could not find someone to love him as he was.

She did not tell him he would be the Beast until the spell was cast, and had merely shrugged when he cried unfair. *You are too pretty, brother. It's impossible to untangle the fey in that, and it might yet dazzle an unwitting heart.*

A filthy trick, with no recourse. The magic could not be undone.

"There was no need to lock yourself away," I venture. "You might have found a bride far sooner otherwise."

"Have you forgotten your own terror when first you met me? No full-witted person would have lingered long enough to see beyond the enchantment. Still others might have tried to have me killed."

I can summon no argument for that.

"But she was right." His hand finds mine in the darkness, and squeezes. "It was a double victory in the end: both the wager and your love."

"And Peregrine? What did she lose?"

The silence stretches between us. "Her name," my husband says at last. "Her true name — it was her stake and so she lost it."

"What does that mean, to lose her name?"

"She cannot utter it, nor can any other soul aside from its keeper." He swallows, and when next he speaks, his voice is hoarse. "And she cannot pass beyond the veil without it."

"She is exiled? From her home?"

"The Fay take wagers very seriously. None would intervene."

"But you can. That's why she came here." Peregrine's sorrowful face floats in my memory, as does the sound of her laughter. The warmth of her hands that day in the garden, as she sat and patiently waited for my tears to cease. Her wicked grin when she bested me at draughts, her sheepish shrug when she didn't. *I am your friend, Bee, as much as I am his sister.* "You must return her name, my love. We both know what it is to be exiled; do you intend to punish her so forever?"

My husband pulls his hand away. A candle on the bedside table flickers obediently to life as he lurches from the bed, turning his bare skin golden.

"First the roses and now my sister. Is there anything you love less than me?"

"I love nothing more than you!"

His laugh is as bitter as rue. "Not even the Beast?"

No, we do not speak of this. We will not speak of this. I will go downstairs and read in the parlour a while, and in the morning we will not speak of this some more. My hand is already on the doorknob when he catches me by the wrist and spins me around. His face is shadowed, but I can see the glint of a tear on his cheek and it stills me. My husband does not cry. He has never cried.

"You changed as much as I did, Beauty."

"How — how is that possible? I have stayed myself."

"No. You loved me — you loved *me* — and then you became a person who loved someone else. Some*thing* else, something I never truly was and cannot be again." He wipes at his eyes, a rough and clumsy motion that cinches my heart. "And I understand, Beauty, I do, I do. I've tried to give you time, and space, and everything you've ever asked of me — *except what I cannot* — but you need to understand that it hurts. I love you, but I am not your Beast, and it hurts."

This moment feels so fragile, as though the ice beneath us will crack if we take just one more step, and every nerve and fibre demands I step back, step away, retreat to the silent safety of the shore. But all that awaits me there are memories and ghosts and girlish fancies. And my husband is here, in front of me, so close, so achingly close. The ice might break, or it might yet hold.

I step forward. My hands find his face, my lips brush his.

"I will not lie," I say. "I loved him first, I love him still. But he belongs to a dream I once had, and you — you are the world I live in. Only do not ask me to cast him aside, my love, when it was he who brought us together."

After so many years, my husband's body should be as familiar to me as my own, yet tonight it feels different. I make it feel different. We move slowly, and I run my hands over the solid muscle of his thigh, arch against the softer press of his belly, navigate his curves and hollows as though he were a new continent, and me shipwrecked without a compass. I want to know this man that I have loved for too long from too safe a distance; I want to know all of him, afresh, with no territory left uncharted.

When we are done, and then done once more, I roll off his hips with a sigh. "Shall I show you again how much I love you?"

My husband laughs. "Let me find my breath first, woman."

I press my lips to his shoulder, tasting salt. The candle gutters and dies, and the room falls to darkness. Just as I'm teetering on the cusp of sleep, I think I hear him speak, his words too soft for me to catch.

"I didn't hear," I murmur. "What did you say?"

"I've missed you," he tells me. "I've missed you for so long."

There will be no return to Paris this summer. My husband has sent for his belongings to be delivered via carriage and intends to spend the remainder of the season at home, teasing out the composition he stumbled upon in his fury. *It feels close to the music of the Beast, my love, only this time it belongs to me.* His face all but glows as he speaks. I fall in love with him a little more.

In the afternoon, he asks for a tour of the gardens.

"You've missed the peak, I'm afraid."

"Nevertheless."

We begin with my customary stroll down the drive to the front gate, where he apologises to my sisters for failing to greet them when he arrived. I wonder if they care for either the slight or the apology in its wake, or even that he is home at all. I snip a handful of dead leaves from Patience; she has only three roses open, already browning at the edges, and no more buds coming through. Is she sulking, or simply weary? Grace, on the other hand, clearly intends to flower until autumn.

"What is that you're humming?" my husband asks as we make our way to the conservatory.

I didn't realise I was, and need to pause to catch the tune. "It's — it's an old song. I doubt you would know it." In fact, it's what Peregrine had hummed that day after we spoke of the enchantment of my sisters. A simple but haunting melody, it's drifted in and out of my head ever since.

My husband stares at me, lips quirked. "Where did you hear it?"

"I can't remember. It feels I've known it forever."

"Beauty, we promised to be honest with each other, did we not?"

Another step. The ice is solid. "I learned it from your sister."

"Why didn't you wish to tell me that?"

"I feared you would be upset, and our morning spoiled."

He says nothing more until we reach the conservatory, where he holds the door open for me to pass. Then, soft as the fall of leaves and near as wistful: "It's one of my own compositions, from before. I didn't expect her to remember."

"You never play that music anymore."

"No," he says. "It feels like it was writ by a stranger's hand."

The roses in here have finished, all but the pair of prolific Chinese bushes, which are on their third bloom already — and one other that catches my startled attention. In the far corner of the conservatory, tucked close beside the savage thorny bush that Peregrine so admired, is a newcomer. The leaves are a dark green, and the single long-stemmed rose that arches from its foliage is white, so bright as to be almost silver, with a pale blue tinge to the edges of its petals. As I move closer, I can spy no more than a dozen or so thorns on the entire bush, each of them as red as heart's blood.

"This one is quite stunning," my husband says from behind me.

"She's new." I glance at him from the corner of my eyes. "But perhaps you recognise her all the same?"

As he studies both the bush and the pot she's planted in — turquoise, with exquisite gold leaf trim — his eyes widen and his lips press to a thin line. He hesitates a moment longer, then bends to press his nose into the open bloom, taking a deep breath. Oh, how I wanted to do the very same from the moment I saw her!

"Is it strong?" I ask. "Is it beautiful?"

He straightens and stalks past me without a word. Only when he reaches the door does he pause, face turned half away. "She can winter here," he mutters. "If she hasn't grown bored by spring, dig her into the ground with *your* sisters. I'm sure they'll all have plenty of gossip to share."

Once he's gone, I let my smile widen and lean in to sample the perfume for myself. The scent is not like any rose at all — or, rather, there is rose, but also lily and a dash of jonquil, and no sooner have I noted this heady mix than it falls away, and in its place is cinnamon and nutmeg and the smell of sugar cookies baking that I remember from my childhood, and now there's the sharpness of an approaching thunderstorm after too many days of flat and rainless heat, and now the intoxicating scent of my husband's skin after a long, hot bath, and now —

I stumble back, dizzy and clutching at the air. Too much, too much.

The rose dips supplicant, three too-white petals dropping to the ground. I stoop to retrieve them; it seems wrong to leave such things to rot. The impulse to pop them into my mouth is bold but fleeting, and I tuck them into my sleeve instead.

"Oh, Peregrine," I chide the rosebush. "What game is it we are playing now?"

. . .

By sunset next evening, there is a drift of white at the base of the turquoise pot. Every last petal has fallen. I take up the shears, intending to clip away the dried, naked pistil, but a faint misgiving stays my hand. Though I've grown used to pruning my sisters, it feels acutely wrong to take an iron blade to Peregrine. It won't hurt to leave it there a little longer. Autumn is coming; she won't be budding again this season.

"I hope she's not ill," I muse aloud at dinner. "That rose was perfectly healthy; it should not have shed so soon."

"Who knows what enchantment my sister wrought upon herself?" My husband spears a chunk of venison from his plate. "Perhaps she wishes you to fret."

"There would be easier ways."

"She has never preferred the *easy* path, my love."

Two more days pass before I'm certain: Peregrine has a rosehip.

It's a small bulge at first, but quickly swells as what remained of her flower shrivels away. Within a week, it grows to the size of a cherry, within another, a sizeable plum. Morning, noon and evening, I slip into the conservatory to check on her progress, astonished at both its speed and volume of growth, and how quickly it outstrips the other hips on the bushes I've cross-pollinated. In less than a month, it might be mistaken first for a pomegranate, then a small melon — though what such fruit would have a skin the colour of clotted blood, I do not know. The hip becomes so large I worry that the cane, already bending, will break and decide to press a sturdy garden stake and an old stocking into service to help carry the burden.

As I ease it into the sling, the warmth of the hip surprises me. It reminds me of Jules as a puppy, his near hairless belly smooth and hot beneath my palm, or else a fresh-boiled egg slipped straight from its shell at breakfast. Unlike either of those, however, the hip is still solid and firm, resisting the press of my inquisitive fingers.

Not that I press too hard.

Barely another month passes before I enter the conservatory to find the stake angled sideways and stocking hanging loose, its precious cargo brushing the floor. The cane the hip has been growing from has split, with half its length dragged down by the weight; it makes me wince to see it. Carefully, I cradle the huge ball in the crook of my arm and reach for my shears. The cane is too damaged; though the first frosts are not yet upon us, there's nothing to be gained by leaving things as they are.

"I'm sorry, Peregrine, I should have noticed sooner."

The stalk surrenders with a snip, and I take a moment to prune the split cane back before bringing the hip over to my work table. There's a sheen to the surface, not so glossy that I can see my reflection, but enough that the fine crack that runs from top to tail is particularly obvious. Concerned, I run my fingernail along the groove; the skin parts a little further. It's time, perhaps past time.

The paring knife is sharp. My husband has honed it twice at my request and I've kept it at the ready. The pots too, a dozen of them lined up along the wall, filled with soil I've mulched by hand. Though with the size the hip has grown, I might need to plant as many as five or six seeds in each and separate them later, depending on how many germinate.

Please, let them all germinate.

My right hand shakes as I lower the blade. I steady my wrist with the left. The two ends of the hip slice easily away, and I'm about to slide the tip of the knife into the crack in the rosehip's skin when a sudden, unnameable doubt gives me pause.

I set the knife down.

Dig my fingers into the fissure instead.

The flesh inside is soft, warm as porridge in winter, and pliant. Grasping hold of the edges, I pull — gently at first, and then more firmly, bracing myself against the table as my fingers threaten to slip. Finally, the hip relents, tearing open with a sigh and there — oh, there! — curled with eyelashes fluttering against her cheeks and hands tucked tight beneath her chin, is a tiny sleeping babe.

She's light in my arms, half the size a newborn should be, but perfectly formed — aside from the greenish cast to her skin. It's not a sickly hue, not at all. On the contrary, her appearance is vibrant. Lush. The green of early spring growth. As I brush away the fibrous hairs that cling to her little body and blow them gently from her face, she stirs and squawks. That tiny mouth opens, revealing the kitten-curl of her soft pink tongue, and instinctively I pop my finger inside. She sucks for only a moment before starting to cry again, high-pitched shrieks that cleave my heart like a blade.

"What do you want? What can I give you?"

Beside us, the cane I cut back on Peregrine seeps a thick, white sap, unlike anything I've ever seen a rose produce. I scoop up a dollop and slide my finger into the babe's mouth once more, delighted to feel her lips latching on. After a third serving, her eyes open and hold my gaze, her mismatched irises bright with the shock of the world in which she newly finds herself — and those eyes! I'd expected Peregrine's cut-glass green but no: the left is blue-grey, the same colour I see reflected in the mirror each morning, while the right mimics the deep, sombre brown of my husband's regard.

Oh Peregrine, oh dear friend. What is this wonder you have bestowed upon us?

I plant a kiss on the babe's verdant brow. "Welcome, little one. Welcome home."

In the middle of the night, I wake to any empty bed — or nearly so. The shallow basket I normally use to gather cut flowers still nudges my hip, the babe soundly asleep within it. From his position on the floor, Jules whines. He has refused to leave the child's side since I brought her up to the house, having duly appointed himself her steadfast guardian.

I reach down to pat his head. "Hush now, she's sleeping."

We might call her Hope, my husband mused earlier. *She has answered ours.*

I shook my head. *Too many girls are given names they need to live up to.*

He squeezed my hand. *Rose, then? It seems fitting.*

Leaning over, I smooth a wisp of golden hair from that sweet, tiny face. "Shall we see where your father has gone, little Rose?"

The basket is heavier on my arm than I remember and indeed its occupant seems to take up more room within it. Perhaps she is growing at the same startling speed as the rosehip did. Shall we have a giantess on our hands come spring? Peregrine filled a small jug with sap before the end of the cane dried over. I don't know if she has given all she can, or if a fresh cut would deliver more. We are mixing only a spoonful into cow's milk and Rose has taken to drinking the solution with gusto.

The house is quiet, its rooms barren and still. There's no response to my whispered calls and my nerves are stretching taut by the time I spot the light through the music room window. A soft yellow glow is coming from the conservatory, the light from a lamp or a candle, and when I peer closer, I can discern my husband's silhouette in the corner where Peregrine stands in her pot. His head is bowed and, as I watch, he reaches out an arm. I imagine his long, careful fingers touching her leaves; in forgiveness or simple gratitude, it is not my place to guess.

In her basket, Rose burbles and I rock her gently from side to side as Jules swishes his tail against my skirts. After a while, when my husband makes no move to return to the house, I carry her back upstairs to bed.

The next morning, a gentle frost spangles the entire grounds silver. From the music room below, a lilting tune drifts to my ears. It reminds me of the song I learned from Peregrine, the song my husband wrote in that long-lost time before, only slightly altered. Reclaimed. The melody speaks now of winter, and of tenacious, late-blooming flowers, and of love. I wrap Rose well in a thick woollen shawl that once belonged to my mother and we stroll along the drive to the front gates, where my sisters shiver in their ice-spun state.

"My dears," I say to them, "I have brought your niece to meet you."

If it is possible for a rosebush to look sullen, Patience carries it off with aplomb. Grace, on the other hand, seems to brighten. Her leaves drip with frostmelt and I could swear she leans closer as I stoop to show off the babe in her basket. Rose looks up with clear, inquisitive eyes. Her green skin almost glows in the sunlight, and her round and chubby cheeks take on a decidedly pinkish hue.

"I hope one day soon your hearts will mellow," I tell my sisters. "If not for my sake, or your own, then for the sake of this little one here. For one day soon, I'm sure, she will want to know her aunts." I hitch the basket onto my hip and turn to leave. Within me, a dogged string tugs, as it always has, and I swallow hard. "But also … I miss my sisters."

Inside the conservatory, the air is crisp and chill. I'll need to attend to my cross-bred hips this week, plant out their seeds and move the pots outside to germinate. But not today. It's too cold to keep Rose in here for long; I've only brought her to visit Peregrine, and to more properly offer my thanks.

But the corner where Peregrine stood is empty, save for my thorny rosebush. Even the pretty turquoise pot has vanished.

"As sudden as she appeared," I murmur. "Oh Rose, I'm so sorry."

Making sure the babe is still warmly tucked in her shawl, I set her basket down on my work table. Still hopeful, I take a hurried catalogue of the conservatory. Perhaps Peregrine has tucked herself away somewhere else, bored with her savage neighbour. Would she really have departed without a proper farewell? To me, or to sweet little Rose? But she's not with any of the other rosebushes, nor even the orchids.

"She's gone, my love." My husband stands in the doorway, his features cast down in sympathy. "I released her name, and she left."

"Oh." I return to the table, heft Rose's basket over my arm.

"Let me take her," my husband says as we approach. He regards the child with such unguarded adoration it reminds me of my father. I wish he were still alive; how he would dote on his granddaughter. "Don't fret, Beauty. My sister will be back, most likely at the least convenient time." He shakes his head, but he's smiling.

I slip my arm through his as we return to the house. Our breakfast will be waiting along, no doubt, with whatever it may be that Rose will need. The Fay have always watched over their own. Beneath my breath, I hum the song my husband was playing earlier, and I can almost hear Peregrine's voice matching mine. It is a beautiful melody, vibrant and strong, and we will teach it to our daughter when she is grown.

Some nights, the three of us curled together in the candlelight of our bedroom, my husband coos and tickles Rose's belly until she giggles. He makes ridiculous faces that smooth to seriousness as he lifts his gaze to mine.

Do you still wish I were the Beast?

I press my hand to his stubbled cheek, and look down at the babe between us. She kicks her little legs in the air, ferociously. Then I say:

Perhaps, one day, we shall all be beasts together.

TRIQUETRA

I shall drown you in the river where the willows grow. Their branches will reach for you and in desperation you will grasp for them but they will break between your fingers like the bones of small birds. As the water fills your throat, the last thing you shall know will be my two hands holding you down.

I only visit my stepmother during the time of the new moon. Although she hasn't been given access to so much as a herb garden since she came to stay in my husband's castle, I don't trust the magic to lie completely fallow in her breast, and would not dare step foot in her rooms when the moon rides full and high in the sky. But now it's noon and I balance the round silver tray on one hand as I rap three times on her door with the other. This is a courtesy only; the door is kept locked and the key, when not borrowed by our housekeeper at mealtimes, dangles from a blood-red ribbon on my belt.

A voice bids me enter and I do so, closing the door gently behind me. For a moment, I hesitate, struck to find the woman standing by the window, staring out at the snow-covered trees.

"Stepmother?"

She turns to face me, hobbling on her birchwood canes. My stepmother is a vain woman still; normally she likes to be seated when I arrive, skirts neatly arranged to hide her feet. "Sit down, fairest." She gestures towards the small, round table where we customarily take our wine.

Setting down the tray, I inquire as to her well-being and she replies, as she usually does, that she is no better, no worse, before plonking herself down with all the grace of a mill-woman. "They're no better either," she says, catching me looking at her feet.

I avert my eyes and pour the wine into our goblets. Thick and sweet, my husband has it brought in barrels from the south, and I've developed quite a fondness for it of late. Lastly, I take up the apple along with the sharp little paring knife and begin to slice it down the middle. The flesh is whiter, crisper, than it has any natural right to be this deep into winter. But the tree behind the stables has borne such fruit, month after month, since my wedding night. One single apple each time, ripening to a bright and glossy red, and no one can pluck it but myself. Which I do, each new moon, pluck it and place it upon my silver tray, and bring it to my stepmother to share.

She takes a slice now, holds it a moment to her nose as she always does, then pops it whole into her mouth. I can hear the crunch as she bites down and my own mouth waters. She always takes the first taste of the fruit. We eat in silence, my stepmother and I, until the apple is gone. She spits the seeds into her hand, arranges them in a circle on the tray, then moves her hand over them in a quick, sharp movement. Does she think I do not notice? Later, I will burn them in the fire. Whatever pitiful magic she attempts, it will be reduced to nothing but ash.

I do this every month.

We do this every month.

"What are your intentions, fairest?" My stepmother sits back in her chair, fixing me with her gaze. Her eyes are brown and glossy as apple seeds.

"My intentions?"

"Regarding your daughter." She leans forward. "And your husband."

Some wine splashes onto my wrist as I return my goblet to the table, and I wipe it hastily on my skirts. "My daughter is happy and healthy," I tell her. "And my husband is travelling on matters of business. You have no need to ask after either of them."

"But that is *why* I ask, fairest. The time to close the barn door is now, before the horse is stolen away."

"Bolted. Before the horse has *bolted*."

"I know precisely what I said."

I gather the goblets onto the tray, still half-full the both of them, and make to rise. The woman grabs my wrist, quicker than a hare before hounds. "Do not close your eyes to this, fairest. You of all people know his proclivities. You know his *heart*."

I wrench myself free. It's not her place to speak to me so, I stammer. If it were not for me, she would have no visitors at all. If it were not for me, she would likely be dead, long dead and rotted in the ground. If it were not for me —

"I would still walk with ease," she says, sticking out a foot beneath her skirts. Although she wears her customary fur slippers, the scars are still visible around her ankles — red and ropey welts where the skin melted as candle wax does. I don't need to see more than that. I know her feet too well. All those months tending to her horrendous wounds, cleaning away the foul-smelling pus and infection as she screamed her agony into my ears, forcing tonics down her throat to break her fevers, allowing her to clutch my hand so tightly that her nails left crescents which did not heal for days. We both bear the scars from those times; she has no cause to remind me.

"I was a child," I whispered.

"And that child chose my punishment."

"He asked me —"

"Make her dance in iron shoes, you said. Make her dance until she falls down dead."

"A child's wish. I — I had no idea of what it meant. I was only *seven*!"

"Seven," she echoes. "The age he made you his bride."

"The age *your* mirror condemned me."

"The age your daughter is now."

My lips ache, I'm pressing them so hard together. Standing, I pick up the tray. It's all I can do not to throw it into her face, goblets and all.

"He thought you were the most beautiful creature in the world when he saw you in that coffin," my stepmother continues. "When you were seven."

"Be quiet."

"What does he think of you now, I wonder? Those broad hips of yours, that bosom which has nursed a babe? Not much *girl* left to you, is there? Not much to catch his wandering eye."

I am half out of the door before she calls out again. "Fairest?" The edge has been shaved from her voice; she sounds almost plaintive now, and I pause, tilt my ear in her direction.

"How?" she asks. "How will it be?"

Without turning around, I tell my stepmother how I will kill her the next time we meet. My tone is clipped; there is no joy in it for me now, despite the many nights I spent concocting my method, choosing just the right words — and the many more I lay awake in anticipation of delivering them. It was particularly vicious this month. My stepmother waits until I am done before telling me of my own murder. I can hear the smile in her voice, the satisfaction, and in any other month I would have been pleased by her inventiveness.

But not now, not after what she has already said to me.

"Next moon, then," I say and step through the door. As I lock it behind me, her voice seeps through the wood.

"Sooner than that, fairest. For your daughter's sake."

I make no reply. I have no reply to make. But I will send word to the kitchen about her supper. My stepmother shall have boiled liver tonight, taken from an old sow. I count my footsteps as I return to my parlour, hoping to distract myself from their cold and empty echoes. The sound reminds me too well of a clock, counting down its minutes until midnight. There are two-hundred and forty-eight steps in all, though admittedly I made my final three small and tidy to avoid crossing the threshold on two-hundred and forty-six.

I dislike figures with sixes in them; they do little to comfort me.

I will lay you naked upon the snow, stretched between four iron stakes. Before your skin can chap too badly, I will take a keen-edged blade and peel it from you as someone might peel an apple. Blood will pool rich and red around your body. I will leave your fingernails until last and spit them into the snow when I am done.

My daughter's hair is like fine-spun gold. She has her father's hair, and his envy-green eyes. But she has my lips, plump and red as blood, and my fine, snow-white skin.

I watch through the window for a minute or two, not wishing to disturb whatever game she's playing in the little courtyard outside the stables. The building is empty now that my husband is away with his horses and the others — including my daughter's beloved pony — have all been sold to repay some debt or another. He has assured me that he'll replace them when this current venture reaches fruition, but such words would be no comfort to my daughter. It won't be her pony that comes trotting back to the stables, if indeed any pony comes at all. These days, my husband's promises run thin as melt-water. She cried herself to sleep the night I had to tell her little Klaus was gone, and for days afterward, when she remembered his absence, her lips would tremble.

Yet here she is, building a snowman outside his very stable, her small face tight with concentration, her nose nipped red by the cold. Children can be so resilient. How astonishing that they are able to bear the very worst of losses and still step forth into each new day as though some fresh delight awaits them there. If I could spare my daughter anything worse than the loss of a favourite animal, I should count myself among the best of mothers.

We must find a match for her soon, my husband told me the evening before he left.

When I protested that she was still a child, he merely glared at me and shook his head. His eyes these days are red-veined and yellowing from the amount of wine he consumes. I couldn't bring myself to meet them and instead bowed my head over my supper. I loved him more than I feared him once, thought him brave and wondrous and strong. How naive I was: a child with no knowledge of the world.

She is the granddaughter of the King, he reminded me. *There will be a wealth of eager suitors, eager enough to plump the coffers of this pauper province I've been saddled with.*

It's a complaint I've heard so often, I could recite it word for bitter word. His two older brothers were given the best lands in the kingdom to govern, my husband insists, while he is forced to preside over lazy peasants and all manner of useless men. Though I've heard it said that these lands where we make our home were prosperous before he took governance of them, that it has been his taxes and sporadic, unannounced levies which have brought poverty among its people and made them fear what each new season might bring. What value is there in the daughter of such a man? Short of a plague running through the rest of the Royal line, she will never wear the crown of a Queen — I should not even think such things, though I am certain my husband would rejoice in such a tragedy.

She's too young to be married, I told him. *She's too young to leave us.*

He laughed. *I would only see her pledged, not handed over. She is unripe fruit; it would not do to have her plucked too early in her season.* He smiled, more to himself than to me, before stuffing a whole rasher of bacon into his mouth. I could see the soft, pink meat being rent between his teeth as he spoke. *Worry not, dear wife. Our daughter will remain under my protection for some years yet. But this is how the world works — not all brides are stumbled upon as fortuitously as you were, arrayed so prettily under glass.*

How I wish it were so. I would rather see my daughter sleeping safe in a glass coffin for a thousand years than have her hurt by the waking world and those who walk within it.

Five times I tap on the window glass, although my daughter looks up at the first knock, grinning to see me standing there. "Mama!" she cries and pushes herself to her feet. As she runs over to the courtyard door, I can better see the creature she has been building. Not a snowman, but some lumpish thing, hunched over and seeming ready to collapse at a breath. It makes my skin prickle with gooseflesh to look upon it.

"What have you been making, my pet?" I ask as she comes charging through the door to hug me. I crouch and fold her gloved hands within my own. Her cheeks are pink. Her teeth chatter.

"Mama, it is Klaus!"

"Klaus?" I stare again at the poor, misshapen thing outside. It could be thought a pony, I suppose, if one squinted hard enough, or viewed it with a mother's eye.

"The fairy told me to make him out of snow and he would come alive and I could ride him again."

"What fairy, my pet?"

"The fairy who came last night."

Sighing, I smooth her hair back from her eyes. "That was only a dream."

"No Mama, look!" She points beyond the window and I follow the angle of her finger to spy a large black bird perched in one of the now leafless trees overlooking the courtyard. Its silhouette, dark against the wintry grey sky, is distinctive. "See, the fairy!"

"That's only a raven, my pet, a feckless bird come to see if we have kitchen scraps to scavenge." I've never liked those birds, with their ink-black plumage and cryptic, guttural croaks. There's often one flitting about the castle grounds, and I never count it as a good day when I happen to spy it. Softly, I kiss my daughter's brow. "Now, remember what I told you? Little Klaus has grown up and gone away to be with all the big horses."

She swallows and her eyes glisten. "When I grow up, will I go away too? Will I get to see him again, when I grow up?"

"I don't know, my pet. Klaus has very many important things to do now. As will you, when you grow up." She doesn't say anything to that, merely hugs me tight and presses her face into my shoulder. I know that she is crying and doesn't want me to see. I rub her back until her small frame ceases to shake. Outside, the tree where the raven perched is empty. Foolish as such feelings might be, I'm relieved to see it gone.

Unbidden, my husband's face swims into my mind. His golden hair, once so glorious, now lank and greasy against his neck. The burst veins in his cheeks spreading like the webs of tiny spiders. Is it memory or imagination, the way his tongue darted across his lips as he spoke of auctioning my daughter to the highest bidder? As he spoke of how young she was, and how fair?

You know his heart, my stepmother said, and she is right.

His heart, and every other dark part of him.

I will keep my daughter safe. I must, I must. But I need to know what threatens her, and there is one thing in this castle that will tell me the truth of it.

I shall feed you honey, spoon after golden spoonful of it. I shall pour it down your throat until you can swallow no more, until it soaks every organ and your veins are stopped with the cloying thickness of it. Then I shall cleave open your breast and catch the gleaming nectar as it drips from your ribs onto my outstretched tongue.

I've never once spoken to the mirror. My stepmother brought it with her when she came to my wedding, so little could she bear being apart from the monstrosity even for the span of a week, and it's been kept it in a small, windowless chamber ever since. I know the sly deeds of which it's capable, how it sniffs out a crack in a person's heart and prises it open. Until now, I've never wanted to seek its counsel — or, at least, not enough to risk its manipulations. But I need to know about my husband. I need to be certain.

The mirror never lies, my stepmother told me once, when I pressed her on the subject. *The trick is to know whose truth it is speaking.*

There's a woman standing outside the mirror's chamber as I approach. Tall and thin and donned in dove grey, I recognised the arrogant set of her shoulders even before she turns to greet me.

"Lady Heron!"

The woman sniffs, her lips a taut line. "I have been waiting for one-half hour. More!"

"I-I'm sorry. I had — I was unavoidably detained." In truth, I'd forgotten utterly about her appointment, a fact which she has no doubt surmised.

She smiles with all the grace of a blade and nods towards the narrow wooden door behind which the mirror awaits. "Shall we?"

I would like to ask her to leave, to return at a later hour or even another day, but there is the matter of the small linen bag that she clutches. I need the coins it contains; they will pay for good meat for our table and perhaps a warm winter cloak for my daughter. After all, the women come more seldom these days; the mirror seems to have exhausted them.

"Of course, Lady Heron." I hold out my hand and she deposits the bag in my palm. It feels lighter than I'd hoped, but perhaps the coins inside are silver. After unlocking the door, I step aside and gesture for the woman to enter. She hesitates for a moment, visibly steeling herself, before sniffing once more and marching past me.

Quietly, I close the door and move to the other side of the hall to wait.

She won't be very long. They never are.

Scarce six minutes pass by my reckoning before she emerges once more, shaken and trembling, a handkerchief pressed to her mouth. "Lady Heron?"

The woman waves me away. "I shall see myself from the castle." Her eyes are red-rimmed and she refuses to meet my gaze. As she walks, her skirts rustle on the tiles in whispered accusation. But how is it my fault? I don't make them come here, these women with their coins and haggard hearts. I don't even know how they learn of the mirror's existence — a network of gossip and half-truth, I suspect. Whatever they expect, whatever they are told, most do not visit more than once.

This has been Lady Heron's fourth visit. Is her heart that ravenous?

I hesitate with my hand on the door knob. One turn and I can be in the room with it. Three steps to place me before its glassy face. A handful of words in return for ... what? I scarce know what I need to ask, let alone how to phrase it.

(Don't I know? Oh, don't I?)

Another day, then. When I have had more time to ponder my question.

Carefully, I insert the key into the lock and turn it. The weighty clatter of the tumblers brings me more comfort, I am sure, than the words of the mirror ever would. But do I imagine it? That barely heard sigh from the chamber beyond, so heavy with disappointment and with desire? Before leaving, I tap my toe three times and brush the tip of my nose.

Am I mad to have even considered such a diabolic audience? My stepmother has twisted my thoughts, most like for her sport. My husband is not a good man but he is not —

(a monster)

He is her father. He would not —

(you know his heart)

I need to occupy myself with practical matters and stop this foolishness. The snow has stopped and I have coins that need to be spent before my husband's return, lest he find a more worthwhile cause for their use. I will take my daughter down to the village and buy her that winter cloak. Already, I can picture her wearing it, a scarlet weave folding soft and billowy around her slight frame, all that golden hair kept safe beneath the hood.

Oh, I know that I won't be able to find such a thing as that. It will be lucky enough if the village seamstress has one of sparrow-egg blue or the bright green of ferns, anything other than muddy hues of brown or grey. If it be trimmed with rabbit fur, then we shall be luckier still. For red, I would have to place an order and all of that would take too long.

My husband returns in a fortnight. The coins will need to be spent by then.

I will hunt you down with dogs. Hungry, vicious hounds that have been starved for days before being given your scent. You will beg for your life when finally they bail you up, circle you with their jaws snapping and slavering, but I will let them have you. I will let them tear you to pieces. I will let them take their fill of your flesh. All that will be forbidden them is your heart. That I shall bring home with me, safe in a locked, lightless box.

The gatekeep steps into our path as we approach, my daughter's mittened hand clutched tight in my own. It takes four more steps to reach him. I do not like four as a number — it is slippery and too easily cleaved in twain — but I dare not take a fifth.

"Weather's closing in, your Highness," the gatekeep says, his shoulders squared.

My daughter squeezes my hand. *Mama*, she starts to say but I shush her quickly. The sky above us is a weak blue and utterly clear of clouds.

"We are only going down to the village," I tell the man. "We will not tarry long."

"The little one will catch a chill." He does not move, though his fingers tighten their grip about his staff. "Best get her back inside."

"Thank you for concern, but we — we are warmly dressed, the both of us." As I tug my daughter forward, the gatekeep too takes a step closer. So close that his broad, leather-clad chest almost bumps my own. His breath fogs as he speaks and I can smell the warmth of it.

"You may go to the village if you wish it," he says. "But the little one should go back inside."

For a moment, I'm too flustered for words. Then I picture my stepmother and the manner in which she used to conduct herself when I was a child. How imperiously she would speak to everyone, even my father himself. I draw myself upright. "Do you propose to tell your Mistress what she might do with her day?"

The words taste flat as failed bread in my mouth and the gatekeep doesn't so much as flinch. "On instructions from His Grace, your master and mine both. He did not wish the princess away from the castle in his absence. The winter is foul and the woods are wild and he would not have his only daughter come to any harm."

He smiles now, a genuine smile, yet my daughter hides her face in my skirts. Part of me wishes to push past him regardless, to see if he will truly dare to lay a hand to his Royal Mistress. But another, more certain part burns with the humiliating knowledge that he would not hesitate to do so. My jaw begins to ache, so hard are my teeth clenched together.

"Mama? Are we not going to the village today?"

I force a smile to my lips. "No, my pet. This kind gentleman thinks that it will storm over so we had best stay warm and dry by the fire."

She kicks at the dirty snow that lies piled at the side of the path. "I wanted to see Klaus."

"Silly poppet, Klaus is not in the village. I told you, he is with all the big horses now."

The gatekeep laughs, a far from pleasant sound. "You'd be best served looking for that old nag in the knackery."

My daughter stares up at me, confused. I glare at the gatekeep but the man merely winks. "That's — that's a place where the big horses live," I tell her quickly. "Come, my pet. We shall go down to the kitchen and have Cook warm you a mug of honey-milk."

"I'm not cold, Mama," she replies, her words frosting in the air. "I want to see the knackery. Please can we visit the knackery?"

The gatekeep's rough laughter follows us up the path as I drag my protesting daughter back to the castle, and I curse him beneath my breath. High in the sky above, a raven flies in a slow circle. I curse it as well, wishing for its feathers to turn to stone, for its abruptly heavy body to fall to the ground and shatter like so many thwarted dreams.

It takes one hundred and nineteen steps before we are inside once more. I don't care for that number, either. It has sharp edges and seems keen to draw blood.

I shall bind you with silken threads, wrapping them around and around your body until every inch of skin is cocooned. Only your eyes shall remain uncovered, so that I might peer into them over the days and weeks it will take for you to wither and waste and starve, stoically, silently, to your death.

My husband doesn't care for the stories of my childhood, of the times before he jolted me from my poisoned sleep and lifted me boldly from the coffin, but my daughter loves to hear them. Each night, I sit by her bedside and tell her tales of the kindly little men who took me into their mountain home when I was lost, and for whom I kept house for several months. I tell her how I would make their beds and darn their socks and prepare their dinner the way they taught me. I do not tell her about poisoned combs or apples, nor about coffins made from glass; she is too young for such horrors.

Neither do I mention my stepmother. My daughter will have too many questions that I'm still unready to answer.

Instead, I relay happier stories of happier days — for there were many happy days betwixt the huntsman and the coffin — as well as the stories that the dwarves used to tell to me. Tales of crafty foxes and wise, well-born hares; dancing princesses and frogs with jewels hidden deep in their bellies; mighty frost giants who once lumbered through the mountains and mischievous pixies with a taste for stolen sweets.

"Can we leave a cake out for the pixies?" my daughter asks me tonight.

"There are no pixies in our part of the world, my pet. It would only be a family of rats who come to nibble on your cake."

"Talking rats?" she asks hopefully. "Magic rats?"

Smiling, I set aside the nightgown I'm hemming. My daughter grows so fast; this is the second time I've let it down and there won't be fabric left for a third. "No," I say. "Fierce and hungry rats who will gobble up their cake and then creep under the blankets to nibble on your toes!" I grab her foot and tickle it until she shrieks.

"Stop it, Mama! Stop it!" She's almost breathless as she struggles to pull away.

Laughing, I release her and begin to straighten the bedclothes. "Come now, fidget. It's past time you were asleep."

She wriggles beneath the quilt. "Can we visit the pixies, Mama?"

"One day, perhaps."

"When? When?"

"They live very far away from here."

"But we can use magic and fly to see them, quick as blinking."

"Hush now." I pull the covers up to her chin.

"But Mama, we can —"

"Hush!" Though her talk is fanciful, I don't like to hear my daughter speak of magic. "It's no small thing, my pet, to use magic. There is always a cost." I kiss her three times, once on the forehead and again on each cheek, before gathering my sewing together. The candle flickers as I pick it up, casting moving shadows on the walls. My daughter cringes to see them.

"Surely you're not still afraid of the dark?" When much younger, she cried whenever her candle was taken away, but many years have passed since then.

"No, Mama," she whispers, her gaze flitting to the corner of the room. "But sometimes he is there when I wake up."

"Who? Who is there?"

"The Night Man. He watches me in the shadows. I don't like him, Mama. I don't like his watching."

"Is he here now?"

"No, Mama. You have the candle. He does not like the light."

"It is a dream, my pet. A nightmare and nothing to fear."

She frowns, doubtful, and I lean over to kiss her again. Forehead, cheek, cheek. "I shall leave the candle then, shall I? Just for tonight?"

I find my way back to my own bedroom by moonlight and memory, keeping one hand on the wall as I creep along the halls. It's a luxury to leave a whole candle to burn while my daughter sleeps, but the way she spoke of the Night Man chilled me.

I do not like his watching.

Has he visited her, this Night Man, while her father has been away? I hadn't thought to ask it and, surely, it is a foolish question. It's only a nightmare. It must be a nightmare.

You know his heart.

I do. I do know his heart.

I will come upon you in darkness, my breath burning hot on your cheek. My ungloved hands will close around your neck and my fingers will squeeze, unrelenting, throttling your startled cries. You will die with your last words lodged, unspoken, in your throat.

I knock my customary three times but do not wait for an answer before unlocking the door to my stepmother's room and swinging it open. The woman is sitting on the edge of her bed, jerking a robe over her bony shoulders. She wears nothing underneath; I glimpse the sag of a breast, the wrinkle and fold of belly-skin pale as fresh cream. Her long, grey hair is dishevelled, hanging in tangles about her face, and her feet are bare. Quickly, I turn away, an apology stammering to my lips.

I've never sought such intimacy; my skin burns with it.

"What did you expect?" my stepmother asks. "I've scarce had warning of your visit."

"But it's past noon!"

"Do you suppose me unduly burdened with morning chores, fairest? Or blessed with a surfeit of company for whom I should make myself presentable?" She waves a hand at the corners of the ceiling. "The spiders here care not a whit for appearances, I can assure you."

I'm ashamed to admit I've not spared much thought for how she spends her days. She is fed; she is clothed. I keep her moderately stocked in embroidery thread, albeit often coarse and dull of colour, and have even brought the occasional book from my husband's ever-shrinking library, as she once expressed a yearning for words. Royal histories, mostly, but also some volumes of verse. If I've ever had cause to think on my stepmother all alone in this room, it has likely been to imagine her daydreaming by the window with book or embroidery hoop in her lap, still elegant despite her fading finery, with all that wild hair swept into its usual immaculate coiffure.

It is a shock to witness her so ... diminished.

"I — I have come to ask — that is, I wish to know —"

"You might meet my eye when you speak to me, Fairest. It would be polite."

I turn around to find my stepmother now risen from the bed, robe tied close around her body, fingers working her hair into a rough braid. I'm careful not to look at her feet, though I glimpse her two canes leaning nearby. "I wish to ask about your — your mirror."

Her eyes narrow. "You told me that you have never gazed upon it."

"I've not had need ... until now."

The woman takes up her canes and hobbles across to the small table where the two of us normally sit. With a soft groan, she lowers herself into a chair then gestures to the one remaining. "I have nothing useful left to tell about that *thing*."

"I've come to ask your aid in ... crafting a question. One that it must answer clearly, without trickery or guile. One that is ... is ..."

"Unambiguous? Fairest, there is no such question. The mirror will know your purpose as soon as the words part your lips. It will twist its own words accordingly."

"If it may only answer yay or nay? How can that be twisted?"

"You cannot impose such restrictions; it will answer as it will, with as many words as it chooses, or as few." She leans forward. "Heed me well, Fairest. When you stand before that thing, when you peer into its depths, you also allow it to peer into you. It will see the very darkest of your fears; it will sup on them and find them delicious. And it will use them against you in terrible ways."

"But I need to know!"

"You already know."

"No, I *suspect*, I *worry*, I *dread* — that's not the same."

"It is enough for you to take your daughter and leave."

The laughter bursts from me like a startled bird. Leave? How simply she puts it, I scoff, as though I might just pack a trunk, snatch my daughter by the hand and waltz out into the world. As though there are carriages and fine horses to carry us wherever our whims direct. As though no burly gatekeep would stand in our path, no armed men hunt us down should we persist.

As though, even if we can find a way to leave, we have a place to go.

"There are always ways, Fairest, if you have the knowing of them. And places."

"This is a waste of my time."

As I stand up, my stepmother reaches forward and grasps my hands. She moves more quickly than I would have thought her capable and this, along with the warm, dry press of her skin against mine, shocks me into place. I can't remember how long it's been since we've touched.

The woman pulls herself to her feet, pulls me closer, her face inches from my own.

"I can help you," she whispers, "but first I have need of some things." Her breath is oddly sweet. It smells of spring blossoms, and of apples. My knees threaten to buckle and I find myself clinging to her as much as she does me. Her eyes locked with mine, she gives me a list, then asks me to repeat it back to her. "Again," she says, and I do, twice more, as her thumbs move in slow circles over my wrists. At last, seemingly satisfied, she releases me.

My arms drop to my sides. I feel muzzle-headed, woolly, as though I've just woken from a troubled sleep. My mouth is dry. "You —" I cough, backing away from the table, away from the woman now supporting herself by its edge. "You spelled me!"

"Only your memory, Fairest. My needs are precise."

"You — you wretched creature! I wish you *had* died on my wedding day!"

Smiling, she sinks back down into her chair. "No, you don't. There is too much kindness in your heart, even now, even for such a *wretched creature* as myself."

I am too furious to speak another word. I want to throw something, break something, break *everything* — but the only thing to hand is a pewter goblet which makes a hollow, unsatisfying clatter as I hurl it against the wall. How dare she? I will leave her to starve. I will tell the kitchen to send her nothing but spoiled milk and rotted meat. I will — I will —

"I can help you," my stepmother says again. "Please — for your daughter's sake."

Jaw clenched to aching, I glare at the woman for one long, cold moment before marching from the room. My hands shake so badly, I drop the key twice as I try to lock the door behind me. As I stalk down the corridor, my stepmother's list rolls unbidden, unwanted, through my mind, each word a barb that catches and throbs. It so distracts me that I completely forget to count my steps.

I shall simmer you slowly, until your skin sloughs away and your flesh becomes soup. Your bones will be boiled for stock so that I might dine with special delight on the consommé drawn from your marrow.

The mirror chamber is cold, windowless and dark. For several moments, all I know is my own breathing, shallow and fast, as I stand in the centre of the room with the door closed firm behind me. Then the glow begins. Faint at first, then brighter and brighter until I might be surrounded by a dozen candles, so forceful is the light that shines from the glass oval on the wall opposite me.

I haven't seen the thing for years.

I'd forgotten how plain it is, had in my memory conjured an ornate, overwrought frame around its edge in place of the thin band of wood that actually bounds it. It's smaller than I remember as well. I could have sworn the glass to be longer than the span of my arms, and near as wide, but in actual fact I could likely carry the thing in two hands without too much effort.

Not that I would touch it in a million moons. My skin crawls at the very idea.

Well met, child.

The voice doesn't seem to come from the mirror. It doesn't seem to come from anywhere in particular, yet it fills my whole head, louder than any thought of my own, almost to the point of bursting. I can't imagine a worse sensation than this.

What would you ask of me?

"I — I want ... my daughter — is she ... under threat?"

Only so long as she draws breath in this world.

"But here, in this castle, is she in danger?"

She will always be in danger, child. You cannot protect her from all the ills that may befall her.

My thoughts are thick and slow. I can't summon the right questions to ask, the right words to pull the answers I need from the glass before me. There's a sudden tightness in my chest and my breath comes too fast to catch. "My husband ..."

He loves your daughter. More than he loves you.

Closing my eyes, I press fingertips to my temples, press so hard into those soft and pliant hollows that stars shatter behind my lids. The pain is an anchor. A compass. "And does he ... does he *desire* her also?" For a heartbeat, I wish I could unsay those words, so solid do they sit in the air, so blunt and inescapable is the echo of them. But it is done. It is said.

It is said.

More than he desires you. The voice of the mirrors swells and gloats. *Beware, child, and tread carefully; your position in this household grows precarious.*

With that it departs, leaving me as empty as a pumpkin shell scraped for seeds — or nearly so. My stepmother's list drifts from my memory like smoke from a snuffed candle, her words wispy and thin but persistent nevertheless. I shake my head. Will my mind ever be my own again? The glow from the mirror is gone; the chamber is pitch black. "Come back," I call out. "I have more to ask of you." There's no reply, no sense that the mirror is even listening. The chill in the room deepens; beneath my sleeves, gooseflesh shivers across my skin. The audience is over. I have been dismissed.

I turn and retrace my steps to the door. But my outstretched hands find nothing more than bare, unbroken stone. No smooth, polished wood or jutting handle of brass, nor any crack or join which might suggest an exit. Frantic, I pace the short length of the wall, palms slapping against stone, as the gorge rises in my throat and the taste of spoiled milk coats my mouth. By what devilry has the mirror trapped me here? For what purpose, and for how long? I thump at the wall with balled hands, demanding to be released, for the door to be restored. I will not rot in this wretched chamber, in darkness and silence behind this newly solid facade, while my husband and my daughter —

Behind me: the creak of a hinge, a shard of yellow light, and a timid voice calling, "Mama? Mama, are you there?"

For a strange, disorienting moment, I can't make sense of it. Then my daughter's head pokes around the edge of the door she has opened — the door! on the wall adjacent! so ridiculously close! — and my cheeks burn with foolishness. I stalk over and, snatching her by the arm, jerk her into the hall beyond. She cries out, the thin, high-pitched squeal of a snared rabbit that sets my teeth to grating, and I give her a rough shake as I pull the door shut behind us.

"You don't ever go into that room! Not ever!"

The girl is starting to snivel, her green eyes wet and bright with shock, and there's a part of me whose heart breaks to see it — but that part feels so very far away, so very small and distant and powerless in the face of the fury that boils in my breast, and I shake her again. "Stop it! You're not an infant any more. You need to start acting like a lady."

She tries to swallow her tears, she does, but her thin shoulders hitch and her mouth contorts with the effort and my fingers dig deeper into her flesh. I want to — I want to —

Nearby, a throat is cleared. "Your Grace?"

Startled, I look up to see Lady Heron standing but a few paces away, hands clasped at her waist. She stares at me in an odd manner, an expression shaded somewhere between pity and fear, before nodding towards my daughter. "Do not berate the lass too harshly, your Grace. I asked her to bring me here, after you were not to be found." The woman taps the linen bag that hangs from her belt. "I wished another visit."

Releasing my daughter, I straighten. "Go to your room," I tell the girl. "Stay there." She obeys, walking as fast as she possibly can without breaking into a run, and I wait until she has turned the corner at the end of the hall before informing Lady Heron that she can expect no visit today. Not today and possibly not ever again. For which she should be grateful.

"Have you stood before the mirror, your Grace?"

"You have no right to question me."

"Shall I instead advise? Do not accept the counsel of the glass. Do not stand before it again."

The laughter that bursts from my throat is coarse and ugly. "Shall I rather take the counsel of a hypocrite? Why do you not heed your own words, Lady Heron, be they so wise?"

The woman bows her head. "I am weak. I wish I were not."

I open my mouth to tell her to go but the words that trip forth are my stepmother's — the wretched list with which she spelled me.

Lady Heron tilts her head. "Your Grace?"

I repeat the list and she echoes me, her grey eyes flat and glazed. There's a curious satisfaction in speaking the words aloud, the feeling of tumblers falling into place, a sense of being *unlocked* — and yet I cannot find any pleasure in it. The manipulations of my stepmother and her mirror have left me drained and shaken, my stomach subjected to sour swells of nausea the results of which I have no desire for Lady Heron to witness.

"Leave," I snap, once my tongue feels again my own. "You're not welcome here." Without waiting to see that she obeys, I turn and march off down the corridor. Bile prickles at the back of my throat and I swallow, hard and hot, with one hand pressed close against my lips.

one-two-three, one-two-three, one-two-three

I cannot keep more count than that, but it doesn't matter. Three is the safest number, after all, and it's a simple thing to match my steps to its calm, protective rhythm. The parlour is closer than my bedchamber; I'll draw the drapes and sit awhile in my favourite chair.

one-two-three, one-two-three, one-two-three

I pass my daughter's room without pause. Pass, almost, without notice. The door is closed. All is quiet beyond. I'll speak with her once I am rested. I love my daughter, with her green eyes and golden hair. My position is not precarious. I love my daughter.

one-two-three, one-two-three, one-two-three

I will bring you before the Mirror; let it tell the hard and glassy truth of your death.

When there comes a gentle rapping at the parlour door, I expect it to be the housekeeper with a fresh bottle of wine. Wine and, perhaps, a plate of cured meats or a bowl of stew, along with yet more earnest supplications for me to eat, eat, eat. But I've had no appetite for food these past two days, not since speaking with the mirror; the mere thought of eating anything, of *chewing* and *swallowing* anything, makes me feel ill. But the wine — oh! — so red and sweet on my tongue. It helps me to sleep, it helps me not to think.

My head is heavy with all that I do not wish to think upon.

But it's not the housekeeper who marches into the room at my summons, stern of face and bearing nought but a small calico sack. Sketching a curtsy so shallow it might nearly be an insult, Lady Heron at least keeps her gaze averted until I have risen from the chair by the window where I have been sitting. My embroidery hoop, forgotten, falls with a clatter to the floor. Neither of us acknowledge it.

"H-how dare you intrude upon me here!" My cheeks feel hot, my knees unsteady.

The woman curtsies once again. "Forgiveness, your Grace — I have your price."

Frowning, I stare at the lumpy, cream-coloured sack in her outstretched hand.

"It is everything you requested," she says. "May I visit now?"

Even as I back away from her, Lady Heron steps forward, pressing her *price* into my grasp and bidding me to look. I don't wish to touch the sack let alone peer inside of it. I can no longer remember the specifics of my stepmother's list and have no desire to invite it into my mind once more. Hastily, I drop the thing onto the little table where my sewing basket sits, then wipe my hands on my skirts. My mouth is dry; I wish my wine goblet were not so empty.

"Why — why do you keep returning here?" I demand of Lady Heron.

She smiles, thin and sharp. "You have stood before it, your Grace. Do you not hear its whisper? Do you not feel its pull?"

No, I want to retort. *No, I am stronger than that. I am stronger than you.* But the woman is not a fool; she would see the lie in my face as quick as blinking. Last night I woke to find myself huddled against the door to the mirror's chamber, fingernails scratching at the wood. I didn't recognise the sounds that came from my own throat — pathetic mewlings like those a starving kitten might make before its head is pushed beneath the water — and it took all my will to force myself back down the hall.

I remember stopping at my daughter's bedroom, easing open the door and slipping inside to stand in the shadows. Like the Night Man. (Like my husband?) I watched her sleep, the swelling moon lighting her face through the window, all those golden curls turned to frost. Her mouth lolled open, a gentle snore easing between her lips. Did she dream of Klaus and of fairies? Or did she dream of becoming Queen?

your position in this household grows precarious

I remember taking a step towards my daughter's bed. I remember the surge of malice in my breast. And I remember running, horror rising with the bile in my throat as my daughter's confused, sleep-bleared voice called out in my wake — *Mama? Mama, is that you?*

This morning, I found my fingernails broken and split, with a narrow splinter of wood lodged beneath my left thumb. I still haven't spoken to my daughter — I'm frightened to look upon her face. Frightened of what I might feel when I do.

he loves your daughter. more than he loves you.

"What does it say?" I asked Lady Heron. "What does the mirror tell you?"

"Words that are mine alone to hear, your Grace." She straightens her spine. "As, having received your own private counsel, you must surely understand."

I hold her gaze for one long, difficult moment before reaching for the keys on my belt. "One final visit then, Lady Heron, after which you may never return. If you have any sense left in your head, you will thank me for it."

"And who shall keep the key from *you*, your Grace?" Her smile twists nearer to a smirk. "Who shall protect *you* when the mirror whispers in the night?"

Making no reply, I stride past the woman and out of the parlour. My footsteps echo in the empty halls; Lady Heron's come half a beat behind, her skirts rustling as she hurries after me. Once this visit is done, no one will come near the chamber again — she can spread the word among all the sorry women who scuttle up to the castle, coin in hand, eyes brimming with hopeful despair.

Whatever words the mirror chooses to speak, they will be mine alone to hear.

I shall ground glass so fine that it glitters like drifts of moonlit sand and then I will use it to salt your supper. The grains will grind through your innards, scouring your tender, secret parts until each movement is torture and you beg to be released from the agony that is breathing.

Lady Heron has been in the chamber for less time than it takes me to pace the length of the hall and back — fifty-nine steps all told — and my palms are sweaty and warm from rubbing too vigorously against one another. I should not have allowed the woman this visit. I should not have left her alone with the mirror. For what if the choice is not mine to make? What if the mirror decides that *she* will be its favoured confidante? What if —

Enough. *Enough.*

I fling open the door, demanding that Lady Heron take her leave right this instant, but my voice falters and I stop barely two steps inside the chamber, unable to properly comprehend the scene before me. The woman is hunched like an old fishwife, mouth contorting in fierce silence as the glow from the mirror grooves deep shadows into her face. In her right hand she wields a small hammer — though wields is perhaps too strong a term for the shaken, struggling manner in which she lifts it, lowers it, lifts it again.

"Lady Heron, what —"

Child, leave us.

The mirror's voice slides into me, fills me, and I stagger forward with arms outstretched. "No," I whisper. "No, please. I must stay. I have questions."

They will not spoil for waiting.

Sensing its imminent withdrawal, I pounce on the first words to trip across my tongue. "Am I safe here in this castle? Am I safe from my — my husband?"

You are safe from nothing, child. And if you do not leave now, you will never again call this castle your home.

The voice burns with fury; the pain is so great that I sink to my knees, hands pressed uselessly to my ears. Before I can beg forgiveness, there comes a great bellowing and a crash so loud it might be cannonfire exploding in my skull, and then

all the world

is dizzy

and dark.

Gradually, I become aware of two things: the cold, hard stone of the floor beneath my shoulder blades, and a strange sputtering noise from nearby. Opening my eyes, I roll over. Something cracks beneath my hip and, in the dim light filtering in from the hall, I can see shards of broken glass littering the chamber floor. On the wall, the mirror frame hangs barren. A few feet away, Lady Heron sits propped in a corner, breathing heavily. She sees me staring and grins with gleaming, dark-stained teeth, before sputtering again. Mindful of the wreckage, I crawl over to the woman. Her grey dress is stained and wet, and a pool of blood has formed beneath her. She has a hand pressed to her side, pressed to the place where a sharp and glittering edge protrudes.

"What have — what have you done?"

"It is over," Lady Heron croaks. "She'll rest now."

"Here, let me help." Carefully, I take hold of the shard in her side and pull it loose. More blood bubbles up through the wound and she groans, catching my free hand in hers. Squeezes hard. Coughs. I wad up some of her skirt and hold it against her side but it soaks red in a breath and Lady Heron is making that sputtering sound — laughing. She is laughing! Though her life now must surely be measured in breaths.

"Thank you," she says, shaking her head when I try to hush her. "Tried so many times. Each time, it held me. But couldn't hold us both. Not together. Couldn't hold me. With you there." She's lifting her right hand, curled in an empty fist. Bringing it down, lifting it again. "Couldn't hold me."

Taking her hand, I press it between my own. The hammer is over on the far side of the chamber, I see now, most likely flung from her grasp once she struck the mirror. My stomach clenches; my cheeks flush with anger.

"No more whispers," Lady Heron says. Though her voice is weak, her speech slick with blood, her eyes are clear. "No more whispers, your Grace."

"You had no right," I snap. "It was not your place."

She smiles. "You would not remember her."

"Remember who?"

"My niece, my darling. Stood before the mirror." Another cough, harsher this time, and the woman's smile fades. "Drowned herself, my darling." Her shoulders stiffen, then relax. "But it couldn't hold me. Tell my sister. Couldn't hold me."

Her gaze is locked with mine when she dies.

Shakily, I push myself to my feet. I try to wipe my hands on my skirts but they are no cleaner, no drier. Everywhere is blood and broken glass. I wouldn't have thought the mirror so large as to produce so many glittering shards — nor Lady Helen capable of containing all that red mess. Have I as much in my own small body? If my throat were slit, would such an ocean surge forth?

you will take the blame for this, child

No, it was — it was an accident.

the wife of Lord Heron lies slaughtered in a room to which you hold the only key

No, I —

you are soaked to the skin with her blood

But —

and a sack of witchcraft left in your parlour for any passing housekeeper to find

I —

see how well you have furnished your husband with your own death warrant

"Stop! Please, stop!" The voice falls silent but doesn't depart; my head might burst from the pressure of it. I stamp down on the nearest shard, a strange satisfaction rippling along my spine at the sound of cracking glass. I break another piece beneath my heel, and another. But even as I do, a sick terror begins to curdle in my belly. Damn Lady Heron to all the unknown hells for her treachery! Damn Lady Heron and — and —

is there another, child? one who might wear the noose destined for your pretty neck?

Dizzy, I lean my back against the wall. All at once, everything draws together. It has been her from the beginning, marking out the pattern, tying off the threads, and how doltish I have been not to see it. "Stepmother," I whisper.

oh yes, child. oh yes and at last. stepmother.

I will bury you alive. Not in a coffin or wooden box. Not even wrapped in a shroud. Bound, on your knees, you will feel the dirt scrape against your skin as I shovel it upon you. And when you are buried, I will salt the earth where you lie so that you might be shunned by each and every living thing.

The old crone looks up, aghast, as I storm into the room. Fumbling with her canes, she starts to rise from her chair but I'm upon her too quickly, grasping her bony shoulders and shoving her back down. She gives a soft, startled gasp and, for the first time I can remember, those brown eyes kindle with fear. "Fairest, whose blood is this?"

"None of it mine," I snap. "As much as you wish it were."

She pushes her face closer, nostrils flaring as she sniffs the air. "I would not be so sure. You are cut —"

I slap her hand away as it reaches for my cheek. "Never touch me again!"

"What has happened?" She touches her chest, hand hovering over the place where her heart would dwell, had she ever possessed such a fine organ. "I felt ... I felt ..."

do not listen, child. this wretch would have you banished from this place. from your home.

"I see you, witch. I see you now for what you are. For what you have always been."

Her gaze sharpens. "You have spoken to the mirror."

it would have been better to have let her die.

"You failed to destroy me once before. You will fail again."

it would be better to kill her now.

"Fairest, I beg you. You must not listen —"

No more, no more of her evil, insidious words, fighting even now to free themselves, even as my hands clutch her pale, wizened throat and squeeze. Eyes wide, she struggles against me, fingers scratching at mine in an effort to loosen my grip. But her nails are as old and brittle as her soul, snapping before they can hope to break the skin, and the pitiful manner in which she writhes only serves to stoke my wrath. I will end this. Now. I will end her —

My hands close around air.

Unbalanced, I tip forward, bracing myself against the abruptly, impossibly empty chair. A raucous, rasping chorus fills the room, goblin laughter bold and burbling, and I whirl around, shielding myself from the sudden mass of black feathers that swoops upon me. The bird caws again, flapping vengeful at my face as it pecks and claws, and I try to move away, turn away, but it is everywhere, dogged and inescapable as death. Covering my eyes — for surely it is those soft and vulnerable globes it seeks to pluck from me! — I stumble blindly for the door, only to step on my own skirts and fall. My knee cracks on the stone and the pain robs me of breath. I cry out, rolling and reaching for my aching knee, and the bird is there, all feathers and fury, its black wings beating a gale as its beak latches onto my cheek.

And then, emptiness.

Warily, I prop myself up on one elbow. The bird, a raven as large as a cat, is on the floor nearby. Catching my gaze, it hops well beyond my reach. The movement is awkward, ungainly; there is something wrong with the creature's talons, an unnatural curl that twists them back upon themselves, and even as I peer closer —

— the raven vanishes. Or, doesn't vanish precisely, but is simply *gone* — with my stepmother now crouched, naked and breathing harder than I am, in its place. Reaching into her mouth, she pulls out a shard of mirrored glass the size of my thumbnail. "You will feel more yourself, Fairest." Her voice is hoarse and broken. "Now this foul thing is removed."

I touch my cheek, feel the blood running fresh from the wound. I remember Lady Heron, and the glass I pulled from her side. The dauntless scarlet flow that leached all warmth from her flesh. *Tell my sister.* My hands begin to tremble. *Couldn't hold me.* My stomach convulses and I lurch onto my side, vomiting a thin burgundy gruel onto the stones.

"Fetch my robe," my stepmother says. "And my canes. Please, Fairest."

Her neck is red, marred with deep crescents that will likely bruise. Shaking, I wipe my chin with the back of my hand. "I — I don't ... I'm sorry ..."

"Hush now." She smiles. "After all these years, what use have the two of us for apologies?"

I fetch my stepmother's robe. And her canes. We sit at the round wooden table, the small shard of glass between us. I fuss at my fingers, trying to scrape away the dried blood crusted around my nails. What a fright I must look. "How — how ... the raven, I mean ..."

"I was a witch long before you were born, before I even laid eyes upon your father. Did you think I had forgotten all my clever tricks?" She pauses, prods the shard with her index finger. Gingerly, as if it might bite. "Though, for a while, I could do nought but mend. It swallows no small part of you, Fairest. I think you have had a taste of that."

I look away. From the shard, from my stepmother. "But how long?"

"Several years now." Her chuckle is raspy, dry as the last leaves of autumn. "Blessed three, I should have gone mad locked in this room without my wings."

"But you could have fled at any time!"

"Is that what you think? That I could leave you to the fate I myself had wrought? You, and then your daughter? The mirror held me for so long, so sweetly and so ruthlessly — but the fault was mine. I stood before it. I asked my foolish question. I opened my heart to its hooks."

"Has this been your penance?" The words taste as bitter as they sound.

"No, Fairest, it has been my justice. And it is not yet done." My stepmother stands and hobbles across to her nightstand. Moving with care, she retrieves the jug of water left for her bathing and returns to the table. Gently, she takes my hand in hers. I flinch but stop short of pulling away. My stepmother works patiently, rubbing at my fingers with an old linen napkin. "So much blood," she murmurs. "And so little of it yours."

I tell her everything, words spilling from my lips like stolen jewels.

My stepmother listens in silence as she cleans, pausing now and then to dip her napkin in the water. Soon the cloth is pink as my daughter's cheeks — and oh, my daughter, my darling one! How could I have spoken to her with such fury? How could my heart have been so quickly hardened against its sole delight that almost I wished her —

"Yet you did not," my stepmother says, wiping at my tears. "And she is not."

"Oh, but what have I done? My husband returns in a matter of days."

"Lord Heron will miss his poor wife sooner than that." Leaning back in her chair, she nods at the mirrored shard between us. "Take that thing and throw it from the window. Its song is faint but still I hear it keenly."

The sky outside is a cold, wintry blue and I fling the shard as hard as I can, the mirrored side glinting in the sunlight as it sails its final arc. My thumb smarts; blood beads from a fresh-made cut. "Good riddance to you as well," I mutter. Despite the chill, I linger by the window a moment more, staring out at the pine forests that border this side of the castle grounds and at the mountains beyond, their crowns hidden in low cloud.

She could have fled at any time. Fled and flown and been free.

"Fairest," my stepmother calls. "There isn't much time."

Squaring my shoulders, I take a deep breath and turn to face her. "Tell me, then. What I must do?"

I shall leave you alone. Without light. Without song. Without the skin of another soul to warm you in the night. You will pass in absolute solitude, knowing only the unsteady beat of your failing, fragile heart.

My daughter is wholly unafraid of the old woman who sits before her, smearing her face with the same clear but strange-smelling ointment that she has already rubbed over my own. The child giggles, wrinkling her nose, and reaches out to run eager fingers through my stepmother's hair. "Are you a fairy?"

My stepmother smiles. "Some might say so." There's a kindness in her voice and in her eyes. Gently, she untangles her hair from my daughter's grasp and sweeps it over her shoulder. "Now stop wriggling, little one."

"Mama says magic is dangerous."

The woman flicks me a glance. "Your mother is right. You should mind her words."

Beneath its ointment, my face itches and my mouth is dry with doubt. She could have fled at any time, I tell myself, fled and flown and been free. Fear is a stubborn habit; it must be broken again and again.

Though my stepmother was well pleased when I returned with what Lady Heron had brought to the castle, she refused to let me watch as she mixed her ingredients. *It is not for you to know, Fairest. One day, perhaps, if you choose such a path, but not this day.* Instead, I was sent to fetch my daughter, who I found curled up on her bed, speaking in whispers to the yellow-haired doll my husband brought back from his travels last spring. Her eyes widened as I entered the room, and she shrank back when I sat down beside her.

I'm sorry, my pet. Please forgive me.

Are you still cross with me, Mama?

Oh no, my pet. I pulled her into my arms, held her and rocked her as I did when she was a babe. *No and never again.* Pressing my face into her hair, I soaked in the sweet, familiar scent of her scalp until she started to twist against me, protesting the tickling of my breath. *Tickling, am I? Tickling?* My fingers found her ribs, and the soft hollows of her knees, wiggled in beneath her arms until she was shrieking with laughter. *Come,* I said at last, smoothing the tangled curls from her eyes. *There's someone who wishes to meet you.*

The doll she left discarded on the bed, its glass-eyed gaze fixed on the ceiling.

"Fairest?" My stepmother asks now. She is holding my daughter by the hand. "We are ready."

"Where — where is your ointment?"

"My enchantment was wrought to last. I have no need of unguents, nor any quills save what fledge from my own skin." She nods at the two feathers lying side by side on the table, sleek and black with promise. Muttering beneath her breath, my stepmother selects the smaller of the two and twirls it between her fingers.

"Will it hurt, Lady Fairy?" my daughter asks, voice faltering.

"No, little one. Quite the opposite."

Quick as a serpent striking, the woman stabs the feather into my daughter's chest and I gasp, rushing forward even as the nightdress she was wearing puddles to the floor. Puddles, then begins to flop and bounce. Chuckling, my stepmother pokes at the linen with her cane until from beneath a fold there flies—a raven, smaller than my stepmother when she takes the form, but so beautiful. As the bird circles the room, swooping and soaring, my fear dissolves into pride. Such mighty wings, such grace! My daughter flies as though she has spent all of her days in the air!

"It might be simpler if you disrobe," my stepmother says. She's holding the second feather in one hand, beckoning me close with the other.

"What if we become lost? What if —"

"Do you suppose I have frittered away all these years without making preparations? Without securing us a haven? You need to trust me, Fairest, one last time."

I shed my blood-stiff garments and take a deep, steadying breath. She could have fled at any time, fled and flown and been free.

"Three days, Fairest, before this magic weakens. We have much ground to cover."

I close my eyes. Already I can smell the mountains, can taste the snow-crisp air. Then a flash quiets my mind, and I feel myself flexing and folding, stretching and sharpening and — flying, flying, oh! Flying so fast, too fast for this too-small space, giddying swoops and banking as a wall rises before me, and another wall, and another, and there — the window and through it to the open air. From behind me, a black arrow shoots. She wheels and caws, and there at her tail is the smaller bird, the beloved bird — oh my beloved bird!

I follow them both, our wings beating us through the clear and boundless sky.

When death comes at last, your hair will be silvered and your bones grown thin with years. I will stay by your side, spinning sweet tales of fairies and goblins, of soft-hearted dwarves and maidens bold and fearful and true. The birds, too, will come to honour your passing, ravens and crows and all the birds of the air. Do you see them, stepmother? Do you see them flying, so fast and so free?

PREVIOUS PUBLICATION CREDITS

Several of these stories have appeared elsewhere, in some cases in a different form:

- 'Burnt Sugar', *Dreaming in the Dark*, ed. Jack Dann (PS Publishing, 2016).
- 'The New Wife', published as a stand-alone chapbook (Brain Jar Press, 2022).
- 'After Midnight', published as a stand-alone chapbook (Brain Jar Press, 2022).
- 'Braid', "Braid" *Review of Australian Fiction,* (Volume 24, Issue 1, 2017).
- 'By The Moon's Good Grace', *Review of Australian Fiction,* (Volume 12, Issue 3, 2014).
- 'Winterbloom', published as a stand-alone chapbook (Brain Jar Press, 2022).
- 'Triquetra', *Tor.com,* (Sept 2018).

ABOUT THE AUTHOR

Kirstyn McDermott has been working in the darker alleyways of speculative fiction for much of her career. She is the author of two award-winning novels, *Madigan Mine* and *Perfections*, along with two collections of short fiction, *Caution: Contains Small Parts* and *Hard Places*. Her stories and poetry have been published in various magazines, journals and anthologies within Australia and internationally, with her most recent work being *Never Afters*, a collection of novellas that retell classic fairy tales. Her next novel, *What the Bones Know*, is due to be published by Mira/HarperCollins in February 2026. She also holds a PhD in creative writing with a research focus on re-visioned fairy tales and for many years produced and co-hosted a literary discussion podcast, *The Writer and the Critic*. Kirstyn lives in Ballarat, Australia, with fellow writer Jason Nahrung and two distinctly non-literary felines. She can be found online at www.kirstynmcdermott.com.

THANK YOU FOR BUYING THIS BRAIN JAR PRESS COLLECTION